Also in the Crime Classics series:

The Sleeping Tiger

A MURDER MYSTERY

DOMINIC DEVINE

ABOUT THE AUTHOR

A hugely underrated and unjustly neglected writer, D.M. Devine (1920–1980) combined his day job (as Secretary and Registrar of the University of St Andrew's) with his writing career. The 13 crime fiction novels he authored all share his trademarks of good writing and excellent plots, qualities which were prized by the Queen of Crime, Agatha Christie, who remained a fan of Devine's throughout his writing career.

This edition published in the UK by Arcturus Publishing Limited
26/27 Bickels Yard, 151–153 Bermondsey Street, London SE1 3HA

Cover artwork by Steve Beaumont
Typesetting by Couper Street Type Co.

AD003690EN

Printed in the UK

PART I

FOREWORD: FROM THE TRIAL

'. . . These were not, members of the jury, crimes of passion, committed while the blood was hot. On the contrary, each was planned to the last inhuman detail many weeks in advance. The first murder took place six years ago, in April 1962; and you will hear evidence that in February of that year . . .'

John Prescott wrote 'February' on the pad they had given him. He added '14th,' then 'Harriet's birthday.' Harriet's birthday . . . He ripped the sheet from the pad, crumpled it, thrust it in his pocket.

From the jury box the thin-faced woman was watching him. Prescott out-stared her this time. Light glinted on her spectacles as she turned her head. The drooping, uncharitable mouth presaged her verdict.

But then the verdict was hardly in doubt anyway. Since the hearing in the Magistrates' Court everyone *knew* Prescott was guilty. The trial was a formality, a ritual decreed by law so that justice might be seen to be done. Prescott's own solicitor had as good as advised him to plead guilty.

Why hadn't he? Not from hope: the future was of indifference to him now. Some last spark of perversity dictated the gesture.

Sir Hugh's voice rolled mellifluously on: '. . . You will hear how on a number of occasions the accused visited Miss Browne in her flat late at night . . .'

Momentarily Prescott was jolted from his apathy. That was a lie. He'd visited Norah once only, and . . . Ah what the hell! Let them say. He returned to his doodling.

'J.W.P.' He embellished with rich scrollwork the monogram he had devised as a schoolboy. Then he wrote 'J. W. Prescott, LL.B., Solicitor.' He added 'Unemployed, of no fixed address'; then 'try H.M. Prisons.' The woman was watching him again. He smiled to her, and was gratified by her expression of outrage.

In the public gallery Prescott's father sat in ashen-faced concentration, as if the burden of the trial lay on his shoulders. All the religious fervour was quenched, he was a shrivelled old man.

In a sense, Prescott reflected, his father was responsible for all that had happened. If only he hadn't been so narrow-minded and puritanical. But that was a futile speculation: his father was as God had made him; and anyway there were worse faults than puritanism. At least he was loyal: he alone believed, or said he believed, his son was innocent . . .

Counsel had moved on five and a half years, to the second murder. '. . . You may think that these facts (which will, of course, be put in evidence) are themselves conclusive of guilt. But any scintilla of doubt is removed by the accused's own words. In a statement to the police on—'

Julius Rutherford, Q.C., defence counsel, was on his feet, gown flapping indignantly. 'My lord, I must ask you to rule . . .'

It was the interview Prescott had had with the Chief Inspector on the night of the murder. The defence claimed he hadn't been properly cautioned and the statement ought not to be admitted.

The jury were dismissed and legal battle was joined. Precedents were bandied, distinctions drawn, Mr. Justice Yardley almost disappeared behind the pile of books thrust on him for his consideration. The familiar shibboleths rolled out: 'my learned friend,' 'with the greatest respect, my lord,' 'alleged statement,' 'judges' rules.'

At length the husky voice of the judge closed the discussion. 'I am bound by Rex v. Stretford,' he said. 'Objection overruled.' And that was that. Rutherford sat down in feigned astonishment, the jury were brought back. Sir Hugh read an excerpt from the statement, reporters' pencils recorded it.

Prescott, catching the eye of Elliot Watson, his solicitor, smiled derisively; he had maintained last night that the Stretford case would be decisive.

Prescott was not impressed by his legal advisers. He had employed a London firm because feeling against him in Cromley ran so high. But in fact he could have prepared his own brief more effectively. Watson was slipshod and perfunctory, as if lacking faith in his client's case. Which was no more than the truth.

And Julius Rutherford was no match for Sir Hugh Lympney. Prescott would never have accepted Rutherford as counsel if he'd had any real interest in the outcome.

He had stopped listening and was examining the courtroom with critical detachment. It was squalid, ill-lit and draughty; and he thought he could see woodworm in the panelling behind the judge's bench. He was mentally re-designing the court when a phrase from prosecution counsel's address caught his attention.

'. . . It may seem, members of the jury, that Mrs. Prescott acted uncharitably, even vindictively. But remember that the marriage she had struggled so long to preserve had been cynically shattered by her husband's unfaithfulness, that she already knew of his fatal attachment to another woman. Perhaps too she had some inkling

of the terrible crime he had committed years before and of the
monstrous design that was now taking shape in his mind . . .'

Again Prescott's indifference was pierced. It was all wrong: his
marriage hadn't collapsed because of Harriet Reece; rather, he and
Harriet had come together because his marriage, after years of slow
disintegration, was dead.

Sir Hugh was in his peroration. '. . . crimes hardly paralleled for
their cold-blooded savagery. What harm had his victims done?
They were in his way, they obstructed his plans: it was their only
offence. The day Norah Browne walked into his life, she was,
although she did not know it, setting the stage for murder.'

The day Norah Browne walked into his life . . . 22nd February
1962. He remembered the date because it was George Washington's
birthday, and Peter Reece had remarked on it. It was the sort of
out-of-the-way information Peter specialised in.

22nd February 1962 . . .

CHAPTER I

Spring was on its way at last. There was warmth in the sun this
morning, last week's snow was gone, crocuses were out in Selwyn
Park.

John Prescott walked to the office, as he always did when it was
fine. As he turned into Selwyn Place, Edward Lowson was getting
out of his car.

'Beautiful morning,' Prescott greeted him.

Lowson locked his car. 'All right for you young chaps,' he said, shaking his head. 'Nowadays when spring comes round, I can't help wondering: will this be my last?'

He didn't mean it. At sixty-three he looked good for another twenty springs. He was portly and benign, bald but for a few silver wisps at each side, and his face had the smooth skin of a much younger man. He wore plus-fours and a deerstalker hat and was usually smoking a cigar. He consciously created the image of the old-style family solicitor.

Lowson, senior partner in W. B. Clyde and Sons, lawyers, was a shrewd man, rather more self-interested than the twinkle of his eyes suggested. Not well-versed in recent legislation or case law; but still pretty sound if you wanted to make your will or buy a house or recover a debt.

Lowson had been responsible for John Prescott's joining the firm. It had been a business transaction, with no sentiment involved, no nepotism: Lowson had put the microscope on his qualifications before making an offer, and Prescott had to borrow heavily to buy himself in. For all that he was made to feel eternally in the older man's debt.

As they climbed the stairs together, Lowson remarked: 'One of these days we must get out of this mausoleum.'

That was another affectation. He liked to talk about moving to the town centre from this Victorian mansion alongside the doctors and dentists. Tim Raven, the third partner, was for it; but when it came to a specific proposal, Lowson always shied off. The cost was beyond their means, he would say. In truth he preferred the old-world atmosphere of Selwyn Place, the dark wood, the musty smell of books. It blended better with his plus-fours.

'By the way, John,' Lowson added, 'are you doing anything

to-night?' And, without waiting for an answer: 'We're having some people in to dinner. Madge and I would be delighted if you could come.'

Someone must have let them down. Prescott remembered Peter Reece's words: 'You're too soft, John. Don't knuckle down to the old bastard.'

'I'm sorry,' he said. 'I can't make it to-night.'

By now they were outside the senior partner's door. Lowson waited for an explanation, and when none was volunteered, said a little frostily: 'Pity. Alice'll be disappointed.' He made a vague gesture of dismissal and went into his room.

Alice'll be disappointed ... Peter had warned Prescott about that too. 'They've been trying to marry her off for years.'

Alice Lowson was twenty-five, a year older than Prescott. She was quite a pretty girl, determinedly vivacious, who laughed a lot but had no sense of humour. Prescott was sorry for her, had taken her out once or twice, and now, conscious of the jaws of the trap closing, was trying to disengage himself.

He pushed open the door at the end of the corridor with his name on gilt letters on the glass. Nadine Smith looked up from her typewriter in the outer office.

'Good morning, Mr. Prescott. Mr. Raven's waiting in your room.'

He went through and found Tim Raven sitting on the desk, reading a letter.

'Morning, John,' he said. 'I see the Laundry Company has raised its offer.'

Prescott suppressed his irritation at having his correspondence read. 'Yes,' he said.

'Going to accept?'

'That's up to Mr. Reece. I'll advise him to, certainly.' Peter's father had had some shirts damaged in the laundry and was tenaciously claiming the full replacement value.

'Damn good work, John.'

In his different way Raven was as patronising as Lowson, his tone subtly conveying the contempt of the amateur for the professional. Raven dealt mainly with property work and employed the old boy network with marked success.

He was ex-public school and Oxford. An elegant man, tall, with a lean, handsome face and black hair, fastidious in his dress; a wit, a conversationalist, much in demand at dinner parties. He was now thirty-four, and no woman had yet ensnared him. Probably none would: his sister, who kept house for him, made life too comfortable.

All the same he enjoyed the company of women. He wooed them, flattered them, sometimes went to bed with them; but avoided entanglements. Which was why Prescott's buxom secretary, Nadine Smith, who was practically offering herself to Raven, was doomed to disappointment.

Peter Reece liked Raven and assured Prescott that his doubts sprang from an inferiority complex. Prescott was half convinced. The three of them, with Frank Hornby, the doctor, made up a foursome on the golf course every Sunday. Raven, the weakest player of the four, somehow contrived to make even that a virtue: one ought not to play games to *win*.

'Speaking of the Reeces,' Raven said. 'Who's the girl?'

'What girl?'

'Peter's latest. She was with him in the club last night. A honey blonde, curved in all the right places.'

'You're ahead of me. I thought it was still Isabel Knighton.'

'No, no, that's *vieux jeu*. This one's from a different stable altogether from the Knighton filly. Really quite presentable.'

Must be a very recent acquaintance, Prescott thought. Peter Reece, never reticent about his girlfriends, had not mentioned her last Sunday.

'I'm going round to-night,' Prescott said. 'I'll ask about her.'

He hadn't meant to call on Peter to-night. But, having refused Lowson's dinner invitation, he felt obscurely impelled to go out.

The Reeces lived on Marsden Hill. 'Dollar Drive,' they'd called it once, where wealth and privilege had their home. The title was less apt now. As suburbia encircled the Hill, the top people moved farther west towards Hastonbury. Their houses were sold and flatted: the Hill had dropped a class.

Ash Grove, one of the few still undivided, was half-way up. The garden was attractively laid out: a wide sweep of lawn, dotted with shrubs and fruit trees, sloped gently down to the plantation of ash trees which gave the property its name. The house itself was Georgian: mellow and dignified, it blended unobtrusively with its surroundings. Even the grey stone garage that Arthur Reece had built against the north gable looked as if it had always been part of the house.

It was half-past eight when Prescott parked behind Arthur Reece's three-litre Jaguar. Harriet answered his ring.

'Oh it's you, John. Come in!' She lowered her voice. 'Peter's brought his new girl home, and do you know who she is? Daddy's secretary! Daddy's absolutely *livid*.' She giggled, then, as Prescott turned towards the sitting-room door, she said hastily: 'Wait till I tell you; this is lush. Peter borrowed the Jag to bring her here and he scraped it on the gate! Can you *imagine*?'

Harriet Reece was just turned fifteen, tall, dark and angular; she looked coltish but could move gracefully. Tim Raven, who claimed to be an authority, said that when she filled out, Harriet was going to be a winner. Prescott couldn't see it. And he found her manner tiresome – the exclamation marks that punctuated her speech, the giggles, the practical jokes, the constant bickering with her brother.

'I'd better not stay,' Prescott said.

'Oh no, John, you must! It's like a *wake* in there.'

He followed her in. Peter's father was sitting by the fire, the *Financial Times* on his knee. Peter himself was on the piano stool. But Prescott's eyes were on the girl.

'Norah, this is John,' Peter said, jumping up. 'John Prescott. Norah Browne.'

'I've heard a lot about you, John,' she said as they shook hands.

'Have you?' As always when meeting someone new, he was tongue-tied and awkward.

'Your ears should be burning,' Peter said. 'Well, how about a drink to celebrate?'

'To celebrate what?' Harriet put in rudely.

Her brother was never at a loss. 'George Washington's birthday,' he said. 'Twenty-second February.'

'Well, I want a sherry,' said Harriet. That brought a reproof from her father and gave Prescott the chance to study Norah Browne.

She was in her early twenties. Honey-blonde hair, blue eyes, full sensuous lips. Prescott couldn't stop looking at her – the long slim legs, the curvy figure, which made Harriet seem from another species. She was the embodiment of his ideal: right age, right shape, right voice. The trouble was, whenever he met such a girl, either his shyness rendered him speechless, or she was already off the market.

Norah was out of the usual run of Peter's girlfriends. He didn't bring them home as a rule. Also there had been something special in the way he introduced her, as if anxious for his friend's approval.

Peter brought in the drinks: brandy and soda for his father, whisky for Prescott and himself, gin and tonic for Norah; and for Harriet, despite her protests, Coca-Cola.

'You're a lawyer, John, aren't you?' Norah said.

'Yes.' Another conversation strangled at birth.

Peter covered for him. 'John's the strong, silent type,' he said. 'There's a tiger sleeping underneath. Don't disturb . . . For God's sake, Harriet, what are you wriggling about for?'

'It's this old thing: it's sore on the behind.' She was sitting on a small sofa, upholstered in faded green tapestry.

'You're speaking of the most valuable piece in this room. Genuine antique. That so, Father?'

Arthur Reece didn't look up from his paper.

'I don't care,' Harriet said. 'It's hard on the behind.'

'It's the behind that's inadequate. Grow a bit of beef on it and—'

'Oh shut up!'

Now their father intervened. 'Stop squabbling, you two. Have you done your homework, Harriet?'

'No.'

'Well, go and do it.'

She made a face, but stood up without protest. 'Good night, John,' she said. ''Night, everybody.' She went out without a glance at Norah.

Arthur Reece laid down his paper and turned to Prescott. 'No more news, John?'

'Yes. I tried to phone you to-day. They've raised their offer to twelve pounds ten.'

'Good. Good. They're beginning to crack.'

'I think you ought to accept, Mr. Reece.'

'Nonsense. Not till they offer what I'm due.'

'For heaven's sake, Father,' Peter said, 'you're not going to haggle over a couple of quid?'

'I'll take them to the House of Lords if need be.'

He would, too. He was a stubborn old devil. You could see it in the set of his jaw, the line of his mouth.

He was in his middle fifties, a widower. He had a successful accountancy business in Cromley in which Peter had joined him after coming down from university.

Peter maintained that his father had been more human before his wife died ten years ago. There was a framed photograph of Mrs. Reece on the piano, which showed where Peter had got his looks.

And his easy-going nature, Prescott guessed. Certainly that didn't come from his father. Arthur Reece was fond of describing himself as a just man. By his own lights it was true; but it was justice untempered by mercy or even by a sense of proportion. Every tradesman's bill was meticulously scrutinised, and he would quibble over a penny. It wasn't miserliness, for he lived in comfortable style: it was simply determination that no one should outsmart him.

'I've another case for you, John,' he said now.

Prescott's heart sank. 'Oh yes?'

'This young ass,' – he waved his brandy glass at his son – 'damaged the car to-night.'

'It's only *scraped*, Father.'

'Take it up with the insurance company, would you?'

Peter said in exasperation: 'It's not worth losing your no-claim bonus. I'll pay for it to be re-sprayed myself.'

His father smiled. 'Ah well, that's all right, then. We'll say no more about it.' He stood up. 'I've work to do. Good night, Miss Browne. Good night, John.'

The tension relaxed as soon as he was gone.

'I'm sorry, Norah,' Peter said ruefully.

'Sorry? What for?'

'He can be so damned rude. Sitting there reading his paper . . .'

'I think he's a dear.'

'A *dear*! That's a new angle.'

'His bark's worse than his bite.'

'But by God he can bark! I'm fond of the old boy myself, but one of these days someone's going to do him in . . . Let's have another drink.'

Norah refused this round. She said to Prescott: 'Peter tells me you're not a local man, John?'

She was doing her best. If only she wouldn't gaze at him so raptly: it made him nervous. Well, not nervous exactly. It sapped his confidence, that was it, revived the bashfulness of his early days, before Peter took him in hand.

However, the whisky helped. 'No,' he said. 'I'm from Fenleigh. Other side of the A.1.'

'Other side of the world,' Peter amended. 'It's fifty years behind the times. Best thing about Fenleigh is the road out of it, to misquote Dr. Johnson.' He spoke feelingly, having once spent an unhappy day in Fenleigh visiting John Prescott at his parents' home.

'But why Cromley?' Norah persisted.

'Leave the boy alone, Norah . . . Come to that, why did *you* choose Cromley?'

'Just chance. I saw the advertisement—'

'Just chance, indeed! You mean, you'd heard that old man Reece was rolling in the lolly, you knew he'd a half-wit son, and you thought—'

'Peter!' Norah's face was scarlet.

Peter laughed. 'I'm sorry, darling. You'll have to get used to my depraved sense of humour . . . You've lovely legs, Norah. Wouldn't you say she'd lovely legs, John?'

'Yes.'

'John says you've lovely legs, Norah. You've gorgeous . . .'

Norah laughed. 'Spare us the anatomy lesson. Anyway, if it was the lolly I was after, I wouldn't waste my time with the half-wit son.'

Peter was delighted. 'You'd set your sights on the old man? Good for you.' Then a shadow crossed his face. 'You wouldn't be the first to try it either . . .'

The longer you stayed out of a conversation, Prescott thought, the harder it was to come in. Anything he said now would be treated with exaggerated respect. It was absurd: he couldn't even find the words to take his leave.

Peter, normally so sensitive to other people's feelings, hadn't noticed the awkwardness: his eyes and thoughts were on Norah. And Norah? She had noticed all right, she'd even tried to bring him into the fold. But she'd given up now.

Prescott was furious with himself, furious with the deficiencies of heredity and upbringing that could still exact this humiliating toll. Unjustly furious even with Peter.

No, not furious: jealous. Peter had so much, all the gifts had been showered on him – money, health, looks, intelligence, and a sunny, carefree temperament. Now he had Norah. And Prescott was jealous . . .

Out of the blue Norah said: 'John, take off your glasses, would you?'

He took them off. They were horn-rimmed. He'd had them since he was at university and he wore them now more from habit than because he needed them.

'That's quite a profile, isn't it, Peter?'

Peter said: 'I've been telling him for years to throw away these damned specs.'

Norah was looking at him thoughtfully. 'He's right, John. They don't do anything for you.'

'They help me to see,' he said, putting the spectacles on. He had meant it humorously, but it sounded pompous.

He looked at his watch, muttered an excuse, and escaped.

CHAPTER II

Prescott drove back to his lodgings and garaged the car. He tiptoed up the stairs, hoping Mrs. Jardine wouldn't hear him.

But her door opened and she called: 'Is that you, Mr. Prescott?'

'Yes.' Who did she think it was?

'A gentleman phoned.'

He went down a step or two, leant over the banisters. There she was, a thin, anxious woman, perpetually dressed in black to remind her of her widowhood. Her peke in its knitted jacket was yapping at her feet.

'Who was it, Mrs. Jardine?'

'Mr. Lowson.'

Checking on him, probably. 'Did he leave a message?'

'No . . . Quiet, Smudge! . . . No, he said he'd see you in the morning. The kettle's on the boil, Mr. Prescott, if you'd like—'

'No, thanks, Mrs. Jardine.' He couldn't face the monologue that would be served with the tea.

He went up to his room. It was clean, tidy, warm; and entirely impersonal. He preferred it to living in his parents' home, but only just.

Prescott was not by nature a bachelor: he wanted to be loved and cared for, wanted a wife. He could have Alice Lowson for the asking, or others of her kind. Unfortunately she didn't meet his specifications.

He sat at the dressing-table and examined his face in the glass. Thick, reddish hair, straight nose, firm chin. He knew he was presentable, even *with* the offending spectacles.

He took them off, squinted sideways at himself. It *was* a good profile.

Yes, in looks Peter had no advantage. Nor in brains. And yet Peter had only to snap his finger and girls like Norah would come running . . . The difference was in personality. For years Prescott had been creating a new persona, ridding himself of the old complexes and inhibitions. But he was still vulnerable, still liable to relapse. With Norah Browne to-night he'd been gauche as a schoolboy. Would he ever break the shackles of the past? . . .

John Prescott's father had been a post-office clerk in Fenleigh; a God-fearing man, but narrow and bigoted. The four children were brought up in the creed that virtue means the avoidance of sin; and sin was widely interpreted.

A more insidious influence was the worship of family. Their world was bounded by Fenleigh and, within Fenleigh, by the Prescotts – brothers, sisters, uncles, cousins; all virtuous, all self-satisfied.

John was less docile than his brothers and sister, and more intelligent. With some misgiving his father consented to a university education for him, and John went up to Liverpool to read law. There he came under the liberalising influence of Peter Reece, who was taking a degree in economics in preparation for a career in accountancy.

Reece was too versatile to be a scholar: athlete (a hockey blue in his first year), pianist, versifier, *bon viveur*, gambler. He was a stocky, dark-haired youth, prone to argue, but with unfailing good humour.

They met after a debate in the Union in which they had taken opposite sides. Peter invited John for a drink and ribbed him for ordering orangeade. From these beginnings an unlikely friendship blossomed.

And yet perhaps not so unlikely, for they had interests in common. Music for a start: they both played the piano moderately well; and hockey, although in that field their performances were unequal. But the cementing bond was, paradoxically, their differences. For Peter loved an argument, loved to chip away his friend's prejudices by sheer force of logic.

Alcohol, sex, gambling – these were the main issues. On the first two John conceded victory. But on gambling he never gave in: he could see no sense in it.

The trouble was, he was at university only twenty-five weeks in the year. In the vacations, he went home to a different world, a world that now seemed impossibly narrow. Several times he spent a holiday with Peter in Cromley. The house in Fenleigh wasn't big enough for him to have Peter back to stay. But he did invite him one Sunday to meet his family. It was not a success.

Peter laughed it off. They were exactly as he had pictured, he said; and he thought John's mother charming. A bigger fiasco was the day John brought home Christine, a student at Liverpool. A few years later he couldn't even remember her surname, although she had seemed important at the time. From the moment she lit a cigarette after lunch poor Christine could do nothing right. In the end she flounced out of the house and out of John's life.

He had a blistering row with his parents that night. But they were on a different wavelength, he couldn't get through. Moreover, his own feelings were ambivalent: he could still see Christine through their eyes. He wasn't yet fully emancipated.

He took his degree in 1958 – an upper second, which was a disappointment. His *viva* probably clinched it, for he had been tongue-tied and hesitant. He was always better with pen and paper. Even in conversation he was inclined to be wooden, afraid to talk naturally, too concerned about the other person's reaction, with the result that people underrated the quality of his mind.

He completed his articles in a solicitor's office in Fenleigh, staying with his parents but living his own life. He disagreed with his father on almost everything now and there was constant friction. His mother was ill much of the time; otherwise John would have left home.

He had a half-serious friendship with a girl in the office, which lingered on, then quietly died. Although the nearest yet to his ideal, she didn't quite measure up.

He kept in touch with Peter Reece and in the spring of 1961 spent another holiday at Ash Grove. One night Peter's father was entertaining Edward Lowson, the lawyer, and John was introduced. The upshot was a letter from Lowson inviting him to join his firm. It occurred to John later that the meeting might not have been entirely fortuitous, especially when he learned how many people Lowson had approached for testimonials.

His parents found it incomprehensible that he should choose to leave Fenleigh, although John guessed that his father was secretly relieved. The Prescott clan rallied round, raised the capital he needed, and insisted that the loan be interest-free. Usury was a vice.

He moved to Cromley in August 1961. The advantages were at once apparent: freedom from domestic tension; more interesting and responsible work; and, of course, his friendship with Peter Reece, now in his father's accountancy business in Cromley.

John spent much of his leisure with Peter. They golfed, they played duets on the piano; and they argued. Often about women.

'Your mistake, John,' Peter would say, 'is to go around *looking* for a wife, measuring each girl you meet against some private yard-stick. Love happens, you can't prescribe it in advance.'

It was a perceptive remark. Prescott did have a prescription, he had a clear mental picture of his future wife.

Peter liked to tease him and once asked: 'What does she look like, this paragon?'

'Fair hair—'

Peter stopped him. 'There you are, you've eliminated half of womankind before you start. One day you'll meet a girl – maybe a brunette or a redhead – but you'll *know* she was meant for you. Too bad if you're already hooked to some brassy blonde who happened to have the right statistics.'

'It's not only her shape, Peter—'

'Ah yes, she must have a beautiful disposition too. Well, good hunting, boy.'

Peter himself seemed in no hurry to settle down. In six months he'd had three different girlfriends to John's knowledge. Not very serious affairs – 'just a romp in the hay' was Peter's own description: they were never allowed to interfere with his golf or his music or his gambling.

But now there was Norah.

*

The grandfather clock on the stair struck midnight. Prescott crossed to the window and looked out. It was a fine, starry night, not cold. He heard the distant rumble of a diesel and presently saw its lights as it rounded the bend at Hastonbury and coasted down towards Cromley Central. It was the last train from the south, running ten minutes late.

Prescott was still obsessed by the humiliating scene at Ash Grove. How they must have laughed after he left! No, not Peter, he wasn't like that. But Norah would have a quiet smile at the inarticulate oaf she'd met.

He remembered every word she'd addressed to him. She'd been very kind. Even at the end she'd seemed interested. 'That's quite a profile,' she'd said.

Prescott swore. Why did Peter have to meet her first?

CHAPTER III

The eighteenth at Cromley is a longish par four, dog-leg to the right, with wild country to trap the slice.

It was Peter Reece's honour, his partner having squared by winning the previous hole.

They were well matched – Reece and Raven against Prescott and Frank Hornby; as often as not the game went to the last green. To-day the weather was typical of April and a boisterous wind made conditions difficult. After a squally shower at the tenth, Tim Raven had wanted to walk in, but was outvoted. He had sulked after that, until he sank that long putt on the seventeenth.

'The widow's mite' was how he described it. And it was apt enough, for he contributed little to the partnership. He didn't have to: Reece was a fine golfer, a four-handicap man who could have been scratch if he'd played more often.

He drove now at the eighteenth with his usual immaculate swing – no fuss, no preliminary flourishes – and sent a low ball boring into the wind, bisecting the fairway.

'God, it gets monotonous,' Hornby muttered to no one in particular.

Raven sliced into the scrub and didn't even bother to look for his ball; Prescott bunkered his second and eventually picked up; and it was left to Hornby to fight it out with Reece. Hornby's second was forty yards short. He mishit his third; the ball never rose from the ground, but rolled on until it pulled up inches from the cup. Hornby was jubilant.

Reece, twelve yards from the pin in two, putted short, leaving himself a two-footer to halve the match. He never missed from that distance: he had the ideal temperament – no nerves, no complexes.

Prescott took out the pin, and Reece lined up the putt. Then he stood aside and said angrily: 'For God's sake, John, do you have to wave that damned flag about?'

Prescott apologised stiffly and walked to the edge of the green. Reece putted and, inevitably, missed. His smile was a little forced as he handed over his half crown.

Hornby and Prescott were behind the other two as they pulled their caddy-cars to the clubhouse.

Hornby said: 'Have you ever known Peter lose his rag before?'

'Never.'

'I think he's overdoing things. Looks to me he's not getting enough sleep.'

'You're the doctor. You tell him.'

Afterwards, over drinks, Reece apologised to Prescott. 'I suddenly *knew* I was going to miss that tiddler.'

'It's the Shakes,' said Hornby. 'They've hit you at last.'

'What's the treatment, Doctor?'

'No known cure. You'll never be the same man again . . .' Then he added sympathetically: 'Have a bad day yesterday?'

Reece looked at him, hesitated, then said lightly: 'Yes. Norah persuaded me to put five quid on Peter The Great. So much for feminine intuition.'

Prescott often wondered how much Peter Reece spent on gambling. Horses, dogs, the pools – he could never resist a flutter.

'As an accountant,' Raven said, 'wouldn't you find it more profitable to play the market?'

'I do that too.'

'Ah yes,' said Hornby, 'but gambling from a distance is no fun, eh, Peter?'

Hornby and Reece went to race meetings together. Peter Reece was, indeed, the common link with the other three, although his friendship with each had a different foundation: with Hornby it was gambling, with Prescott music chiefly. With Raven? Prescott wasn't sure what the shared interest was there. Women, perhaps.

'Same again, everybody?' Hornby was saying. He was always first to finish his drink.

Frank Hornby was in his early thirties, a short, thickset man with fair hair and an engagingly ugly face; his misshapen nose was a battle scar from the rugby field. He had come to Cromley five years ago as assistant to Dr. Parry, was taken into partnership last year, and was now carrying the major burden of the practice.

A convivial man, he was to be found most nights in the golf

club, drinking whisky and exchanging bawdy stories. He was said to have a violent temper when roused, although Prescott had no direct evidence of it. At any rate the pugnacious set of the chin made it plain he was not to be trifled with. He was happily married, with one child and another on the way.

'I meant to tell you, Peter,' Hornby said. 'Your friend Norah Browne has registered with me.'

'I know. I advised her to.'

Tim Raven said: 'For a pessary?'

A second time Reece's temper flared. 'That's a filthy suggestion.'

Raven laughed. 'My God, Peter, don't play the innocent. We all know your record—'

'Boys, boys!' Hornby broke in. 'Behave yourselves.' He passed round his cigarettes. 'You can certainly pick them, Peter.'

'I haven't even met her yet,' Raven said.

Again Reece was quick to recover his composure. 'You shall, Tim, you shall. Father's giving a party next Saturday. The twenty-first. I hope you'll all come.'

'What sort of party?' Prescott heard himself ask. But he had guessed the answer.

Reece was smiling. 'Actually we got the ring yesterday. But we're keeping it unofficial till Norah's written her mother.'

Prescott joined in the ribald congratulations, but with a sense of defeat. Until now he'd deluded himself that Norah might be another of Peter's passing fancies, soon to be discarded . . .

'This calls for champagne,' he said and crossed to the bar to see about it. They were a long time producing a bottle; when he returned an argument was in progress.

'My dear Peter,' – Raven was at his most condescending – 'I'm only saying accountancy wouldn't appeal to *me*.'

'You've a damned insulting way of putting it: "cleaning up shop-keepers' grubby accounts".'

Hornby said: 'Get that bubbly poured, John, before they come to blows.'

But Reece wasn't finished. 'There would be a hell of a sight more dishonesty if it weren't for people like us. And it's not only *shopkeepers*...'

Prescott had poured the champagne. Frank Hornby pushed a glass across the table to Reece. 'Here, take that, and get off your soapbox.'

Reece stared at him, then slowly grinned. 'Thanks, Frank. I'm on edge to-day. I haven't been sleeping. Overworking, I think.'

Raven opened his mouth to say something, thought better of it.

'Come to my surgery to-morrow,' Hornby said. 'I'll give you something for it.'

'Maybe I will.'

After that the celebration fell flat. Hornby and Raven soon left. Prescott wanted to go too, for it was after seven o'clock, and Mrs. Jardine made a production of Sunday supper. But Reece asked him to stay and help him finish off the bottle.

'I made an ass of myself, didn't I, John?'

'What's the matter, Peter?'

Reece shrugged. 'This and that. Problems at the office, among other things ... If it weren't for Norah I'd be round the bend altogether.'

Again Prescott experienced disappointment. He had half convinced himself that Norah was the cause of Peter's jumpiness, that all was not going smoothly between them.

'I'd never have thought you worried about your work.'

'I don't as a rule. But this could be rather . . . awkward.' Abruptly Reece changed the subject. 'Have you been round to Ash Grove recently?'

'Once or twice.' He'd gone partly from habit, partly to use the piano (there was none in his lodgings). And partly, too, though he was reluctant to admit this, in the hope that Norah might be there. She wasn't; nor was Peter. Harriet told him Peter was out every night, either working late at the office, or with Norah. The golf continued only because Norah was busy with domestic chores on Sundays.

'What did you think of the old man?' Reece dropped the question out casually.

'Your father? He was out one of the nights too.'

'You don't know where?'

Prescott stared at him. 'What is all this, Peter?'

'Nothing. Forget it, John . . . Anyway Harriet would be glad to see you.'

'Harriet's a bloody nuisance. I had to help with her Latin prep.' Reece laughed. 'She's got it bad.'

'I'd rather she transferred her adolescent crush to someone else.' Then he added impulsively: 'She doesn't like Norah.'

'Give her time, John. Give her time.'

CHAPTER IV

The formal invitation, when it came on Monday, was to 'Mr. John Prescott and Partner,' and it appeared that it was to be more than a cocktail party. '21st April, 8 p.m. onwards,' it said: and 'Dancing.'

The choice of partner caused him some concern. 'Anyone but Alice Lowson' was his first reaction; in the end he was almost driven to her for lack of alternatives. Then he thought of his secretary, Nadine Smith, who was the sociable type and loved parties. She accepted his invitation with alacrity, probably because she guessed that Tim Raven would be there.

The party was in the ballroom of the Regent Hotel. When Prescott arrived with Nadine thirty or forty people were already there, many of them business friends of Peter's father, for whom an engagement party was an exercise in public relations. Drinks were already circulating.

Peter and Norah were receiving the guests, Norah radiant in a deep blue dress. As Prescott shook hands Peter whispered to him: 'You haven't seen the old man?'

'What?' Prescott had been feasting his eyes on Norah.

'Father hasn't turned up.'

'I haven't seen him. Want me to phone or something?'

'No, no. Better if he doesn't come at all than—' He broke off as Dr. Parry came up. 'Evening, Uncle David. Sorry Aunt Lucy couldn't make it . . . Yes, I did rather want a word with you. Three o'clock Sunday? Fine . . . You've met Norah, of course . . .' Prescott moved on.

He found Nadine a gin and french and an arm-chair. Then he spotted Harriet Reece standing by herself, defiantly sipping sherry.

'Just a minute,' he said to Nadine. 'There's someone I want you to meet.'

He brought Harriet over and introduced her.

'What a pretty dress,' Nadine said, and sounded as if she meant it. Prescott warmed to her.

The dress was a disaster. It made Harriet look thinner than ever;

and black was too sophisticated for her. She could have done with the advice of a mother or an older sister.

By half-past eight all the guests were assembled. Close on sixty, Prescott estimated. Waiters were edging dexterously through the crowd, carrying trays with drinks and savouries. On the platform the band was quietly improvising, almost inaudible above the hum of conversation.

Peter and Norah were mingling with the guests, although Peter kept glancing at his watch. At 8.35 Arthur Reece entered. Prescott watched Peter's expression: it showed relief tinged with anger.

Arthur Reece clapped his hands for silence. His speech was short. He apologised for being late but gave no explanation. He said he was glad his son approved his choice of secretary; and he told an irrelevant story about a previous secretary. He hoped his guests would have a pleasant evening.

The applause was uneasy. But then old Dr. Parry stepped into the breach. Speaking, he said, as the man who had brought Peter into the world and now as one of his clients, he would like to add a word or two to Arthur's felicitous phrases. He proceeded to say all the things Arthur ought to have said. The chestnuts rolled out and gradually the right mood was set for the toast to Peter and Norah.

Then dancing began. Prescott had the first two dances with Nadine, who was proving agreeable company. Then he took pity on Harriet.

It was a waltz. He realised after the first few steps that she was a natural dancer. She floated; and she seemed to anticipate every move he made.

'Where did you learn?' he asked.

'To dance? We have lessons at school. And Peter sometimes tries out steps with me ... Or he used to. It's fearfully *square*, though, isn't it?'

'What? Dancing?'

'This old-fashioned stuff.'

'Don't pose, Harriet: you love it.' No one could move like this and not enjoy it.

She grinned. 'With you, John, it's heaven! Let's dance cheek to cheek.'

'Harriet, behave yourself!'

She mimicked him: 'Harriet, behave yourself! Don't be a fuddy-duddy, John ... Anyway, look at *them*.'

It was Tim Raven and Nadine Smith, not literally cheek to cheek, but companionably close. She had been quick off the mark.

Harriet screwed up her face. 'That man makes me want to throw up.'

'It's not the common reaction.'

'I know. Girls are stupid, most of them.'

'Listen to the voice of experience.'

'John, I wish you'd take me *seriously* for once.'

He almost could. Her face was flushed, her eyes sparkling. For the first time he had a glimmering of what Raven had meant when he said she would be a winner one day.

The music stopped, and Harriet was once more a gawky fifteen-year-old in a dress too old for her.

There was a splutter of applause and the band started up again.

'Have you danced with Norah yet?' Harriet asked.

'No.'

'Are you going to?'

'I don't know.' He would if he could summon the courage.

'I wish she'd never come to Cromley. I wish Peter had never met her.'

'Don't be silly—'

'She's a bitch, that's what she is. A bitch.'

He was angry. 'Watch your language, Harriet!'

'Bitch, bitch, bitch, *bitch*!'

'And you're a spoiled brat. You need your bottom spanked.'

They danced in silence for a bit, then Harriet said: 'Everything's been lousy since she came. Peter's in a foul mood all the time. And as for Daddy, goodness knows what's eating *him*!'

'Why was he so late to-night?'

'I don't know. He made me go on ahead with Peter to – to collect Norah. He hadn't even *started* to dress. Peter was furious.' She paused while they executed a spin. 'Of course, they had a fearful row this afternoon.'

'Who did?'

'Peter and Daddy. They were shouting at each other.'

'What about?'

'I was in the kitchen. I turned up the radio so I wouldn't hear. It was *horrible*.'

The dance ended. 'Thank you, John,' Harriet said primly. 'You've done your duty. Now you can make a pass at Norah,'

'You little bitch!' he said involuntarily.

'Watch your language, John!' She smiled sweetly and walked away.

The party wasn't getting off the ground. The coolness between Peter and his father communicated itself to their guests.

Arthur Reece retired to one of the small tables at the end of the room and sat morosely drinking with Dr. Parry. Peter and Norah went over once, smiling, bearing the olive branch, Prescott guessed. But after a rapid exchange of words they retreated, Peter's face grim.

'That's a *horrible* man,' Nadine said to Prescott.

'Who?'

'Old Mr. Reece. Look at him.' He was in characteristic pose, lower lip thrust out aggressively, finger wagging at Dr. Parry to emphasise some point.

'He's not so bad when you know him,' Prescott said, to impress Nadine. He was, in fact, more than a little in awe of him.

'Who'd want to know him? They say he has more enemies to the square mile than—'

'They?' Prescott interrupted.

She laughed. 'All right, *Mr. Raven* says. He also says the old boy's a bit of a wolf. Apparently there's a girl in Hastonbury . . .'

John was annoyed. Tim Raven had no right to be spreading that kind of gossip.

Later he tackled Raven.

'My dear John,' was the reply, 'it's common knowledge. Why do you think Peter's so disgusted with him?'

'Who is the woman?' Prescott asked.

'Ah, that we don't know! My spies tell me she's a dish, though . . . Excuse me, I see my opportunity.'

A tango had been announced. Raven crossed the floor to Norah Browne. Prescott saw her smile to Peter and get up.

Raven specialised in the tango. His technique involved spectacular flourishes interspersed with quieter passages of close communion with his partner. Norah looked slightly startled the first time she was drawn into his embrace, but he soon had her smiling.

'Don't look so disapproving, John. Norah can take care of herself.' It was Peter.

'I dare say, but—'

Peter laughed. 'Still the old puritan . . . Norah's complaining you haven't danced with her yet.'

'I will.' But he had now no intention. 'Damn good party, Peter.'

'It's a rotten party and you know it . . . God, I'm tired.'

He looked it, too. 'Did you go to Frank?' Prescott asked.

'What?'

'For sleeping pills.'

'Oh that! Yes, I did.'

'Are they helping?'

'I suppose so. They give me hellish nightmares, though. I dreamt last night Father had been murdered.' He looked down the room. Arthur Reece was with Edward Lowson now, and they were arguing hotly. 'Might be prophetic at that,' he added.

'Come off it, Peter. You've been working too hard. Relax.'

Peter smiled. 'It's damn funny getting a pep talk from *you*. I had a blow-up with the old boy this afternoon—that's what's depressing me.'

'Harriet told me.'

Peter's eyes narrowed. 'Harriet? How much did she hear?'

'Nothing. She just heard you shouting at each other.'

'The truth is, John, Father's making an ass of himself and I'm trying to avoid a scandal.'

Hesitantly Prescott said: 'It may not be such a secret as you imagine.' He repeated what Tim Raven had told him.

'Oh hell! . . . You're sure he doesn't know who the girl is?'

'So he said.'

'That's something at least. I don't mind Father sowing the odd wild oat. But this girl is – well, let's just say she's highly unsuitable. For an intelligent man he can be extraordinarily dense – he actually meant to bring her here to-night.'

'I don't see why *you* should lose sleep over it.'

'You don't know the girl. Anyway, that's not my only worry. John, there's something I'd like to discuss with you – Oh, here's Norah!'

The tango had ended. Tim Raven was piloting Norah across the floor, his hand solicitously on her arm.

'She's superb,' he said, as he delivered her to her fiancé. 'We were *en rapport* from the first step, weren't we, Norah?'

'Very close indeed,' Norah agreed dryly.

Peter laughed. 'I've captured your tiger for you, darling.'

'What? Oh John! At last! Where have you been hiding?' She had turned her back on Tim Raven; and after some hesitation he walked away.

They danced. Although Norah didn't float like Harriet, she was more exciting to hold.

'Does he always behave like that?' Norah said.

'Who?'

'Your partner.'

Prescott looked across at the bald head of Edward Lowson, whose argument with Arthur Reece was still going on.

'No, not him,' Norah said. 'I mean that gigolo.'

'Oh *Tim*! What about him?'

'I only met him to-night and he acted as if – as if – well, he must be thoroughly familiar with my shape by now. He almost squeezed me to death.'

Prescott slackened the pressure of his arm and eased fractionally away. He was in danger of committing the same blunder.

'Tim's all right,' he said. 'He has his standards: he wouldn't try to—'

'Seduce me?' Norah suggested.

'That's right.' She gave him an odd look but didn't comment.

It was true about Raven. He would no more have an affair with a friend's fiancée than with a girl in his office. Not from moral scruples, but because of the inevitable complications. So Norah was safe, just as Nadine was safe.

'I see you've left off your glasses,' Norah remarked.

'Yes.'

'Because of what I said?'

'Partly.' He only wore them in the office now.

He was becoming tongue-tied again, but it was easier when you were dancing: you didn't *have* to talk all the time.

'Ouch!' Norah grimaced.

'*So* sorry!' Harriet Reece swept past, smiling sweetly.

Norah was angry. 'She did that on purpose. I saw her.'

'Oh no, Norah, I'm sure you're mistaken.' But Prescott lacked conviction.

'She needs a good spanking, that girl.'

'I've told her that already to-night.'

'One of these days she'll get it . . .' Then she smiled and said: 'No, it's not fair. She's never had a chance, poor child, with no mother and that terrifying man for a father.' It was a more charitable judgment than Harriet's on her.

'You find Peter's father terrifying?'

'He scares me rigid. He has us on tenterhooks at the office. The least mistake and he's roaring for blood.'

'You said the other night he was a dear.'

'A figure of speech.'

When the dance ended, Norah said: 'Come and talk to me, John. We've never had a chance, have we?'

'But Peter—'

'He's doing his duty over there.' Peter was in a laughing group which included his sister and Nadine Smith.

'All right. Let me get you a drink.'

Norah hesitated. 'A still orange, then. I've had two gins already. That's my limit.'

The more Prescott discovered about Norah, the more he liked her. She was not nearly so sophisticated as he had imagined.

When he returned with the drinks, Norah was massaging her ankle. Prescott still had enough of his father in him to look away: girls with a plunging neckline ought not to bend down.

'Painful?' he asked.

She smiled ruefully. 'Dear Harriet's signature will be with me for some little time . . . Thanks, John.'

He raised his glass: 'Good health! When's the wedding?'

'The autumn. Provided Peter can find the time . . .' She sounded resentful. 'Is he always as busy as this?'

'Busy as what?'

'He's back at the office till all hours two or three nights a week. If he'd only let me *help* him. . .'

'He seems worried,' Prescott said, wondering how much she knew.

Nothing, apparently. 'Worried? Not really. Just overtired. But let's not talk about Peter, let's talk about you, John. The strong, silent type always fascinates me. I'm curious to know what lies beneath the still waters.'

'In my case mud and sludge,' he said. 'Fears and inhibitions and memories.' He was suddenly more articulate, less in awe of her.

Norah stared at him. 'What a strange thing to say! Peter says you're fighting your past. Is that true?'

'Aren't we all?' But that sounded ponderous, and he added: 'Yes, it's true.'

'Peter says—'

He interrupted, suddenly angry. 'Peter says, Peter says . . . Why don't you form your own judgments?'

She was taken aback. 'Goodness, you looked so *fierce*, then, John.'

'I'm sorry—'

'Oh no, but I *like* it! Put that face on again, please.'

He couldn't; and they both laughed. 'Anyway,' he said, 'you're right to listen to Peter: he knows me better than I do myself.' He added casually, not meeting her eyes: 'I only wish you'd met me before you met Peter.'

She seemed not to hear.

It was twenty minutes to midnight. The party had come alive: there was a noisy crowd round the bar and the band was playing beat music for the younger guests.

A policeman came into the ballroom and spoke to Arthur Reece. They turned and stared across towards where Prescott and Norah were sitting. He knew before the policeman came over that it was a message for him: his mother was dead.

His offside rear tyre was flat.

Peter said: 'Are you driving there to-night?'

'Yes. I'll need to pack a case first—'

'Right. We'll change the wheel while someone drives you to your digs. Frank, would you—'

'There's no hurry, Peter.' There was all the time in the world now.

But Frank Hornby was already shepherding him to his car. 'No trouble, boy, no trouble at all.'

Prescott analysed his feelings. Grief? Yes, although his mother's death was not unexpected. And guilt; he'd meant to go and see her last week-end. But how could he have known? She'd been under the shadow for years.

His chief emotion was bitterness at the waste of it all. When she was young his mother had been gay, had loved music and dancing and parties. Then she met and married John's father, became a Prescott; was indoctrinated, brainwashed, crushed . . .

Frank Hornby's Zephyr swung out of the Regent car park and, with barely a pause, crossed the traffic of Mason Street and roared off towards the Tunnicliffe crossing.

Prescott was jolted out of his reverie when he saw the red lights ahead. 'Steady on, Frank,' he said.

The brake was slammed down, the car shuddered to a halt, front wheels on the line.

'All a matter of timing,' said Hornby. He was off again as soon as the amber joined the red.

'Sorry about your mother, John,' he said. 'What was it? Heart?'
'Yes.'

'Ah well, it comes to all of us . . . Now where the hell are my fags?' He fumbled in his pocket. The car's course became erratic.

'Frank!' Prescott said sharply. 'Keep both hands on the wheel. And *slow down* . . . Here, let me drive.'

'You wouldn't be suggesting I'm tight, would you?'

Prescott didn't answer. Hornby as a rule could hold his liquor. To-night he must really have hit the bottle hard: he hadn't danced, but had sat in a corner with one or two acquaintances and soaked it up.

The accident could have happened to anyone. Hornby had turned into Flanders Street and was slowing as he approached Prescott's lodgings when two youths ran, unheeding, across the road. There was a scream of brakes, a thud as one boy was struck a glancing blow, the car swerved wildly, mounted the pavement and came to rest against a wall.

Prescott was jarred but not hurt. Hornby opened his door and scrambled out; then put his head back in and hissed. 'Get into the driving seat, John.'

'What?'

'The *driving seat*. Quick! There's a copper coming.' And when Prescott still didn't move: 'For God's sake, it's my livelihood, don't you understand?'

He saw it now. 'I'm sorry, Frank. I can't do it.'

Hornby stared at him. 'Old Holy Joe, eh? . . . O.K., let's go see if the boy's hurt.'

CHAPTER V

John Prescott's mother was buried on the Tuesday, just two weeks after her sixtieth birthday. The whole Prescott clan had gathered for the funeral.

John was made to feel an outsider; in some obscure way he was blamed for his mother's death.

'Why didn't you come last week-end, John?' his father said. 'You promised to come. It broke her heart, that did.'

Why hadn't they told him she was so ill? They never wrote, his father, his brothers, his sister – never replied to his letters. It was his mother who'd always written, and she never mentioned her health.

As he stood at the graveside his mind was only half on the committal service, on the coffin lying by the open grave. He was looking out over the trees and shrubs of the cemetery to the rooftops of Fenleigh, to St. Michael's spire, the chimney of the dyeworks, the rugby posts on the Grammar School playing fields. All this was part of him, had moulded him, made him what he was. Just as these people gathered round the grave were part of him: his father, a little bent now, beginning to look old; his brothers; his sister, quietly sobbing into a handkerchief.

You couldn't escape from your past, it was a mistake to try. When the pinch came, the old values reasserted themselves. As on Saturday night, when Frank Hornby asked for help. The accident hadn't been caused by Hornby's drunkenness, even sober he couldn't have avoided it. He stood to lose so much: a doctor couldn't afford a scandal. Yet John had refused to tell the white lie that would have saved him; just as his father would have refused, or his brothers, or his cousins. He was a Prescott.

He drove straight back to Cromley from the funeral, was home by seven o'clock. Mrs. Jardine wasn't expecting him and was out. So he had a meal in the Southern Hotel.

He was restless and needed company, couldn't bear the thought of returning to his lodgings. He thought of Alice Lowson and phoned from the hotel lobby. He got Edward Lowson, who sounded happy to tell him Alice was otherwise engaged.

What now? Ash Grove was the remaining hope. He could always help Harriet with her Latin prose . . .

But as he drove up Hammond Road, he saw a light in the

window of Arthur Reece's office and recognised the silhouette of Peter's head. He stopped and got out.

It was a three-storied building, of which A. H. Reece and Son, C.A., occupied the middle floor.

Prescott climbed the stone stair, pulled the brass bell and heard its peal reverberating inside. He had to ring a second time before the door was opened.

'Oh it's you, John,' Peter said. 'Something wrong?'

'No, I was passing, and I noticed the light . . .'

Peter was looking at him uncertainly. Then he pulled himself together and said: 'Come in, then. Nice to see you.'

The office had been gutted and reconstructed two years ago. No expense spared. It contained all the latest gadgetry and everything was planned for maximum efficiency.

The door of Peter's room was open and Prescott saw the desk was heaped with papers.

'We'll use Father's room,' Peter said. 'It's less cluttered.'

He opened a door on the left and switched on the light. It was a small room, equipped with a row of maroon filing cabinets, desk with electric typewriters, telephone, and internal communication panel.

'Straight through,' Peter said, indicating the communicating door. 'Just a minute, though.' He pulled out the top drawer of the desk and started rummaging.

'This'll be Norah's room?'

'Yes.' There was no trace of her occupation, all was functional and impersonal, and immaculately tidy.

Peter was still searching. 'What are you looking for?' Prescott asked.

'Her office key. She asked me to see if she'd left it in her desk
. . . She's been ill, you know.'

'Norah has?'

'Yes, she had to get the doctor. But she's all right now. She'll be
back at work to-morrow.'

He straightened, closed the desk. 'Not here . . . Never mind,
let's go through.'

The inner room was large and richly furnished, with deep-piled
wall-to-wall carpeting, curtains on the windows, the walls oak-
panelled. The desk was walnut, the chairs upholstered in green
leather.

'Does himself well, doesn't he?' Prescott remarked.

'Yes.'

'That's one of his own, isn't it?' He indicated a water-colour on
a wall, depicting a cricket match on Selwyn Park. Painting was
Arthur Reece's hobby, and he had some talent.

Peter shrugged. 'Of course.'

Prescott detected impatience. 'I'm being a nuisance,' he said.
'I'll push off.'

'No, John. Sit down and talk . . . How were things at Fenleigh?'

Seeing him now in the light, Prescott was disturbed. He looked
more than tired, he looked ill: there were shadows under his eyes
and he'd lost his good colour.

Peter seemed to guess what was in his mind. 'I had another row
with Father to-day. He's impossible. Thinks he can do what he
damn well pleases and to hell with the consequences.'

'You mean he won't give up this girl?'

Peter nodded. 'He's getting careless – it's bound to leak out
soon. And I don't believe the old devil would care . . .'

Prescott was puzzled why Peter was so concerned.

'Have you ever had a premonition, John, that – well, that some-thing terrible was going to happen?'

'All the time. I'm a pessimist by nature.'

'No, I'm serious. I had that dream again last night. That Father was dead – murdered. I know it's silly, but—'

'It *is* silly.'

'He's so bloody cantankerous. He's even fallen out with Edward Lowson, the one real friend he has.'

'Do you see Lowson as the potential murderer?'

Peter smiled. 'No, I'm just depressed, that's all. And dead beat.'

'What are you doing here at this hour, then?'

'Working.'

'On what?'

Peter hesitated. 'I'm not sure of my facts, John, I must be certain of my facts first. After that I'd appreciate your advice.' He looked at his watch. 'Like to do me a favour?'

'Surely.'

He had left Norah at Ash Grove, where they'd had dinner – it was her first time out since the week-end. She and Harriet were watching television.

'I said I'd be back by nine o'clock, but I'm not nearly through. Go and keep her company, John, and if I'm not there by eleven, run her home, would you?'

'You ought to pack it in, Peter—'

'I can't. *Please*, John . . .'

Harriet impulsively threw her arms round Prescott. 'Oh John! I was so sorry to hear about your mother.'

'Thanks, Harriet. Where's Norah?'

She disengaged herself. 'In the sitting-room,' she said coldly.

The television set was off and Norah, looking bored, was leafing through a magazine. The sparkle returned to her face when she saw who had come in.

'Ah, it's the tiger!' she said.

'The what?' said Harriet.

Norah smiled sweetly. 'Private joke, darling.'

'Don't darling me!' Harriet muttered, not quite under her breath, as she sat down at a card table where her school books were spread out. Then aloud: 'Just you two chat. Don't mind me.'

Prescott described his visit to Peter's office.

Norah was annoyed. 'Might not be back till after eleven!' she repeated. 'He should take his bed to that office.'

'I thought he looked tired.'

'Of course he looks tired. He's working like a slave.' She smiled. 'However, he's sent a very acceptable stand-in.'

'Norah!' Harriet said, without looking up from her books.

'Yes?'

'What's the French for "bitch"?'

Silence, then Norah said evenly: 'I told you already, Harriet, I don't know any languages.'

'I thought you might know that particular word.'

It was too much. Prescott said: 'I think you should apologise for that remark, Harriet.'

'I didn't mean anything. There's a sentence here about a female dog—'

'Don't prevaricate. Say you're sorry to Norah.'

She tossed her head. 'Sorry, Norah.'

'You don't sound it. You're an insolent brat. You need—'

She stood up, the tears flowing. 'I need my bottom spanked.

That's all anyone ever says to me.' Blindly she gathered up her books; the card table crashed over. 'Well, don't say I didn't warn you, John.' She flounced out and slammed the door.

'Don't take it to heart, Norah. She's just a spoiled child. She'll grow out of it.'

Norah's hand trembled as she lit a cigarette. 'No, John. I've made every allowance, I've *tried* to like her. But she's impossible. Do you know what she was doing before you came in? Baiting me because I don't know any Latin or algebra or French . . . I was earning my living at her age.'

She described her earlier life. She came from Ellswick, a small town twenty miles east of Cromley, where her father had been an electrician. He died when she was twelve. As there were three younger children in the family, Norah insisted on leaving school and taking a job as soon as she legally could.

'It was no great loss to scholarship,' Norah said, smiling. 'I wasn't clever. Unlike Miss Know-all up there.' She raised her eyes to the ceiling; they could hear Harriet stomping about upstairs.

Norah worked in the Electricity Board office in Ellswick, attending classes in the evening. Three years ago, at twenty, when her family was no longer dependent on her earnings, she took up her roots and moved to London, where she found a job as secretary to a consultant surgeon.

She returned to Ellswick last Christmas when her mother had a serious illness. After the mother recovered, Norah found she didn't want to go back to London. Arthur Reece had just advertised for a secretary; Norah applied and she was appointed.

If Prescott had been inventing a setting for his ideal woman, it would have been on these lines: a girl of humble origin who had made her own way in life, who had supported her widowed mother, who after sampling life in the metropolis still preferred the slower pace of the provinces.

'That's a very pretty dress,' he said suddenly. It was pale blue in a soft woollen material.

'It's too tight for me – I've put on weight since I came to Cromley.'

'You look all right to me.'

Norah laughed. 'Thanks, John. But Dr. Hornby's advised me to take more exercise.'

It reminded him. 'Peter said you've been ill?'

'Just a tummy upset.' She looked at him curiously. 'Dr. Hornby was telling me about his accident. I believe you were in the car?'

He'd almost forgotten. 'Yes, what's happening about that?'

'He's been charged . . . Was he drunk?'

'If he was, it wasn't the cause of the accident.'

'But if he *was* drunk, if he's found guilty—'

'It could be serious.' He explained about the Disciplinary Committee of the General Medical Council.

They heard a car change gear as it turned into the drive.

'There's Peter now,' Norah said.

'No, it's the Jaguar. It'll be the old man.' They heard the car being put away, then the front door opened.

Arthur Reece, still in his overcoat, looked into the sitting-room. 'Where's Peter?' he asked.

'At the office,' Norah said flatly.

Reece frowned. 'What the hell is he up to?' he muttered. Then he turned to Prescott. 'Well, John, I was right and you were wrong, eh?'

The laundry company had thrown in the towel. Rather than face the publicity of a court action they were meeting the claim in full.

'Yes,' Prescott agreed. 'You were right.' Right in the tactical sense; not morally.

'You're young, John, you'll learn. Be tough, that's the lesson.' He yawned. 'God, I'm whacked. I'm off to bed.'

Prescott wondered if he'd been visiting his mistress.

Reece paused at the door and said to Norah: 'You'll be back to work to-morrow, will you?'

'I hope so,' Norah said.

'Young people are soft nowadays. A tickle in the throat and they're off for a week.' He went out.

Norah smiled. 'Charming man, isn't he? Of course, he doesn't approve of me.'

'Why not?'

'I'm a typist. I'm not good enough for his son ... Here, John, look at the time! What can be keeping Peter?'

It was 11.20. 'I'll run you home,' he said.

Norah had rooms in a bungalow on Westerlands Avenue almost opposite the Lowsons' house.

'You'll come in for a drink, John?'

When he hesitated she laughed and said: 'Worried about your reputation?'

'No – yours.'

'For heaven's sake, this is 1962! Still, perhaps you're right. My landlady's in Scotland at the moment.' She opened the car door. 'Thanks for the lift.'

The temptation was too great. 'Well, just for a few minutes,' he said.

As they stood in the doorway while Norah got the key from her bag, a girl's footsteps clip-clopped along the opposite pavement, stopped, and a gate creaked. Prescott looked across. It was Alice Lowson. He wondered if she'd seen him.

Norah opened the door and they went in. As she was putting her key back in her bag, she said: 'Peter didn't mention my office key, did he?'

'Yes. He looked in your desk but it wasn't there.'

She seemed puzzled, but didn't comment. She took him into a small sitting-room, switched on the light.

'I'll get you a drink,' she said. 'I'm afraid I've only sherry.'

'I like sherry,' he lied.

The room was warm; it had electrical central heating. The decor was pleasant but anonymous: only the photographs on the mantel pointed to Norah. One was of Peter, the other of a woman who was clearly Norah's mother.

Norah was away a long time. When she reappeared, carrying a tray with glasses and a decanter of sherry, she was in a short blue housecoat.

'That dress was killing me,' she said. She laid down the tray. 'Now let's be really cosy.' She switched on a table lamp, put off the centre light.

As she poured the sherry, she said: 'What I like about you, John – there you are, I warn you it's foul – what I like about you is you're so dependable. I mean, here's the stage set for a seduction, and yet I know I'm safe.'

Not to-night, she wasn't, Prescott thought. He was in a mood of scarcely controlled excitement: reaction, no doubt, from the strain of the past few days. And the stage *was* set for a seduction . . .

'Cheers!' Norah said and made a face.

'Cheers!' he echoed. She was right; the sherry *was* foul.

Norah laid her glass on the hearth and curled herself on the rug beside his chair. Her face was in shadow; the pool of yellow light shone on her bare legs. Shapely legs. He wondered what she was wearing under the loosely tied housecoat . . .

'How long have you known Peter?' Norah asked.

Peter's name sobered him. 'Six years. Nearly seven,' he said.

'Has he always been moody?'

'Moody? Peter? Never!' Then he realised he was speaking of the past. 'I've never known him like this before. Something's upsetting him.'

'*I'm* upsetting him.'

'Nonsense.'

'He's avoiding me. Look what happened to-night. I think he's regretting our engagement.'

When Prescott tried to reassure her, he found himself saying instead: 'If only I'd met you first, Norah . . .'

She was looking up at him, not speaking. Her face was still in shadow, but he thought he recognised an invitation. He should have despised her, but he was past the stage of logical thought.

She was not, as he had imagined, naked under the housecoat. That was the first cold douche. Also, although she didn't actively resist, she was limp and uncooperative.

Prescott quickly broke away. 'I'm sorry, Norah,' he said.

'My fault entirely.' Norah's voice was shaky. 'I should never have tempted you.'

'How could I have imagined that you—'

'Forget it, John. Drink your sherry.' She handed him his glass. His only thought was to escape, but he took the glass from her.

Norah grinned. 'I felt the claws of the tiger to-night.' She was massaging her arm. 'That'll be black and blue to-morrow.'

*

It was 12.45 when Prescott left. Deliberately he looked across at the Lowsons' house. In the light of a street lamp he thought he saw a face at an upstairs window.

CHAPTER VI

The last Sunday in April began like any other. Details were impressed indelibly on Prescott's mind, not because they seemed important at the time, but because of what happened before the day was out.

Mrs. Jardine brought him breakfast in bed, as she did every Sunday. She was dressed for church in her Sunday black, which differed from her week-day clothes only in being blacker.

She handed him the tray and the *Observer* and the *Times* with her usual comment on the weight of the papers. She asked, as she always did, if he wanted another egg; he gave the expected negative reply.

She hovered. 'Mr. Raven phoned.' She had departed from the script.

'What did he want?'

'He's not able to play golf to-day.'

There would only be Peter and himself, then. Frank Hornby had called off yesterday.

Prescott browsed over the papers till the church bells were ringing, then shaved and had his bath. Those bells stirred his conscience: although he was an agnostic nowadays, it was with a backward look over his shoulder.

Mrs. Jardine returned at 12.30 and began the leisurely preparation of lunch. Prescott had long since given up offering to help: she didn't approve of men in her kitchen.

He had the sermon with the soup and a catalogue of the congregation with the joint. He suspected her of proselytising.

'Alice Lowson was there,' she said to-day.

Well, *that* was no recommendation.

'And that dark girl – your friend's sister—'

'Harriet Reece?'

'Yes. Going to be very pretty, that one.'

'You think so?'

Mrs. Jardine nodded emphatically. 'Mark my words, she'll suddenly blossom, like a flower.' She tossed a scrap of meat to Smudge, who attended every meal, snuffling in expectation. Then she coughed delicately: Prescott recognised her advance apology for a piece of scandal. 'They say as how her father is doing a line in Hastonbury.'

'Doing a line, Mrs. Jardine?'

She coloured. 'Of course I can't vouch for the truth of it. But Mrs. Potts said . . .'

If Mrs. Potts knew, everyone in Cromley would soon know. Prescott wondered if Mrs. Potts could put a name to the girl.

It was Prescott's turn to pick up Peter Reece. The day was warm and sunny, although rain was forecast for later.

As he drove up Marsden Hill, he savoured the names on the gates: Long Row, Glandersley, Abbotsford, Shepherd's Fell, Ash Grove . . .

No one answered when he rang. But, hearing the sound of racquet on ball, he went round the side and found Harriet practising tennis strokes against the wall. She was in a sweater and white shorts.

'Peter's gone out,' she called. 'He left you a note.' She went on slamming the ball against the wall, whipping it viciously back. She had a good eye, like her brother.

As Prescott waited, she added, still not looking at him: 'It's on the hall table. The door's not locked.'

It said: 'Sorry, John – can't make it to-day. Just remembered I hadn't told you. Come round to-night and I'll give you the gen. Nine o'clock do? P.'

Prescott went out and rejoined Harriet, who ignored him. Eventually he intercepted the ball and wouldn't let her have it.

'I'll only keep you a minute,' he said.

'That's as much as you can stand of me, isn't it?' She must still be smarting from Tuesday night.

'Where did Peter go?' he asked.

'I don't know. He got a phone call and went dashing off.'

'Why didn't he ring me?'

Harriet shrugged. 'He seemed in a tearing hurry.'

Ah well, he'd get the explanation to-night. It would have to be good . . . 2.35: he could probably still get a partner at the club.

'Please may I have my ball back?'

The unhappiness in her voice came through to him. In previous years when he'd visited Peter, Harriet, if she was there at all, was one of a gang of noisy, obstreperous children. Even last summer she hadn't lacked for company.

He gave her the ball. 'Where are all your friends, Harriet?'

'I haven't any.'

'Don't be silly.'

She was bouncing the ball on her racquet. 'They've no time for me any more. All they think of is boys.' '

Aren't you interested in boys?'

She didn't answer. He saw a tear running down her cheek.

Prescott abandoned thoughts of golf. 'The Hastonbury courts opened yesterday,' he said. 'If I could borrow some gear of Peter's . . .'

Harriet continued to bounce the ball. 'I don't want your pity,' she said haughtily.

'Don't you?'

She grinned. 'Yes, I do.'

They played three sets. Prescott was impressed by the power and agility of this fifteen-year-old. The appearance of awkwardness that the thin legs and arms gave was an illusion. He should have known from the way she danced . . .

'You're *terrific*, John,' she said as they came off the court.

'No, just ordinary. In two years' time you'll leave me standing.'

She wouldn't have it.

'Want an ice-cream or something?' Prescott suggested.

'No, let's go home and have a picnic on the lawn.'

They were driving along Hastonbury's main street, with Harriet chattering happily, when Prescott suddenly interrupted. 'Is that Tim Raven?' he said, indicating the pavement on their right.

Harriet looked out. 'That man in the brown suit? That's not the *least* like Tim! Anyway I think it was Tim that Peter—Here, where are you going, John?'

He had turned down a side street. 'Sorry. Have I turned off too soon?'

'It's nearly a mile to the junction. Goodness, that's not like you! Never mind, you'll get back up farther along.' She continued to chatter.

He'd been successful in his ruse to prevent her seeing what he had seen: on the near pavement, arm in arm, Arthur Reece and a woman. She was in a green suit and green shoes. He hadn't seen her face properly, but she looked young – not much older than Norah Browne . . .

They had their picnic at the foot of the lawn, in the sunshine, sheltered by the ash trees from the gentle breeze. Tea and chicken sandwiches.

'The chicken was for supper to-night,' Harriet confessed. 'But they can just go hungry.' Sunday was the housekeeper's day off and Harriet was in charge.

After they had eaten Harriet sat on the swing that was suspended from a branch of the tallest tree and got him to push her.

'Higher, John, higher!' she kept shrieking. And when she finally tired of it and came to rest, she said 'I've never been so happy. Never in all my life.'

They walked down the path between the trees to the gate. Stone steps led down from it to Mason Street.

'Does anyone ever use the back way?' Prescott asked.

'Oh yes! This is how I go to school every day.' It was the quickest route into town if you hadn't a car.

Prescott leant on the gate and looked out. The sun was still bright, although clouds were banking to the west; the smoke rose almost straight from the chimneys. It was a peaceful, idyllic scene: Cromley on a Sunday afternoon in spring.

He couldn't account for his uneasiness. Perhaps it was guilt over Harriet: he was aware of her schoolgirl crush and should have discouraged it. Also he couldn't obliterate from his mind the picture of her father with that girl . . .

Harriet noticed that the door of the toolshed was open. It was a wooden shed hard against the fence that bounded Ash Grove from the neighbouring property.

Prescott went over and found that the lock was burst: last week's gale, probably. He glanced inside. It contained a lawnmower and

other gardening implements, several folding chairs and miscellaneous bric-a-brac. He effected a temporary repair and closed
the door.

He refused Harriet's invitation to stay for supper. When he left
at ten past six, Peter had not yet returned; nor had his father.

At five minutes to nine Prescott turned into the drive of Ash Grove
for the third time that day. It was already dark, and the first spots
of rain were falling. Peter's Mini was outside the front door; there
was no sign of the Jaguar.

Harriet came to the door. She had changed into a pinafore dress
and had obviously gone to some trouble with her hair and make-up.
A big purple brooch was pinned to her dress.

'You're out of luck,' she said. 'Peter's not here.'

Prescott was really angry this time.

'Calm down, John. He won't be long. He went out not long ago
he didn't even put a coat on.'

'It's beginning to rain—'

'He'll be back all the sooner, then . . . Recognise the brooch?'

'No. Should I?'

Harriet didn't answer. She took him into the sitting-room.
'It's not Peter I'm bothered about,' she said. 'It's Daddy. He's not
home yet.'

'Any idea where he is?' Prescott asked cautiously.

'Not the slightest. But he said he'd be in for supper . . .'

She'd lost all the sparkle of the afternoon. 'I just don't matter to
them,' she said. 'Peter scarcely uttered a word at supper – I might have
been part of the furniture. I wish Daddy would let me board at school:
I *loathe* being at home now that Peter's engaged to Norah Browne.'

It was the first mention of Norah to-day. Prescott had been

trying to shut her from his thoughts: last Tuesday was too un-comfortable a memory . . .

By half-past nine neither Peter nor his father had returned. The rain was now battering on the window panes.

'Where on earth can they be?' Harriet said.

'Which way did Peter go?'

'He heard a knock at the back door. He went out and didn't come back. I thought Tim Raven must have called for him.' Raven lived with his sister in Mason Street.

'If you're anxious, why not phone Tim?'

Margaret Raven answered. Prescott could hear her words: 'Peter? . . . No, I'm sorry, dear, he's not here.'

Harriet put down the phone.

For no tangible reason Prescott was alarmed. 'Have you a torch, Harriet? I'm going down the garden.'

'I'll come with you.'

'No, stay here. No use both of us getting soaked, and anyway one of them might phone.' He tried to speak lightly.

The wind had risen and was whipping rain into his face as he picked his way down the lawn between the shrubs. It was totally dark apart from the thin pencil of light from his torch.

An irregular banging ahead told that the door of the toolshed had burst its lock again.

He reached the end of the lawn and found the path between the trees, which were creaking and groaning in the wind. Almost at once his torch picked out, just off the path, a wooden chair lying on its side. That hadn't been there this afternoon.

As he bent to take a closer look something struck him lightly on the small of the back; and again a second later. The swing, he thought, as he swivelled the torch.

It wasn't the swing. It was a shoe, two shoes, two trousered legs, dangling, swaying obscenely twelve inches off the ground.

A moment of horrified incomprehension, then Prescott was gripping the legs, supporting the weight. 'Harriet!' he shouted; the wind swept the sound into the blackness. He began to swear.

But Harriet appeared at his side almost at once: she must have followed him down the garden.

'What's happened—'

'An accident. Get the garden shears.'

She began to scream.

'Shut up,' he shouted at her. 'Get the shears!'

She continued to wail but disappeared into the darkness. Prescott was sweating and swearing under his burden. It was too late, he knew it was too late, but he had to try.

He heard sounds coming from the toolshed. She'd never find anything in this blackness, he should have given her the torch. But presently she was back, panting and sobbing.

'Put that chair up,' he ordered her. 'Now can you hold him?' Harriet gasped as she took the weight.

Prescott took the shears, stood on the chair, shone the torch on the rope. Then, throwing down the torch, he started hacking at the rope with the shears. They were blunt.

Below, Harriet was wailing: 'Oh Daddy, Daddy!'

'Look out!' he shouted as the blades rasped through the last strands. The body slipped gently to the ground.

Prescott jumped down, retrieved the torch. The face was suffused, the eyes bulging, the skin cold as a pebble. Nothing could be more dead than that, he thought. But he went through the motions, cut away the rope round the neck, applied the kiss of life.

Harriet had lost control, wasn't even looking. She lay drumming her heels in the ground and screaming: 'My daddy's killed himself! My daddy's dead!'

At that moment Prescott felt no pity for her, only irritation. 'It's not your father,' he said sharply. 'It's Peter.'

CHAPTER VII

The second shock silenced Harriet. Afterwards Prescott thought she grew up in that moment.

She stood up, came over beside him, picked up the torch and watched.

'He's dead, isn't he?' she said.

'Yes.' But he went on breathing into the lifeless mouth.

'He was always so good. He never did anything mean, did he, John?' She began to weep, but quietly now.

'Phone the police, Harriet,' he said.

'No, I want to stay.'

'There's nothing you can do here now.'

'I want to stay,' she repeated stubbornly.

After ten minutes Prescott gave up. He knew – had known from the start – it was a corpse that lay stretched on the grass.

He stood up, put his arm round Harriet. Through her macintosh he felt her trembling.

Headlights silhouetted the house as a car came up the drive. Arthur Reece had returned.

'Let me break it to him,' Harriet said.

'Are you sure you want to?'

'I'm all right now.' She walked towards the house, pointing the torch at her feet.

Prescott stayed by the body. His mind was numbed, hadn't fully grasped what had happened. Later the feeling of guilt would come: he should have guessed – they all should have guessed – that this might happen. Peter had shown the signs of intolerable strain.

Prescott took out his cigarettes, put one in his mouth. In the gusty rain he had difficulty lighting it. He was drawing on the third match between cupped hands when its flicker showed something white protruding from a pocket of Peter's jacket. He pulled it out. It was a sodden envelope, sealed. He lit another match: the one word 'Father' was typed on the envelope.

The house was all lit up now. Prescott saw the back door open and close. The beam of a more powerful torch moved towards him.

Arthur Reece gazed down at his son's mottled face. 'Christ!' he said wearily. 'Why did he have to do it?'

Prescott said nothing: what was there to say?

Reece gazed a long time, then turned away. 'Thanks for all you did, John. Harriet told me.' His voice was flat.

'The police . . .?' Prescott murmured.

'Harriet's phoning them.'

Prescott gave him the envelope. His reactions were slow. He stared at it, then stuffed it in his pocket.

They walked back to the house together.

The machinery of the law swung into action. Cars rolled up with uniformed police and C.I.D. Old Dr Parry, who was police surgeon for Cromley, arrived and joined the flashing cameras down at the plantation. He looked more shattered than Arthur Reece himself:

he had been fond of Peter. At half-past eleven the body was carried up the garden, put in the mortuary van and driven off.

Meanwhile in the house the questioning proceeded. The C.I.D. had commandeered Arthur Reece's study and took statements in turn from Harriet, from Prescott, from Reece himself.

When Prescott came out, Reece said to him: 'Did you tell them about the note?'

'Damn it, no, I forgot!'

'Never mind – I'll let them see it.'

'Did it give any reason?' Prescott asked.

Reece hesitated. 'You'll hear soon enough,' he said.

Back in the sitting-room Harriet was sitting silent, dry-eyed, deathly white. A uniformed constable stood, as if on guard, at the door.

Prescott spoke to him. 'You won't need Miss Reece any more, will you? She can go to bed?'

'I could ask Inspector Hayman, sir . . .'

'I'm not going to bed,' Harriet said. Her tone brooked no argument.

The minutes ticked past.

'What about Norah?' Prescott said suddenly.

No answer.

'She'll have to be told.' And when Harriet's lips remained un-compromisingly closed: 'Damn it, she's Peter's fiancée, she has the right—'

'She has *no* rights,' Harriet burst out. 'If she'd never cast her spell on Peter, he'd be alive to-day.'

'That's not fair, Harriet.' He turned to the constable. 'Ask Inspector Hayman if it's all right for me to go and tell Miss Browne, would you?'

'You couldn't just phone her, sir?'

'Not with this kind of news, no.' The urge to go to Norah had become overwhelming.

The man went out. Harriet said: 'I warn you, John, if you visit that – that woman to-night, I'll never speak to you again.'

Permission was given.

'Good night, Harriet.' Prescott bent over to kiss her. She jerked her head away. 'Don't touch me!' she spat at him.

It was 12.45 when he rang Norah's bell. To-night he didn't even glance across at the Lowsons'. He wondered if the landlady was still away. He rang again. A light came on and Norah's voice called: 'Who is it?'

'Let me in, Norah,' he said. 'It's John Prescott.'

She opened the door. 'What's wrong?' And then, seeing his face: 'It's Peter, isn't it?'

'He's dead, Norah,' he said gently.

He caught her arm as she swayed and helped her into the sitting-room. She was wearing the same blue housecoat. He made her lie on the couch while he told the story.

She took it quietly to begin with, then the tears began to flow.

'I knew it couldn't last,' she sobbed. 'He was too good for me.'

'Don't say that, Norah.'

'It's true! I've done rotten things but – but I would have made him a good wife. I would have *tried* . . .'

It was like a confessional. On and on she went, never quite specific, veering from the point, repeating herself; but he could piece it together. In London she had been more than a secretary to the surgeon: she had been his mistress. Then, sickened of the life, she came home to start afresh. Her one ambition was to find a decent husband, to have a normal home life, bring up a family.

She met Peter Reece, he fell in love with her, proposed to her. She told him of her past; he was prepared to take the risk. And now this . . .

Prescott was moved. He was in no doubt that her story was genuine, her grief for Peter real.

One question remained. 'Last Tuesday,' he said, 'when I was here, did you—'

She nodded tearfully. 'I didn't mean any harm,' she said. 'I wanted to prove to myself that you weren't—'

'Queer?' he suggested.

'No, not that. You were a challenge. You seemed so *cold* . . . I thought you despised me. I just wanted to be reassured . . .'

Norah talked of Peter, of what they'd done together, the fun they'd had. She needed reassurance there, too: Prescott had to keep telling her she wasn't the cause of Peter's suicide.

'Why did he do it, then?'

'I don't know. He left a note for his father. I expect—'

'Not for me? There you are: that shows how little he cared for me.' And she was off again.

He let her talk. Twice he made a move to go but she wouldn't let him. He was sitting uncomfortably on the floor beside the couch holding her hand.

At 2.15 the telephone rang. Norah jerked upright, frightened.

'You answer it, John,' she said.

'At this hour? I can't possibly . . . I expect it's the police.'

Norah crossed warily to the telephone and lifted the receiver. 'Yes?'

Prescott heard a harsh, angry voice at the other end of the line. He saw Norah go white, clench her knuckles.

'I know,' she said. 'John's told me . . . John Prescott.'

Another metallic stream of words, then Norah said: 'Oh my God! He can't have!' The flow continued; several times she tried to interrupt, glancing over her shoulder at Prescott. Finally she managed to say: 'John's here . . . That's what I'm telling you, he's *still here*. What! *Now? To-night?* But what can I . . . Yes, I suppose so, but . . .' The man's voice crackled some more, then there was a click.

Norah, looking dazed, replaced the receiver.

'Who was it?' Prescott asked.

'Peter's father,' she said slowly, as if rehearsing a part. 'Peter's been embezzling money from the firm.'

'I don't believe it!'

'He admitted it in the note he left. His father wants me to go round to the office now to check with him.'

'*To-night?* He must be crazy.'

She looked frightened. 'I think he is a little crazy . . . He said he had to wait till Harriet was in bed and asleep . . . But I'm going.'

'Don't be silly, Norah.'

'I have to. I owe it to Peter . . . Come and help me dress. I've to be there in twenty minutes.'

He saw she was shivering. 'Have you brandy in the house?'

'No, only that dreadful sherry. There's no time anyway.' She went out, crossed the passage, switched on another light.

'John!' she called. 'Come and talk to me, John.'

Her bedroom was small and compact. Fawn curtains, brown carpet, light oak furniture. Not Norah's choice, he was sure. The bed clothes were rumpled; she'd obviously been in bed when he arrived.

She had taken off her housecoat. Under it was a short, pale blue nightdress. That was coming off too.

She was unconscious of Prescott except as a straw to cling to, a last link with sanity. She was near to hysteria, words were pouring from her mouth. Wild words: about embezzlement, and Peter's gambling, and his generosity and how it was all her fault.

'Control yourself, Norah!' he said sharply. But her voice rose, she became more frenzied still.

He slapped her face.

That silenced her. She drew her hand slowly over her cheek, staring at him. Then she said: 'I'm sorry, John . . . Hand my skirt over, would you?'

He had to fix it for her, her hands were shaking so much. But the hysteria didn't return.

In the car she clung to him, still trembling. He realised this was more than grief and shock, there was fear as well.

'You don't have to do this, Norah,' he said. 'He can't make you.' She didn't answer.

He stopped on Hammond Road, outside the Reeces' office. There was no sign of Arthur's car and no light in any of the windows.

'I'll have to wait for him,' Norah said. 'I've lost my key.'

They sat in the darkness. Norah had snuggled close; he felt the pressure of her shoulder on his, of her thigh on his.

The kiss and the embrace were spontaneous and inevitable. He knew he was going to hate himself for it; but he couldn't resist. This time Norah's lips were soft and compliant.

They didn't hear the Jaguar pull up behind them. It was only when a car door slammed that Norah gasped and broke away. Arthur Reece was already on the pavement striding into the building.

Could he have seen? Prescott thought not. There was no light in the car, and Reece would have been driving on his side-lights.

A light went on in a first floor window. Norah had begun to tremble again.

'Wait for me, John,' she said as she got out of the car.

'No. Let him drive you home.'

'*Please*, John!'

'No, I daren't . . .'

She nodded, seemed to understand. 'Thanks for everything,' she said.

He watched her disappear into the building. He rolled down the car window, listened to her footsteps on the stone staircase, faintly heard the bell ring, a door open and close. Then he drove away.

He was thinking of Peter. Of Peter arguing good-humouredly over a pint of beer – he'd always loved an argument; of Peter at the piano, on the golf course, the hockey field. He'd had such a zest for life, and such a gift for friendship. 'He never did anything mean,' Harriet had said: an epitaph to be envied.

Prescott's thoughts turned to Norah. Peter would understand what happened to-night. 'It didn't mean anything, Peter,' he said aloud. 'Just two unhappy people sharing their grief.' It was a lie; but Peter would understand that too . . .

CHAPTER VIII

The inquest was held on the Wednesday in a packed court-room.

Dr. Parry gave the medical evidence. It was his swansong, for in the summer he was retiring from practice and from his police appointment. None too soon, Prescott thought: he had aged a lot in the last year. To-day he looked especially frail.

He described his examination of Peter Reece's body at Ash Grove and the subsequent post-mortem. In medical language he explained the cause of death.

The coroner, himself a doctor, said, glancing at the jury: 'In lay terms, Dr. Parry, what you're saying is that the deceased died from strangulation? Am I right?'

'That is so.'

'From your observation and from your professional experience did you form any conclusion as to the manner of death? Could it, for example, have been an accident?'

'I have no doubt at all that it was self-inflicted.'

'You mean suicide?'

'Just so.'

'One final question, Doctor: did the post-mortem reveal any other injuries besides the ones you have described? Or any disease?'

Years afterwards Prescott was to try to remember Dr. Parry's manner as he answered. Had there been hesitation? His impression was 'yes.'

The actual reply, according to the records, was: 'There was no other relevant injury and no sign of organic disease.'

No one at the time saw significance in the word 'relevant,' no one recognised the first warning that all was not as it seemed.

Prescott himself was the next witness. He described finding the body, cutting it down, and his efforts to revive it. He was impressed by the coroner, who had the rare gift, in holders of that office, of sticking to the point.

As he gave his evidence Prescott was watching Harriet Reece, who sat in the front row, staring at her feet. He willed her to look up, but she didn't.

She continued to avoid his eye when she herself was testifying. She had little to add, except that the chair found near the body had come from the toolshed, and the rope likewise. She was asked about the knock on the back door. She hadn't heard it, she said. Peter had been in the hall and had called to her that someone was at the door and that he would answer it. A few minutes later she heard the door close. She never saw Peter alive again.

Police evidence was presented next: mostly on measurements, heights, distances. And fingerprints – Peter's prints had been found on the chair. Detective Inspector Hayman gave his opinion that not only were all the signs consistent with suicide, they were conclusive of suicide.

Cause of death; circumstances of death; evidence of suicide. And now, logically, reason for suicide. The one piece of drama in the whole proceedings came when Arthur Reece read out the letter his son had left for him. He read it in his clipped, toneless voice, rapidly and without emotion.

'My dear Father,

If you have not already suspected defalcations in our accounts, you must very soon become aware of them. I make no excuses: I have gambled and lost; gambled again and lost more heavily. Or should I say our *clients* have lost – it was their money.

I think Norah suspects. I am too weak to confess to her, much too weak to confess to you, Father. So I am taking the easy way out. Please don't think too harshly of me.

Be kind to Norah.

Your loving son,

Peter.'

It was the second clue, and it was ignored like the first. Peter was neither weak nor dishonest: his whole life was testimony to that. But he had hanged himself, hadn't he? That was the act of a weak man, and a confession of guilt . . .

Arthur Reece testified that the signature was his son's, and that the letter and the envelope had been typed on the electric typewriter in his office. The letter was handed to the jury along with a sample typed on that machine by a police officer. Certain irregularities in characters common to both specimens were pointed out.

Reece also described the investigation he and his secretary had made into the accounts. They found a total discrepancy of £932 17 4d. Peter had been fraudulently converting monies entrusted to him for investment.

'Mr. Reece,' said the coroner, 'suppose your son had come to you and confessed his crime, what would you have done?'

'I'd have given him a hell of a bawling out, but I'd have made good the losses . . . I *have* now made good the losses.'

'Had you no suspicion of what was going on?'

'None at all. It was all in the last six months, you see – we haven't had an audit. But, of course, he was always a gambler, Peter. Couldn't resist it. A nice boy – I must put that on record – but no backbone.' The third and last pointer.

In later years Prescott analysed his blindness. Having swallowed the suicide, he had found the other implausibilities easy to take: they were simply further evidence that he had misread Peter's character. It didn't occur to him to reverse the argument: the minor discrepancies were evidence of an error in the major premise . . .

Norah wasn't called. The jury, after a token retirement, delivered the inevitable verdict: 'Suicide while the balance of his mind was disturbed '.

Peter Reece was cremated on Thursday, 3rd May 1962. On 20th May Arthur Reece and Harriet left Cromley: the business was being wound up, Ash Grove was put on the market.

On 14th June John Prescott and Norah Browne were married in a registry office.

PART II

FOREWORD: FROM THE TRIAL

'How long have you known the accused, Mr. Lowson?'

Edward Lowson took off his spectacles, polished them with a handkerchief, glanced across at the dock. 'It must be – let me see – nearly seven years.'

'Where did you first meet him?'

'At the home of my friend, Arthur Reece. Prescott was staying as a guest of Arthur's son.'

'And as a result of that meeting, you offered him a partnership in your firm?'

'As a result of that meeting *and* of certain further enquiries. One does not take such a decision lightly, Sir Hugh.'

'Indeed not.'

'Even so,' Lowson added sadly, 'one can make mistakes.'

He was a good witness. Bald, rubicund, twinkling-eyed, he had an air of bluff honesty. Even his dress contributed to the image: for the occasion he had forsaken his plus-fours and was wearing a dark blue suit of good material but going shiny.

He was careful not to overplay his hand. Yes, he agreed, Prescott was a competent lawyer – 'far cleverer than I,' he added with an engaging smile. Yes, he had liked him to begin with, had thought him a modest, rather shy young man. He and his wife had entertained him in their home, had treated him like a son. They had been delighted when John Prescott and Alice, their daughter, showed an increasing fondness for each other.

The dated, courtly language was persuasive. From the dock Prescott consulted his weather-vane – the thin-faced woman on the jury: she was wearing her approving smirk.

The popular belief that juries were swift to detect insincerity was a myth: an actor like Lowson could pull the wool over their eyes every time. His lies were not the kind you could easily controvert, they were contained in subtle shifts of emphasis, omissions, misleading innuendoes. And he studied his audience.

Having prepared the ground, Lowson was now describing Prescott's perfidy.

'. . . and this at a time when he was still paying court to my daughter.'

'You actually *saw* him visit Miss Browne's apartment?'

'My house is across the road from where she—'

The hoarse voice of the judge interrupted: 'That was not counsel's question, Mr. Lowson.'

'I apologise, my lord. Myself, I saw him only once, but my daughter—'

Counsel interposed hastily: 'Never mind what your daughter told you, Mr. Lowson. What did you see yourself?'

'It was a few nights before Peter Reece was murdered—'

The judge corrected him again: 'Before Peter Reece *died*. It is not yet established that he was murdered.' It seemed that Mr. Justice Yardley at least did not like Edward Lowson.

The rebuke did not disconcert him. 'You must forgive an old man, my lord.' A penitent smile, then: 'I saw him leave at twelve forty-five a.m.'

'You took particular note of the time?'

'Indeed I did. I was watching for him, you understand. He had gone in with her at eleven-thirty.'

'You saw him go in?'

He evaded that one. 'I recognised his car outside.'

The judge opened his mouth to speak, thought better of it, scribbled a note instead.

Counsel continued. 'Did you see Miss Browne?'

'She came to the door when he was leaving.'

'How was she dressed?'

'In one of these modern dressing-gowns. Knee length . . . There's a street lamp outside the door, you understand . . .'

Prescott yawned. He wondered if boredom was usual in one on trial for murder. Presumably not . . .

Edward Lowson was now being questioned about Peter. 'When did you last see him alive?' counsel asked.

'The afternoon of the day he died.'

'Would you tell the court the circumstances?'

'I telephoned him after lunch and asked him to come round.'

'Why?'

The spectacles came off again and Lowson rubbed them vigorously. Although he had only recently taken to wearing glasses, they were already a formidable part of his conversational armoury.

'After anxious consideration I had decided that Peter must be told of his friend's treachery.'

'And did you tell him?'

'I did indeed.'

For Prescott it was the first shock of the trial. It brought a moment of panic: could Peter have died believing that he and Norah . . .? But no – Peter would never have believed that.

'What was his reaction?' counsel was asking.

'Extreme anger. He said he had an appointment with Prescott that evening and would have it out then.'

Prescott wondered how much of Lowson's story was true. The phone call and the meeting with Peter certainly – he'd never dare invent these. What they talked about, however, was another matter; Peter wasn't here to dispute Lowson's account.

A vindictive old man, Edward Lowson. All this because years ago Prescott had rejected his daughter ... To be charitable, he probably believed Prescott was guilty. Manipulation of the facts to ensure a conviction might then seem to him justifiable.

'Did you communicate to anyone else your suspicions of the accused's misconduct with Miss Browne?'

'I told Arthur Reece.'

'How did he take it?'

'He didn't listen to my warning. I reminded him of it after – after Peter was dead. He knew it then, all right. His daughter had guessed.'

Harriet had guessed? An over-simplification. Harriet had been confused, hadn't known what to believe. She hated Norah.

What did it matter? That was six years ago. Harriet had forgiven him long since; forgiven him, and then – He closed his mind to the thought ...

'Despite your disapproval of his conduct, Mr. Lowson, the accused remained with your firm?'

'He did his work. His morals didn't affect that.'

'You were satisfied with him as a partner?'

'He was adequate.'

A grudging testimonial.

'You didn't, of course, suspect he was a murderer?'

'Indeed not, although one was horrified by the callous haste with which he married poor young Reece's fiancée. But one naturally accepted the verdict of the inquest.'

'Quite so . . . And now, Mr. Lowson, I move on to more recent events. Did you keep in touch with Arthur Reece after he left Cromley?'

'Naturally. He was one of my oldest friends.'

'Did you see him often?'

'Never. He was abroad. But we corresponded.'

'Would you tell the court about your most recent correspondence with him?'

'Certainly. I received a letter from him on 10th September last. I remember the date because . . .'

10th September 1967. Prescott remembered the date too . . .

CHAPTER I

The Ravens' car was already in the drive when John Prescott got home from the office.

Norah came out to the front door as he let himself in. 'Do you realise what time it is?' she said without lowering her voice, although she had left the sitting-room door ajar.

'Sorry, dear,' he began. 'I—'

'You might make the *effort*. I had to do the drinks myself. Tim's always in time.'

Yes, but Tim didn't do his share in the office . . .

'I'm sorry,' he repeated. No use trying to explain. 'I'll just have a quick one, then, and—'

'There's no time. Go up and change.'

These Friday evenings with Tim Raven and his sister went back five years and more. Dinner and bridge, home and away in alternate fortnights. The evenings bored Prescott; and his dislike of Raven had hardened with the passage of time. It was difficult to pin down the reason: perhaps the hint of patronage in Raven's manner; and, of course, the collusive glances he would exchange with Norah.

Raven was pushing forty now, elegant as ever, still a bachelor, still a rake. The time was, perhaps, coming when women would be repelled rather than flattered by his attentions. But not yet.

Norah was under his spell. In his company her whole personality changed, she sparkled. To-night, as Prescott topped up the wine glasses, she was laughing at a malicious anecdote of Raven's.

'Where do you get all your stories?' she asked.

'A lawyer's office – thanks, John, damn good claret – a lawyer's office provides an inexhaustible supply.'

'John never brings any home.'

'Ah well, John's the serious one, he does the work . . . But that reminds me: who do you think's coming back to live in Cromley?'

'Do you think you ought, dear?' Margaret put in timidly, her spaniel eyes on him. She seldom spoke when her brother was present; she was content to admire.

'There's nothing secret about it . . . *You* know him, Norah.'

Norah said: 'I loathe guessing games, Tim.'

'All right: it's Arthur Reece.'

Prescott saw the colour drain from his wife's face. She muttered: 'Oh God no! He can't be!'

Margaret said to her brother with unusual asperity: 'I warned you . . .'

Raven was all remorse. 'My dear Norah, I've upset you. I never dreamt that after all these years . . .'

That was a lie, Prescott thought. Raven must have known he was on delicate ground.

'I'm all right,' Norah said, and drank some wine. 'Is he home yet?'

'Let's forget Reece . . . There's a marvellous story going round that—'

'No, Tim. I want to know. Have you seen him?'

'No. Edward Lowson got a letter to-day from Brittany. Very shaky writing – he's been ill, apparently. "Get the tenant out: I'm moving in." Just like that. Still the *grand seigneur*. Damn lucky for him there's no tenant at the moment.'

They'd never managed to sell Ash Grove. There had been offers, but never quite up to what Reece believed it was worth. Against his lawyers' advice he'd refused to compromise. So the property had been let instead to an American geologist who was doing some work on the Hastonbury rocks.

But the geologist had recently died and his wife had returned to the States. The house was vacant.

'Arthur hasn't married again, has he?' Prescott asked.

'Don't think so. The daughter's coming back too, to look after him. Hilary, isn't it?'

'Harriet,' Norah amended.

'Very pretty girl,' said Margaret.

Prescott thought she was off the mark. He remembered Harriet Reece as long-legged, thin, undisciplined; certainly not pretty. But that was more than five years ago, when she was still in her teens. She must now be – twenty? twenty-one? Impossible to think of her as grown up.

After dinner they played bridge: as always Prescott partnered Margaret against his wife and Raven. The pairs were unequal: the men were of a standard, but Norah outclassed Margaret Raven. She had the flair and the ruthlessness, and alone of the four was a member of a bridge club.

To-night the cards didn't run well for her. Prescott and his partner quickly won a couple of rubbers, and on the first hand of the third Margaret made a small slam.

When the hand had been played, Norah, who hated losing, turned to her husband and said tartly: 'Why didn't you put her up to seven?'

'We didn't *make* seven,' he pointed out.

'That's beside the point.' She glanced rudely at the placid Margaret. 'There were thirteen tricks sitting if she'd set up her diamonds.'

Raven joined in. 'Yes, I must say, John, you were a bit timid. I agree with Norah . . .'

He always did agree with Norah. Prescott controlled his temper. 'Your deal, Tim,' he said.

A few hands later, when they were now game and sixty, Margaret dealt and, after the customary pause while she counted her points, passed. Third in hand, Prescott bid a light no trump which was passed out. Dummy went down with twelve points and he easily made eight tricks.

'Seventy and seven hundred, partner,' he said, marking his score card.

'Just a minute.' Norah's voice was shaking. 'You didn't have a bid there. Couple of aces and a queen. You only bid because you knew Margaret had a good hand. You took advantage of her hesitation.'

'Oh no, Norah!' Margaret said pacifically. 'I'm always slow, you know that. I have to count—'

'Are you accusing me of cheating?' Prescott asked.

'Don't fly off the handle, John,' said Raven. 'Norah only meant—'

'I meant,' said Norah speaking very distinctly, 'exactly what I said: you took advantage of your partner's slow pass. That's un-ethical. Cheating, if you like.'

Prescott gathered up the cards, restored both packs to their boxes. 'Will you have a drink, Margaret? Tim?'

But they made their excuses and left.

It was a long time, Prescott reflected, since he and Norah had had a major row. Come to think of it, they'd quarrelled more often in their early days.

The immediate cause of to-night's conflict wasn't important. Norah knew he would never cheat, and when she was calmer she would admit it. She'd been in a sour temper because she was losing; and even before that the news of Arthur Reece's home-coming had upset her.

It was five years last April since Peter Reece's suicide. Although his name was never mentioned, he was a constant shadow between Prescott and his wife.

Their marriage might have worked if they'd had a family, but after several miscarriages Norah was warned by her doctor not to try again. They had both wanted children, Norah even more than her husband. With nothing to fall back on, she became discontented.

It was hard to name a date when the marriage finally dis-integrated: the process was too gradual. Even now Prescott was not wholly without feeling for Norah: but it was pity, not love.

To-night, however, marked a turning point. It was the first

breach in the facade they still presented to the world. Norah had never before spoken to him in front of others in the tone she had used to-night.

The quarrel didn't develop immediately after the Ravens left. Norah went upstairs. To bed, her husband thought; but presently she came down wearing a housecoat and slippers. She lit a cigarette and sat gazing into the fire.

The housecoat – blue, her favourite colour – touched in Prescott a memory of a night before they were married . . . He felt sorry for her now as she sat hunched in her chair, her blonde hair falling loosely on her shoulders, her face turned away from him. At twenty-eight she was still an attractive woman, but only when congenial company stimulated her and smoothed away the lines of discontent.

Norah looked round, and her expression banished sympathy.

'Go on, say it,' she said. 'You didn't cheat, you haven't the guts to cheat. What do you want? Will "I'm sorry" do? Or must I go down on my knees?'

'Why do you hate me, Norah?'

She stubbed out the half-smoked cigarette, lit another. Her hands were trembling. 'You really want to know? You're a bore, John. A great, bloody BORE. Since the day we met you haven't said a single thing that interested me. Sometimes I could *scream.*'

'Then why did you marry me?'

'God knows! I must have been mad.'

'If I'm a bore now, I was a bore then. I haven't—'

She stopped him. 'Listen to yourself! Making debating points as if we were . . . Oh hell, I don't know. I married you, I suppose, because I thought – well, you were his *friend* and . . .'

It was the nearest she had been for years to mentioning Peter Reece by name.

'You thought I was like him?'

'"The sleeping tiger," he used to call you.' She laughed shortly. '"Dead mouse" is more like it.'

They'd both been disillusioned, they'd both married an ideal rather than a person. Prescott, for his part, had been shattered to find how shallow Norah was, how narrow and self-centred her interests.

She lit another cigarette.

'You smoke too much,' Prescott said.

'Shut up!'

The quarrel fizzled and died. It was futile to bandy recriminations: arguments had no point when they had no power to persuade.

After a while Norah said, gazing into the fire: 'I wonder why he's come back.'

'Arthur Reece? He belongs here. He didn't sell his house'

She wasn't listening. 'He said he'd never come back. Never. Not after what happened.'

Prescott said gently: 'Does it matter, Norah? You got a shock when you heard his name again. But does it matter whether he's here or in France or in Timbuktu?'

She turned on him: 'For God's sake, shut up! You don't know the first thing about it.'

It was, he decided, as good a time as any to grasp the nettle. 'Do you want a divorce, Norah?'

Her eyes were suddenly wary. 'I didn't say that.'

'But we can't go on like—'

'I didn't say I wanted a divorce,' she repeated sharply. 'Anyway, you've no grounds. I've been faithful, haven't I?'

Had she? Even of that Prescott was no longer sure. The way she sometimes looked at Tim Raven told him she had been unfaithful in thought if not yet in deed. Not that it mattered any more . . .

'I would arrange to give you grounds,' he said.

'I don't want a divorce.' Norah's mouth was set obstinately. 'We've put up with it so far. And nothing's changed, has it?'

CHAPTER II

It had been a poor summer; and winter set in early. The third Wednesday of October was cold and bright, with the wind from the east. Frost had filmed the grass and there were reports of snow in Scotland.

Norah was down with flu and had to be given breakfast in bed. As a result Prescott was late getting to the office.

He smelt coffee brewing as he climbed the stairs. Must be after ten already.

As Sandra Welch looked up from her desk he forestalled her question. 'Domestic chores,' he said. 'My wife's ill.'

He went through to his own room. Sandra got up and followed him in.

'I've put the draft lease of the Simpson property on your desk,' she said. 'I've marked one clause I think you should look at.'

They made a good team, he and Sandra. She had succeeded Nadine Smith two years ago, when Nadine finally abandoned hope of Tim Raven and married the boy next door.

Mrs. Welch had more intelligence than Nadine, and more initiative; already she had picked up a useful knowledge of law. She was in her early thirties, had been married and divorced, and now seemed bent on making a career. In the office she dressed quietly, submerged her personality. When Prescott ran across her one night in the Chilton, he hardly recognised her: in the right clothes, in the right setting she was an attractive woman.

She was a native of one of Cromley's dormitory towns, had left the district on her marriage and returned after the divorce. So much she had told Prescott at the time of her appointment; it was all he ever learned of her background, for she didn't encourage exchanges of confidences. But they respected each other, they had the same philosophy of work, they both preferred solid accuracy to erratic brilliance. Or, to put it another way, they both disapproved of Tim Raven.

Sandra said: 'Will you do your mail just now?'

'No. Later, Sandra.' His head was aching. He'd been doping himself with aspirin, fighting Norah's virus.

She nodded. As she was going out, she remarked: 'You'll see on your pad, there was a phone call from Miss Reece.'

'*Harriet* Reece?'

'Yes. She's going to ring again.'

'You should have put her on to Mr. Lowson.'

'She particularly wanted you.' It was half-past twelve before she telephoned.

'John? It's Harriet Reece.' Her voice stirred no memory.

'Nice to hear from you again, Harriet. How are you?'

'Oh, I'm fine . . . John, I'd like you to come and talk to me.'

He hesitated. 'On business?'

'Kind of.'

'I thought Edward Lowson was handling your affairs.'

'Not *my* affairs,' she said sharply.

'I meant your father's. And anyway your father. . .'

'I know. He hasn't forgiven you.' For marrying Norah, she meant. 'But he sleeps in the afternoons. Come at half-past two. He'll never know.' And when he didn't answer, she added quietly: 'It's important, John. It's about Peter.'

While he hesitated, Edward Lowson knocked on his door and came in. Seeing Prescott on the phone, he made a pantomime of inquiry; Prescott motioned him to a chair. The aroma of cigar smoke filled the room.

'*Please,* John,' Harriet was saying.

He made up his mind. 'All right, Harriet. Two-thirty this afternoon.' He replaced the receiver.

Lowson was looking at him with interest. 'Harriet?' he said. 'Not Harriet Reece, by any chance?'

'Yes.'

'Grown up, hasn't she?'

'I haven't seen her.'

'You'll find her . . . changed.' He laid his cigar on an ash tray, took out his spectacle case. 'I called on Arthur on Saturday.'

'How is he?'

Lowson shook his head. 'Very frail, poor old chap. On the way out, I'd say.'

He took his glasses from the case and carefully put them on. They had solid black frames. 'Tell me honestly, John, how do they look? Now I want your honest opinion.'

At sixty-nine Edward Lowson had at last been compelled to consult an oculist. He was much concerned about the effect of spectacles on his image.

'Very distinguished,' Prescott said. 'Ambassadorial.'

'You're sure? You don't think I'd be better with rimless?'

'No, these are more effective. Especially for waving at people.'

'Like this, you mean?' He took them off and brandished them, as if to emphasise a point. There were times – not many times – when Prescott found an engaging Churchillian flavour in Lowson's little vanities.

Although it was not obvious on the surface, their relations had deteriorated. Edward Lowson had not forgiven Prescott for spurning his daughter, who was now, at thirty, gathering dust on the shelf. Prescott for his part was disenchanted by the hypocrisy of his senior partner, by the hard, selfish core that underlay the avuncular geniality.

'Did Reece tell you why he's come back?' Prescott asked.

'My dear boy, if you were old and ill and in a foreign land, you'd—' He broke off, looked thoughtfully at Prescott, then said: 'No, one must be honest. I think he has other reasons for coming home . . . Matter of fact, it was about the Reeces I came to see you. Have you the file on the inquest?'

'Why should I have it?'

'Miss Burroughs was sure you'd borrowed it.'

'Then Miss Burroughs is wrong . . . What did you want with it?'

'Nothing much, nothing much.' He looked puzzled. 'Are you *sure* you haven't—'

'Damn it, Edward, how many times do I have to—'

Sandra Welch put her head round the door. 'I couldn't help overhearing,' she said. 'I've got that file. I lifted it yesterday by mistake.' She handed it to Lowson and went out.

'There you are,' said Prescott. 'You're too damn' quick in jumping to conclusions—'

'My dear boy, you're extraordinarily touchy these days. I think you're overworking.'

'I'm off colour to-day.' He'd been feeling more groggy as the morning progressed.

Lowson looked pleased. 'Never had a day's illness in my life,' he boasted. 'A bottle of stout with your lunch – that's the secret . . . Speaking of lunch, look at the time!'

As they went out together, Lowson said: 'One of these days we must get out of this mausoleum. We really must.' One of these days . . .

Norah was padding round in her dressing-gown when Prescott got home. She had made his lunch.

'Frank said I could get up.' She looked at her husband. 'You're not so frisky yourself, are you?'

'I'm all right.'

She shrugged. 'If you say so.'

They had observed an armed truce since the quarrel, each careful not to spark off a fresh explosion. It was a situation that could only deteriorate.

Over lunch Prescott mentioned Harriet's phone call. He did it to see his wife's reaction, hoping (was it possible?) that it would hurt her. It bothered him, this streak of cruelty, the desire to pay her back in her own coin.

Norah reacted predictably: apparent indifference, then vicious counter-attack.

'She's still carrying the torch, then?' she said.

'What?'

'Come off it, John. She was crazy about you – and you know it.'

'That's rubbish!'

Norah laughed and said: 'Have it your own way.'

'She was a schoolgirl, Norah.'

She smiled derisively. 'So what?'

CHAPTER III

Since Peter's death Prescott had avoided Marsden Hill except when business took him there; and even then he'd always passed Ash Grove without a glance. Too many memories and frustrated hopes were locked up there.

To-day he drove slowly, letting the familiar scene tug at his emotions. He read those evocative names on the gates: Long Row, Glandersley, Abbotsford, Shepherd's Fell, Ash Grove . . .

The gravel scrunched under his tyres as he swung in between the stone pillars. It had always been an awkward entry: he remembered the time Peter scraped the paint off his father's Jaguar. That was the night Prescott met Norah.

The garden was smaller than his picture of it; and the house also. Curious how time could distort the memory. He could have sworn, too, there had been a lily pond; perhaps the tenant had filled it in. At least the garden had not been neglected: the lawn was lush and weed-free as ever.

A furniture van stood outside the front door, and as Prescott pulled up behind it two men in white aprons were carrying in a sofa. He crossed to the porch and rang the bell. Through the open door he saw two more men manhandling a mahogany bookcase across the hall to the staircase, watched by a girl in black sweater and jeans.

Hearing the bell, the girl turned: her face broke into a smile, she rushed to the door, threw her arms round Prescott, and kissed him.

'John, darling!' she said. 'How marvellous!'

He disengaged himself awkwardly, conscious of the grins of the workmen.

'You look terrific, Harriet,' he said.

The words were an understatement. It was hard to believe that this was the same girl, that the substitution of curves for angles could make all that difference. She had dark, unruly hair and laughter in her eyes. Her lips had been soft and cool on his.

Harriet turned to the men with the bookcase. 'Second on the left at the top of the stairs,' she said. 'And try not to make too much noise, would you? My father's sleeping.'

She took Prescott into the sitting-room, where the sofa had just been installed. She sat on it and the springs creaked. 'I can't think why Daddy prizes this so much. It's ugly as sin and—'

'And it's sore on the behind.'

She laughed. 'I wasn't going to put it quite so crudely.'

'You did once.'

'Did I? . . . Sit down, John.'

He took the arm-chair by the fire. Although the room was hot, he was shivering.

'Has it all been in store?' he asked, vaguely indicating the furnishings.

'No. The house was let furnished. Daddy only put our few treasures into store.' She looked down wryly. 'Such as this.'

From upstairs came a crash of a heavy object falling. A petulant voice called: 'Harriet!'

'I knew it!' Harriet said. 'Excuse me.' She hurried out.

Prescott crossed to the window that overlooked the lawn at the back. The sun was shining; it might have been that Sunday afternoon five years ago. He could see the spot where he and Harriet had had their picnic. He imagined he could pick out the tree on which . . . He turned away.

The room had been re-decorated, he noticed, and the night-store heater and electric radiator were new. Otherwise nothing had changed. Even that old framed photograph of Mrs. Reece was back on the piano.

The piano itself was a link with the past. There was music on the stand – a Bach partita. He sat down and began to play; clumsily, for he was out of practice. Like so much else, he'd let his music slide since his marriage.

Harriet came back. 'No, don't stop, John. It's nice to hear it played properly. I can't—'

'It's not played properly. Anyway it's too cold over here.' He went back to his chair by the fire. The shivering was getting worse. He'd been a fool to come out – must be running a temperature.

'I'm sorry I embarrassed you with my welcome,' Harriet was saying. 'I'd forgotten how self-conscious you were. Remember how Peter used to talk of the sleeping tiger? I see he's still dormant.'

She spoke naturally of Peter. Unlike Norah, whose avoidance of the name was pathological.

'You were always so solemn,' Harriet went on. 'Remember that night when—' She checked herself. 'I musn't reminisce.'

'Tell me about yourself. You've been nursing?'

'Yes. I got my State last June. I had to do something useful with my life. A kind of penance for Peter's death.'

'You weren't to blame.'

'Wasn't I? I think we all were, we all failed him, Daddy and Norah and I. Even you, John. No one should be so – so alone that he has to kill himself.'

She was right. The signs had been there: the uncharacteristic moodiness, the flashes of temper, the long hours in the office at night. They'd remembered them afterwards; but afterwards was too late.

'All the same,' Prescott said, 'there's no sense in dwelling on it. Try and forget—'

'Someone isn't letting us forget.'

'What?'

'It's why I asked you to come. Just a moment – they're in my room.'

Harriet went out, leaving the door open. He watched her bound up the stairs with the easy grace of an athlete. The jeans were tight enough to do her curves justice. Yes, she had changed.

She was soon back. She handed him a buff-coloured foolscap envelope.

The postmark was Cromley and the date 17th August last. It was addressed in childish block capitals to M. Arthur Reece, 18 Avenue Penfoulic, Fouesnant, Brittany, France.

'He's had three of these that I know of: maybe more. It's because of them he came back to Cromley.'

'What's he been doing all this time?'

She told him. After leaving Cromley five years ago, her father had stayed a few months with a brother in Eastbourne and then gone abroad. Harriet had been installed in boarding-school.

'Not that he lost any sleep over me,' Harriet said. 'Peter was always his favourite. In fact, I think he resented me for having survived Peter.' Her tone was matter-of-fact, without rancour.

Prescott was attracted by her unselfconsciousness, the absence of false pride and self-deception. He liked her voice, too, and the way her nose crinkled when she smiled, and the gesture by which she kept pushing her fingers through her hair. Undoubtedly he had a temperature.

'I only saw him twice after that,' Harriet was saying. 'He came over once on business – I think it was to see a specialist. And the following summer – that would be '64, I think – I spent a week in his house in Brittany. That was a mistake.'

'Why?'

For the first time she hesitated. Then she shrugged and said: 'He was living with a woman. Oh! not while I was *there*. But the evidence was all over the house. I could – I could *smell* her.' She frowned. 'I thought I was broadminded, but ... well, one's own father! I mean, he was nearly sixty ...'

'Did you know, Harriet, that even before he left here—'

She nodded. 'The woman in Hastonbury? Yes, I never guessed at the time, but I worked it out later. I was very unobservant as a child.'

'Innocent,' he suggested.

'You might call it that. I was a little horror, though. You used to get mad, John – you used to threaten to spank me, remember?'

'Yes.'

'I was wrong, you were right every time. Except on one thing.'

'What was that?'

But she wouldn't answer. She didn't have to – it was Norah. She hadn't even asked about her to-day: she must loathe her as much as ever.

'All right,' he said. 'Go on with your story.'

After the disastrous week in Brittany, Harriet and her father lost contact, apart from Christmas cards. And he always remembered her birthday.

Near the end of August of this year she received a cable from
France to say that her father was seriously ill in hospital. She had
just qualified as a nurse and taken a post in a maternity hospital in
Southampton. They gave her compassionate leave.

'Why Southampton?' Prescott put in.

She blushed. 'If you must know, there's a doctor there, a friend
of mine . . .'

She flew over, stayed in her father's house in Fouesnant. He
was in hospital in Quimper, fifteen kilometres away, and she used
his car for her daily visits. He'd had a moderately severe cerebral
haemorrhage, but was progressing. His speech was already almost
fully restored and the paralysis, the doctor assured her, was yielding
to treatment.

'What about the woman? Was she still in evidence?'

'No, she'd disappeared years before, the neighbours told me.
They had an almighty row one night – the whole village heard
about it. Next day she was gone . . . She was English, they said,
which surprised me.'

'The Hastonbury woman?'

'I suppose it might have been.'

'Why France anyway? What made him settle there?'

'He always was a Francophile. When I was a child, we used to
go to Paris every spring. He was so interested in painting, of course.'

'Does he still paint?'

'He can't. Or so he says, although Dr. Hornby—' She broke off
and laughed. 'Don't sidetrack me, John.'

She continued her story. She had been in France a week when
a letter to her father with a Cromley postmark was delivered at the
house. The address was in ink capitals and the date stamp showed
3rd September. She was puzzled, because she understood her father

had cut off all connection with Cromley. However, she took the letter to Quimper that afternoon.

When she gave him it, she could tell he was upset. Without a word he put it, unopened, under his pillow; and he was unusually silent for the rest of her visit. Next day he told Harriet he was going back to Cromley; he refused to discuss his reasons.

'Is he home for good?' Prescott asked.

'I don't even know that. He hasn't sold his house in Brittany.'

'Why did you come with him?'

'He asked me.' Harriet smiled. 'And oddly enough I'd begun to like him more. We'd talked a lot in that hospital. He still thinks I'm less than the dust but – well, I suppose blood's thicker than water.'

Arthur Reece came out of hospital in mid-September, had a fortnight's convalescence at Fouesnant, then crossed to England with his daughter. He stayed with his brother in Eastbourne while Harriet went ahead to get the house ready; and he joined her a few days later.

'How is he?' Prescott asked.

'Physically not bad.' She put emphasis on the first word. 'Terribly tense, though, and irritable. There are reminders of Peter everywhere, you see. It's been worse since yesterday.'

'What happened yesterday?'

'Another of these letters came. By the second post, unfortunately, so Daddy was downstairs and took it from the postman. He stuffed it in his pocket without a word.'

'Didn't you ask him about it?'

'Of course. But he flew off the handle and told me to mind my own business. I had to let it drop. I've been warned not to excite him.'

In the afternoon, while her father was asleep, Harriet searched for the letters. In a pocket of one of his suits she found the envelope with the August postmark. Empty. And in the fireplace in his bedroom the ashes of burnt paper; the smell of smoke still hung about the room.

'He wasn't thorough enough,' Harriet said. She opened the folder she had in her hand and took out a scrap of paper; one edge, untouched by the flame, was pale blue.

Harriet passed it to Prescott. 'If you look closely, you can read— Here, watch how you hold it: it's fragile . . . Oh *blast!*'

Another shivering fit had come on and he couldn't keep his hand steady. The paper slipped from his fingers and dropped to the floor; a small bit flaked off.

Harriet's tone changed. 'John, you're not well,' she said.

'A chill,' he muttered. 'It comes and goes.'

Harriet was contrite. 'Why didn't you say? Never mind, Nurse Reece will take over.' She went out of the room and came back with a thermometer. 'Put that under your tongue,' she said, shaking it. 'And give me your hand.'

'My hand?'

'Don't talk: you'll bite the thermometer . . . I'm going to take your pulse,' she explained briskly.

Prescott felt relief at not having to pretend any more, as he sat shivering, teeth chattering, head throbbing. He was soothed by the touch of Harriet's fingers on his wrist. He looked up, but she was concentrating on her watch.

'Right, Mr. Prescott,' she said presently, releasing his hand. 'Let's see how we are to-day, shall we?'

She took the thermometer from his mouth and studied it. 'Good heavens!' she said, 'and it's the undertaker's half holiday!'

She sounded concerned all the same.

'How much is it?' he asked.

'Nearly a hundred and two. John, you really are an ass . . . And your pulse is racing like an outboard motor.'

'Ah! but that's because of you, Harriet.'

'Don't get fresh with the nurse. It's straight home to bed for you, my boy. Who's your doctor?'

'Frank Hornby. But—'

'I'll ring him. And I'll give you something to stop that rigor before you go.'

She left him. He heard her voice on the telephone, then sounds from the kitchen.

The scrap of paper was on the carpet where it had fallen. He stared at it, trying to focus. The glow from the radiator shone on the blackened paper and picked out those now familiar capital letters. Only four lines survived, and even they were partly mutilated.

NOT COMM   CIDE BUT W

DERED.   H   FELLED BY A BL

N THE   BACK OF THE HEA   AND THEN

GED.   I HAVE IRREF   OOF.

Harriet came back.

'Drink that,' she said, handing him a steaming cup.

'What is it? Coffee?'

She smiled. 'Irish coffee.'

He took a mouthful; it went down like a ball of fire. More whisky than coffee, he judged. He drank more. The shivering stopped.

'You're an angel,' Prescott said.

'No, not that. No angel. . Don't romanticise: you made that mistake before.'

It was an oblique, and perceptive, reference to Norah, whom he'd invested with qualities she didn't have.

'I've been reading this,' he said, indicating the paper.

'What do you make of it?'

'". . . did not commit suicide but was murdered. He was felled by a blow on the back of the head and then hanged. I have irrefutable proof . . ." I suppose it must mean Peter?'

'Who else?'

'Do you believe it?'

'That Peter was murdered? Of course not . . . But that's not the point. Daddy would believe it. He would believe anything rather than that Peter killed himself. Someone is trading on that.'

'Who?'

'Drink that while it's hot, John. I don't know who. I thought you might help me find out.'

'Why me?'

She regarded him reflectively. 'Let's say I have hopes of releasing that tiger.' When he didn't answer she said: 'I thought of you because you knew Peter so well. Now, off you go. Are you fit to drive?'

'Yes.'

'Don't dally, then.' She was shepherding him to the door.

'I'll come back in a day or two—'

'You won't, you know. Dr. Hornby'll have you in bed for a week, or I've never read a thermometer. If you're a good boy, I'll visit you.'

It was twenty-to-four when Prescott got home. The stimulation of the alcohol was wearing off; he felt cold.

As he got out of the car, he happened to look up and saw the front bedroom curtains move. Simultaneously his subconscious released the registration number of the blue Hillman he'd seen parked fifty yards down the road: EFG 480 D. Tim Raven's car.

He felt physically sick as he stood shivering in the doorway. Then, making up his mind, he put his key in the lock and opened the door.

'Are you there, Norah?' he called and tramped noisily through to the liquor cabinet. He poured himself a stiff whisky. His hand was shaking, and it was not solely from influenza.

In five minutes Norah came down in a dressing-gown. She specialised in dressing-gowns, his wife. 'What's the matter?' she said. 'I've been resting. I didn't feel so good.'

Not bad, he thought. Not bad, you slut. The second step from the bottom creaked. They both heard it – and ignored it.

Norah said: 'I told you not to go out. You look like death. I'll put on your electric blanket while you finish your drink.'

He felt too ill to have it out with her; and too nauseated by the vulgarity of the situation.

'Shall I phone Frank?' Norah called.

'He knows. He'll be looking in.'

Presently she came back, fully dressed now. 'All set,' she said.

He saw the mockery in her eyes.

CHAPTER IV

While the antibiotics were dealing with the virus, John Prescott had the chance to take stock, to stand aside from his daily round and have a good, hard look at the wider prospect.

He didn't like what he saw. Here he was, twenty-nine, nearly thirty: junior partner in a reputable firm; not rich, but already earning more than his two elder brothers together. And, with it all, desperately unhappy.

What was wrong? His marriage? Yes, partly, but Prescott was honest enough to recognise it as a symptom rather than a cause. The fault lay deeper, it lay in himself.

He lacked roots. He had broken away from the deadening influence of Fenleigh but couldn't fit into a new environment. The emancipation that Peter Reece had begun for him had never been completed. Perhaps if Peter had lived . . .

But it was dangerously easy to find explanations and excuses. As well say: perhaps if he hadn't married Norah. The point was, he *had* married Norah, he'd married her because of a fundamental flaw in his character, because he was the kind of man he was. He couldn't turn round now and blame some malevolent quirk of fate.

The five wasted years of marriage were not his loss alone. Norah was equally disillusioned. He bored her. She'd said so outright the other night, but he'd guessed it long before. And not only Norah: other people found him dull, too. He'd lost his confidence, he'd gone back into his shell.

Now, if he wanted, he could break with Norah. She'd blundered, taken one risk too many, been found out. But what then?

A dreary life of bachelorhood stretched ahead: he'd never have the courage to marry again.

Someone was calling his name.

Prescott stretched, yawned, opened his eyes. Frank Hornby was looking down at him.

'That's right, don't hurry – it's only the doctor.'

'What time is it, Frank?'

'Ten past four.'

He must have dozed off after lunch. He'd been dreaming. Of a girl with dark, unruly hair and laughing eyes . . .

Hornby was shaking a thermometer. 'Stick that under your arm, though I can see you're better.'

He felt cool and rested, and the aching in his bones had subsided.

'Do you often work on a Saturday?' Prescott asked.

'Twenty-four hours a day, seven days a—' He took the thermometer back, read it. 'Uh-huh. That's more like it. No, I'd another call, John. Thought I'd look in while I was passing.' It was his third visit in four days.

He gave Prescott a perfunctory prod or two with his stethoscope. 'You'll live. Keep on with the tablets. Up for an hour to-morrow if you feel like it. I'll be back on Tuesday.' As he was closing his bag, he said: 'Young woman was asking for you.'

'Harriet Reece?'

Hornby gave him a sharp glance. 'How did you guess? I was out seeing her father . . .'

Prescott said: 'Are you in a hurry, Frank?'

'No, you're my last. And no surgery to-night. Why?'

'Stay and have tea. Norah'll—'

'Norah's not here. I let myself in.'

Damn. She'd be at her bridge club.

'Well, how about whisky?'

The doctor hesitated. 'I don't as a rule prescribe alcohol for influenza.'

'I'll only take a thimbleful to keep you company.'

There was no further objection. 'Where do you keep the stuff?' he asked. Prescott told him.

He was soon back carrying a tray with a bottle of scotch, a jug of water and two glasses. He laid it on the bed beside Prescott, who poured two generous portions.

'Damn great thimbles you use in this house,' Hornby growled. He added a splash of water. 'Cheers, John!'

At thirty-seven Frank Hornby was beginning to go to fat. 'Not enough exercise' was his explanation; 'bends his elbow too much' his critics said.

He drank no more heavily than he had ever done. The difference was that people noticed now, and talked. He hadn't lived down that night, years ago, when he crashed his car and injured a pedestrian. He'd been fined and had his licence endorsed; and he was called before the Disciplinary Committee of the GMC. They let him off with a warning, but ever afterwards the threat was there: the dog had had its one bite.

A few of his more straitlaced patients deserted him after the court case. He would have lost more had it not been generally agreed that, drunk or sober, Frank Hornby was incomparably the ablest doctor in Cromley.

He was a sociable man, generally popular, although his temper, when roused, was a force to be reckoned with. On one occasion he knocked a man out in the golf club lounge for repeating a slanderous story about his wife. The spectators, while they admired his loyalty, thought it misplaced.

Tessa Hornby did not share her husband's popularity. Born in the impoverished fringes of the nobility, she had pocketed her pride and married beneath her; and never tired of reminding Cromley of the sacrifice. She was pretentious, snobbish, arrogant. And extravagant. Hornby had to keep a tight rein on the purse strings.

Yet the marriage survived, even prospered. It prospered,

Prescott believed, because Frank was determined that it should. He was, in his way, an ambitious man: he wouldn't want his career endangered by a broken marriage as well as by the undeserved reputation for drunkenness. They had four children; an insurance policy, perhaps . . .

Prescott sensed beneath Hornby's tough exterior a kindred spirit: a man in search of security, sensitive to criticism. They still played golf together every Sunday and the occasional game of billiards. The one blot on their friendship, was the memory of the car smash; Prescott still felt occasionally his friend's unspoken reproach . . .

Hornby was filling his pipe.

'How is Arthur Reece?' Prescott asked.

'Damn it, John, he's a patient. I can't—'

'It's not a medical bulletin I'm after. What brought him back to Cromley, do you think?'

'I wish I knew. Why?'

'Oh, nothing.' He'd hoped that Reece had confided in his doctor.

Hornby drew on his pipe until it was going, looked around for somewhere to put his match. 'John,' he said, 'if you've any inform-ation, you'd better tell me. Something's on his mind and it's not doing his blood pressure any good.'

Well, why not? He described his conversation with Harriet.

Hornby nodded. 'I thought it must be something to do with Peter. Anonymous letters, eh? That's a police matter.'

'He doesn't seem to think so.'

'No. You know, it makes you wonder—' He stopped.

'What?'

'Mind if I . . .?' Hornby indicated his empty glass.

'Sure – help yourself.'

'Thanks. It almost makes you wonder if Peter's suicide was – well, as straightforward as it appeared.'

'You can't get round the evidence.'

'Which evidence?'

'Dr. Parry said there was no other mark on Peter's body.'

Hornby looked at him oddly. 'I think you've missed out a word, John.'

So he had: 'no other *relevant* injury' was what Parry had said. But surely a bruise on the back of the head . . .

Hornby asked: 'How did the anonymous letter say it was done?'

'It said he was knocked out by a blow on the base of the skull and then hanged.'

'There would certainly be bruising, then . . . Parry was damned cagey about that post-mortem. He generally discussed his police cases with me. But not that one: not one word did he say about it.'

Too late now to cross-examine: Dr. Parry had died two years ago.

'You don't seriously believe Peter was murdered, do you?'

Hornby said slowly: 'I've always felt, John, that Peter's suicide was psychologically wrong.'

What he meant was that Peter Reece was too well adjusted, too much of an extrovert.

'Especially for such a paltry sum,' he added. 'His old man could have paid it back out of his pocket money.'

'You've been reading too many detective stories,' Prescott said.

Hornby laughed. 'I expect you're right.' He finished his drink and stood up. 'Thanks for the whisky, John.'

'Have another.'

'No. Tessa's expecting me . . . By the way, warn Norah not to excite the old boy.'

'What?'

'When she goes for tea to-morrow.'

'*Norah*? To Ash Grove?'

'Didn't you know? Harriet told me – she's *furious*.'

Prescott was inclined to discount Frank Hornby's misgivings about the suicide; he was more intrigued by Norah's invitation to Ash Grove.

After Peter's death Norah had fallen out with Arthur Reece. The cause of the quarrel never became known, for Norah wouldn't speak of it. But the breach was so total that she wasn't even invited to the funeral. Yet now she was going to tea . . .

Prescott stretched for his cigarettes and found the packet empty. It was only six o'clock; Norah might not be back for another hour. He got up and put on a dressing-gown. He tried Norah's room first, for she usually kept cigarettes by her bed.

Norah had moved into the guest room six months ago. 'For a few nights,' she said: to help her insomnia. The nights stretched into months, and neither suggested that she should return.

Prescott had never cared much for the decor of the guest room: the yellows and greens (Norah's choice) were too bold for his taste. Now he had additional reasons for disliking the room. He would never see it again without thinking of Tim Raven.

There were cigarettes in the box on the bedside table. Tipped, but they would serve; he took two. The table drawer was not quite closed. With his instinct for tidiness Prescott tried to shut it, but it resisted. He pulled out the drawer to get more purchase.

Inside were Norah's sleeping pills, a bottle of aspirin, the spare car key, a lurid paperback, a shopping list, a pencil. And a letter.

The envelope, marked 'Private' was addressed to Mrs. J. W. Prescott and had been posted last Tuesday. He recognised Tim

Raven's almost illegible scrawl and guessed it was a note confirming Wednesday's assignation.

Without compunction he took the letter from its envelope and began to read:

> Dear Norah,
>
> It gives me no more pleasure to write this than you will have in receiving it. Five years ago—

Puzzled, Prescott turned over the page to the signature: 'Arthur Reece.'

It was a lesson in auto-suggestion: he'd recognised the writing because he was half-expecting to find a letter from Tim Raven. In fact the similarity was superficial, for this was in the shaky hand of an old man. Anyway he should have known Raven would never commit the folly of writing to his mistress.

He read on.

> '—Five years ago I expressed my contempt for you, and nothing has caused me to revise my opinion. Nevertheless we have common interests to protect; and these are now threatened.
>
> I must talk to you. And, since I am immobilised, you will please come to Ash Grove. Next Sunday at 4 o'clock will suit; Harriet will not be there.
>
> I expect you at that hour.
>
> > Yours,
> >
> > Arthur Reece.'

The style was characteristic. Someone – Tim Raven, was it? –
had once remarked that even a letter of thanks from Arthur Reece
would give offence.

However, it was not the style but the content that interested
Prescott. He was so absorbed that he didn't hear Norah until she
was in the room.

'Well, well,' she said. 'So this is what the mouse does when the
cat's away!'

She didn't sound particularly annoyed. She'd had a good session
at the club; he could always tell from the animation, the sparkle in
her eyes. Presently, if they didn't quarrel, she would be analysing
the hands, describing her triumphs.

As a rule he encouraged her, praised her, glad there was something, however trivial, that could occupy her.

To-day he said: 'It's an interesting letter, Norah.'

'The word "private" doesn't mean anything?'

'I'm sorry . . . I thought it might be from Tim.'

He saw her flush. Although not yet ready for the showdown,
he wanted to make it plain that he *knew*.

'Tim?' She raised her eyebrows. 'Why on earth should *he* write?'
Then, briskly: 'You'll catch your death here. Get back to bed.'

'In a moment.' He was cold, and his legs were shaky after four
days in bed. But he wanted to take advantage of her unpreparedness.
'Will you go to Ash Grove to-morrow?'

She shrugged. 'I haven't made up my mind. He can't order *me*
around.'

'You're frightened, aren't you?'

'Don't be stupid!'

'"Common interests to protect": *what* common interests?'

And when she didn't reply: 'It was the night Peter died, wasn't it? Something happened in the office that night.'

Arthur Reece had summoned her to the office after midnight. The only record of their meeting was contained in Reece's evidence at the inquest. Norah never spoke of it.

Something had happened, something big enough to cause lasting hatred on both sides: and fear on Norah's.

She turned away. 'Do you really imagine I would tell *you*?' she said.

CHAPTER V

Norah returned from Ash Grove on Sunday at 6.15, and said not a word to her husband about her visit. She looked pale, he thought, but perhaps that was auto-suggestion again.

Prescott had dressed in the afternoon and he had supper downstairs. Afterwards Norah spent some time with the telephone directory. At half-past eight she put on a coat.

'Where are you going?' he asked her.

'Out. Any objection?'

There was no answer to that. He heard the engine of the car roar as she reversed, too fast as usual, out of the garage; the jarring stop, the clash of gears as she moved into first; then she was away. Norah had no feeling for cars, maltreated them and complained when things went wrong. In the early days Prescott used to tease her about it: now it was an additional source of grievance.

Four days had passed since his discovery that Norah and Tim Raven were lovers, and he had done nothing. His very inaction was tantamount to a decision: you don't wait four days before taking cognisance of your wife's adultery – not unless you intend to condone it.

He was even beginning to doubt the facts. Had it really been Raven's car he saw last Wednesday? Had he imagined the creak of the stair? The truth was that he wanted an excuse to procrastinate: to sue for divorce was too positive a step, too forthright a condemnation of Norah when he felt almost equally to blame.

He was tired to-night, and restless. He'd been out of bed too long. 'An hour,' Frank Hornby had said; but he'd been up since mid-afternoon.

Yet he couldn't bear to go back to bed. He tried television, switched off after five minutes, yawned over the Sunday papers.

Finally he rang Ash Grove. Harriet hadn't kept her half promise to visit him and he was unreasonably disappointed, even irritated. Must be the depressive effect of these damned pills Frank had prescribed.

'My daughter's not here,' Arthur Reece said when he answered the phone. 'Who's speaking?'

His speech was slower than it had been, and very slightly slurred; but the arrogance still came through.

'It's John Prescott.'

Silence. Then, curtly: 'I see . . . Harriet's away for the week-end.'

'How are you, Mr. Reece?' Prescott felt he must make an effort.

'I'm alive.'

'Perhaps some time I could call and—'

'My doctor forbids me to entertain.'

Prescott was at last stung by the rudeness. 'You did see Norah, though, this afternoon?'

'That was on business. Good-bye, John.' The line went dead.

*

When Prescott returned to work on Friday, he found the backlog gratifyingly small.

'How did you cope?' he asked Mrs. Welch.

'Mr. Lowson was helpful,' she said.

But when he read the correspondence, he recognised that Edward Lowson's contribution had been minimal. He was fortunate in his secretary.

'Miss Reece rang twice,' Sandra said.

He grunted.

'She wanted to know when you'd be back. She'd like you to call her.'

Well, she could wait, Prescott decided: he hadn't forgiven her. That was 10 o'clock. He rang at 10.20.

He should have guessed the explanation. She'd called at the house twice and been told by Norah both times that her husband was asleep.

'Didn't you get the books?' Harriet said.

Norah hadn't given him any books . . .

'Daddy said you rang last Sunday,' Harriet added. 'I was in Southampton.'

'Visting your doctor friend?' he couldn't resist asking.

'Yes.' Well, it was no business of his.

'John,' she went on, 'there have been developments since our last talk. Are you alone?'

'Yes.'

Even so she picked her words carefully. 'The idea we discussed doesn't now seem quite so – so impossible.'

She must mean the suggestion that Peter was murdered.

'What have you found?' he asked.

'Not on the phone, John. I must see you.'

She didn't want him back at Ash Grove. Too awkward, she said, with her father there: he'd been doing without his afternoon sleep recently.

They arranged an appointment in his office for Monday afternoon.

He'd kept out of Tim Raven's way all morning. But the meeting couldn't long be postponed.

As Prescott parked in Selwyn Place after lunch, Raven was getting out of his car a few yards away.

Raven waited for him. 'Nice to see you back, John. You look fit.'

Now was the opportunity, the confrontation.

'Thanks, Tim,' he said. Immortal words of the cuckolded husband: 'Thanks, Tim.'

It wasn't cowardice, he told himself, but lack of confidence in his own observation. After all, he'd been ill that day, with a high temperature, he could have imagined it.

In any case, who was he to judge and to condemn? If Norah and Tim were lovers it was because he had failed as a husband.

So he said: 'Thanks, Tim.'

'We'll be seeing you to-night?' Raven said.

Prescott had forgotten it was Friday: dinner and bridge with the Ravens. That would be turning the knife in the wound, but what could he do? There were no half measures.

'I'm looking forward to it,' he said.

Saturday was the Cromley monthly medal competition. Although still not entirely fit, Prescott was tempted by the sun.

His partner had to leave immediately after the game, and Prescott went into the bar alone. When he had his drink he looked round for the most congenial group to join.

Ron Williamson left the bar at the same time. Detective Inspector Ronald Williamson of Cromley C.I.D., but Ron to his friends.

The pair of them sat down at an empty table. 'How did it go to-day?' Prescott asked.

Williamson laid down his beer. 'Not so hot,' he said. 'Net 77.'

He was a former club champion, handicap three. Prescott had met him off and on for years in the club and on the course. He liked him, although he could never achieve the easy familiarity that others did.

They commiserated with each other on the day's misfortunes on the course.

Then Prescott said: 'Remember that match of yours against Peter Reece when he—'

Williamson laughed. 'When he sank his pitch at the eighteenth? Yes.'

It was the semi-final of the club championship the year Prescott came to Cromley. He watched the last few holes. They came to the eighteenth level. Williamson laid his third stone dead, whereupon Peter won the match in the grand manner by holing a chip from thirty yards.

'Cost me five quid, that did,' Williamson said. 'He asked if I'd lay forty to one in half crowns he wouldn't sink it. I was glad afterwards he won that particular bet. *And* the final.'

'Who would have guessed,' Prescott said, 'that within a year—'

Williamson nodded. 'Terrible waste.'

'I suppose there's no doubt he *did* take his own life?' Prescott had been half-intentionally leading up to this.

He could see the mask come down, the transformation of golfing acquaintance into C.I.D. inspector.

'I'm not sure I understand you, John.'

'I mean – could someone have faked the suicide?'

'Asked Peter to stand on the chair and put his head in the noose, then pulled the chair away?'

'Perhaps he knocked him out first.'

'According to the medical evidence there was no other injury.' No other *relevant* injury, Prescott silently amended.

'And what about the suicide note? That was faked too, was it? And the murderer conveniently knew about Peter's embezzlement?'

Put like that, it sounded in the highest degree implausible.

'All right, Ron, you win.'

Williamson seemed to come to a decision. He said: 'What are you drinking? Scotch?' He went over to the bar.

When he brought back fresh drinks, he said: 'Interesting you should raise this now. We had a letter the other day telling us Peter was murdered . . .'

Prescott waited.

'. . . As usual, it was unsigned. We get a lot of them. From cranks and busybodies, sometimes people with a grudge. Not often five years after the event, though.'

'Do you just ignore them?'

'We daren't ignore anything, John.'

Prescott was tempted to ask if the letter had been in ink capitals.

'So you're reopening the case?' he said.

'Let's say we're re-examining our files. Of course this possibility was gone into at the time.'

'Murder?'

'Oh yes! I wasn't on it myself – it was Jim Hayman's case – but I know there were certain . . . *odd* features.'

'Such as?'

From another part of the room came a burst of laughter. Frank Hornby, Tim Raven and some others were swapping stories.

The inspector didn't answer Prescott's question. 'Jim was satisfied in the end it was suicide.'

Prescott waited. This had become more than a casual conversation: it was an interview.

Williamson sipped his beer. 'If we *were* reopening the case, the sort of question I'd ask – just to tie up loose ends, you understand – is why you took twenty-five minutes to drive a quarter of a mile. Your landlady, Mrs. – what's her name?'

'Jardine.'

'That's it. She told us you went out at half-past eight.'

And he'd reached Ash Grove at five-to-nine. 'I went into a cafe for cigarettes. The place was crowded and I had a long wait.'

'You remember details like that after five and a half years?'

'I remember everything that happened that day.' He could even see the face of the woman in the cafe who'd held everyone up while she argued over her change.

'The note you found, the suicide note – where exactly was it?'

'Half sticking out of the breast pocket of Peter's jacket.'

'You didn't, of course, put it there yourself?'

Prescott stared at him. 'No, I didn't put it there myself.'

'Had anyone else been near the body before you found the letter?'

'Only Harriet. Perhaps *she* planted it,' he added ironically.

The inspector smiled. 'Please don't take offence, John. I was going to call on you anyway, but when you brought up the subject yourself . . .'

'Go on. Don't mind me.'

'There's not much more, actually. Later that night you called on your wife – Miss Browne, as she was then?'

'Yes. To break the news.'

'And you stayed till when?'

'I stayed with Norah till half-past two. She was hysterical.'

'Quite so. And you then drove her to the Reeces' office, I think?'

'Yes.'

'Good . . . Oh, one other thing: you didn't actually go into the office?'

'No. I waited outside with Norah until Mr. Reece arrived and—'

'Had you ever been in the office?'

'Occasionally.'

'Recently? – I mean, just before Peter's death?'

'I don't think so – oh yes I was: the night I came back from my mother's funeral.' He described the incident.

'But you never at any time had a *key* to the office?'

'No, I hadn't a key. What the hell are you driving at, Ron?'

'Don't get excited. We're asking everyone these questions. Well, that seems to be it, then.' Prescott could almost hear an invisible notebook snap shut. 'Now how about a game of snooker?'

On Monday Harriet arrived punctually for her appointment. Prescott's temperature that day at Ash Grove had not affected his judgment: she was every bit as attractive as he had found her then. She had learned about clothes during her absence from Cromley and the very short skirts in current fashion might have been designed with Harriet in mind.

'You've a new secretary, I see?' she remarked.

'Not *new*: Sandra's been with me two years.'

'Is she local?'

'More or less. Why?'

'Her face seemed familiar. But if she's local, that explains it.' She sat down, took off her gloves. 'John, the police have been round. Twice.'

Last Tuesday Inspector Williamson had spent an hour with her father. Two days later he was back, this time accompanied by Chief Detective Inspector Lacey. They had a further talk with Arthur Reece and afterwards questioned Harriet herself.

'What about?' Prescott asked.

'Mostly about what happened the day Peter died.'

'They've had a letter.' Prescott described his own conversation with Williamson. 'They have to make a show of investigating it.'

Harriet said slowly: 'This is no pretence. My impression is they're taking it very seriously indeed.' She hesitated, then added: 'A lot of their questions were about you, John.'

'What sort of questions?'

'They wanted to know what you did that day. Exact times and so on. They also asked if you often called on Norah while Peter was working late.' She smiled. 'I lost my temper then.'

Someone must have told them of the one occasion he did take Norah home late. Alice Lowson, probably; or her father.

'Do the police know of the letters your father's been receiving?' Prescott asked.

'Not unless he's told them, and I'm sure he hasn't. But that's another thing, John: he's being blackmailed.'

Harriet had spoken again to her father about these letters. Again he angrily refused to discuss them. So she kept an eye on his mail, listened when she could to his telephone conversations.

One day she heard him instruct his stockbroker to sell certain shares and pay the proceeds into his current account. He then gave Harriet a note to post to his bank manager. She steamed it open: it was a request to send him, by messenger, £500 in single notes. Next day Reece hovered by the door until the messenger arrived. He took the package to his room.

Harriet saw it later in a drawer in his dressing-table. But when she returned from her week-end in Southampton the package was gone.

'I suspect he gave it to Norah,' she said.

'You're not suggesting Norah's blackmailing him?'

'She hasn't the guts.'

It was true: Norah was too frightened of Arthur Reece to extort money from him. Anyway the letter Prescott had found in her room clearly implied that she was not the blackmailer.

'My idea is,' Harriet continued, 'that Daddy was using Norah to deliver the money.'

That was more plausible. He remembered how, on her return from Ash Grove, Norah had looked up addresses in the directory and then gone out. Had she taken a bulky envelope with her? He hadn't seen it; but naturally she would hide it from him.

The telephone rang. It was a client consulting him about a road accident he'd been involved in. Prescott explained the legal position and advised him what to do.

Harriet was watching him as he put the receiver down. 'You know, John,' she said, 'you're two different people: the crisp, confident lawyer and . . .'

She didn't have to go on. She meant that in his personal relations he was timid and ineffectual. The explanation was simple: he was on top of his job, he could speak with authority, without fear of seeming a fool: whereas in his private life he felt everyone else was better integrated than he.

'You know what you need?" Harriet said. 'Someone to tell you you're wonderful. Four times a day after meals. You've never had that, have you?'

No, and never would.

Harriet sighed. 'Ah, well, back to business. Will you tackle Norah?'

He had expected that. 'She's no more forthcoming than your father, Harriet.'

'At least she's not liable to take a stroke if you get rough. I daren't bully Daddy.' And when he hesitated: 'John, we do have a lever: tell Norah you'll go to the police unless she spills the beans.'

Harriet hadn't followed the argument through. If Peter had been murdered, and if Arthur Reece was being blackmailed, it wasn't hard to suggest a connection . . .

She was furious when Prescott pointed it out. 'If you think,' she said, 'for one moment that Daddy murdered his own son, I'll never—'

'I'm only telling you how the police would look at it.'

'Well, don't tell me again. I won't listen.'

Time had altered Harriet's character less than her physical appearance. She was still fiercely loyal to those she loved; at the expense, if need be, of reason and logic.

'I'll talk to Norah,' he said.

'Good. And, John—'

'Yes?'

'Wade into her, give her the works.' She grinned. 'Sorry – I keep forgetting she's your wife.'

CHAPTER VI

Prescott was late home from the office. Norah had left a cold meal and a note: 'Playing in bridge match. Will be late – don't wait up.'

She came home at 1.20. She was wearing a fine wool dress and had her fur stole over her arm. She looked elated, glowing.

'You shouldn't have waited up,' she said.

'How did the game go?'

'We lost. But Thelma and I had a good score.' Thelma Russell was Norah's regular bridge partner. 'I went round to Thelma's for a drink afterwards, to discuss the hands,' she added casually.

Too casually. Prescott remembered Margaret Raven mentioning last Friday evening that she was spending this week with her married sister in Cardiff. Tim would be alone . . .

'Suppose,' he said, 'I were to phone Thelma to-morrow, would she confirm that?'

Norah said: 'What the hell are you talking about?'

'You heard me.'

She rummaged in her handbag, thrust a yellow sheet at him. 'There's the score sheet, if you don't believe me.'

'I don't doubt you played in a match. But it didn't go on till one o'clock.'

'I told you: I went to—'

'I know what you told me. Sit down, Norah.' And when she ignored him: 'SIT DOWN!'

She sat down. 'My, my!' she said. 'Listen to the mouse squeaking!' But her hand shook as she lit the inevitable cigarette.

He hadn't meant to bring up the Raven affair tonight. But she'd looked so damned *smug* when she came in.

'I'm not blind, Norah. And I'm not a *complete* idiot.'

She drew on her cigarette, expelled the smoke. 'I admit nothing,' she said. 'But, my God, if I *were* driven to someone else's bed, would it be so surprising?'

She had hit the right note, touched on his own feeling of guilt. His anger gave way to a feeling of helplessness.

'I did offer you a divorce,' he reminded her.

Norah knew she had won. 'And I told you, John, I don't want a divorce.' She yawned, looked at her watch. 'And now—'

'Don't go yet, Norah.' If he didn't speak now, he never would. 'Who's blackmailing you?'

She had half-risen, but slumped back down in her chair. 'Nobody's blackmailing me,' she said.

He kept his voice flat. 'Ten days ago Arthur Reece drew five hundred pounds from his bank: You went to see him on Sunday and he gave you the money. You delivered it that night. Right?'

'You're crazy.' Now she did get up and walk towards the door.

Prescott moved past her and stood with his back against the door. 'You're not leaving this room till you tell me.'

Norah laughed. 'Squeak, squeak!' she said, her face raised tauntingly.

The crack of his hand on her cheek was like a whip lash. And as she stood unmoving, incredulous, he struck her a second time.

Norah cowered away. 'Don't touch me!' she hissed.

'I'm—' But the apology died on his lips as he saw something in her eyes he hadn't seen for years: respect.

He hadn't known he was capable of such rage. Later it would be on his conscience; but now he had to press home his advantage.

'I'm waiting,' he said.

'My cigarette . . .' Norah muttered. It had fallen from her hand and was smouldering on the carpet. Prescott stamped it out, offered her another. Red weals were appearing on her cheek where he had struck her.

'I'm not being blackmailed,' Norah said in a shaky voice. 'It's Reece. And he doesn't know who the blackmailer is.'

'Who did you deliver the money to?'

She explained that Reece had received a demand for £500. It was to be left in the telephone kiosk outside the Midland Bank on Howlands Road at precisely 9 o'clock that Sunday.

Norah found an 'Out of Order' notice hung on the outside of the box, no doubt to keep other people away. She left the package and drove off.

'Didn't you wait to see who picked it up?' Prescott asked.

Reece had been warned that no attempt must be made to identify the recipient. Norah had, however, turned into a side street, parked her car, and walked back to Howlands Road. A car was standing at the phone box and someone was getting into it. He drove off in the opposite direction.

'"He"?' Prescott said. 'It was a man?'

'I've no idea. It was too far away and it was dark.'

'What sort of car?'

'Fairly small one, I think.'

Prescott said reflectively: 'Arthur Reece is an invalid. How was *he* expected to deliver the money to Howlands Road?'

She didn't answer.

'I asked a question, Norah.'

She said sulkily: 'The letter told him to get me to deliver it.'

'So that whatever hold this blackmailer has on Reece concerns you equally?'

'Not *equally*.'

'Don't quibble.'

'Well, don't act the bloody cross-examiner.' It was the first sign of returning spirit.

'What is it, Norah? Something about Peter?'

Norah stubbed out her cigarette, immediately lit another. 'Yes,' she said. 'It's about Peter. And don't ask me to say any more, because I won't.'

'Oh yes, you will—'

'No, John. Hit me again if you like – it won't do any good.'

He had no temptation to hit her again. 'Norah, the police now suspect Peter was murdered—'

'But he wasn't murdered. I *know*.'

'Then what in God's name is Reece being blackmailed about?'

She shook her head stubbornly.

Prescott tried another tack. 'Surely he must have some idea *who's* blackmailing him?'

Norah hesitated. 'He's not certain. He says it's worth five hundred pounds to keep things dark. But if there's any further demand—'

'What'll he do then?'

'God help anyone who doublecrosses him,' she said.

Prescott didn't believe Reece would disgorge even £500 without a fight. 'Whose address were you looking up in the phone book?' he asked.

'When?'

'That Sunday evening.'

'It wouldn't mean anything if I told you,' she said. 'You don't know this person. And anyway the name wasn't in the book.'

*

Prescott couldn't sleep. His imagination tingled at the blows he had struck Norah; and with satisfaction, not guilt. He couldn't convince himself he had been wrong: if ever a woman had asked for it . . .

The violence had produced results too: Norah had talked, had admitted the blackmail, had admitted it concerned Peter's death.

Prescott cast his mind back. When he broke the news that Peter had hanged himself, Norah showed the normal reaction: shock, hysteria, the tears of grief. But later, when Arthur Reece telephoned, her response changed: the predominant emotion was now *fear*.

Why had Reece phoned? To order her into the office, at 2.30 in the morning, to check on the funds Peter was supposed to have been embezzling. Making every allowance for the shock of his son's death, was that a reasonable thing for him to do? It was not.

All right, what *were* they doing in the office that night? Something for which, years later, they were being blackmailed. Sex? No, even Norah wouldn't, on the night of her fiancé's death, make love to his father. Anyway, that angry voice on the telephone had not been in the accents of desire.

A small incident provided the clue. Prescott recalled his interview with Inspector Hayman at Ash Grove after Peter's body was found. When he came out Arthur Reece had asked if he'd mentioned the suicide note to the police. He hadn't: it had slipped his mind in the excitement and shock. 'Never mind – I'll let them see it,' Reece had said.

But *when* did he show it? That night? Or the following day? Suppose Reece and Norah went into the office not to check on Peter's embezzlement but to create false evidence of them; and to type the 'suicide' note. The corollary must surely be that Arthur Reece, with Norah's connivance, had murdered his son. Why else fake evidence of suicide?

For one moment Prescott was blindingly sure this was the answer. Then he remembered the first note – the one he had himself found on Peter's body and passed to Arthur Reece. Addressed to 'Father.' What had that contained?

At breakfast Norah made no reference to the previous night. She buried herself behind the *Daily Express*.

He felt less confident this morning, had to force himself to speak. 'Norah!'

She lowered her paper. Her face was still faintly marked where his hand had struck.

He said: 'The night Peter died—'

She interrupted, wincing. 'For God's sake, not again!' She no longer looked frightened, only bored.

'Just one question: did Peter really steal from the firm, or did you and his father cook the books afterwards?'

Did she flinch? He wasn't certain.

She took her cigarettes from her dressing-gown pocket. 'You know what, John? It's high time you saw a psychiatrist.'

She lit her cigarette, dropped the match in her saucer, where it continued to burn.

'Use an ash tray,' he said.

'Shut up!' She yawned.

He wanted to tell her she was a slut. He hated to see her lounging in her dressing-gown at breakfast. But he couldn't make the effort, couldn't face another quarrel. Their old relationship was restored; and Norah knew it.

Prescott called at Ash Grove that evening. Harriet was surprised to see him.

'I warned you not to come to the house,' she said.

'All right, I'll go away.'

She laughed. 'Don't sulk. Come in – the sitting-room's all right. Daddy's in the study with Mr. Lowson.'

She had been playing the piano, she told him; trying to master a Chopin study. She played it to him. She was quite good, but not as fluent as her brother had been. Or Prescott himself.

'One of these days I must buy a piano,' he said.

Harriet was astonished. 'You haven't *got* one?'

He shook his head.

'Why not?'

It was Norah: she would never have let him enjoy it. She resented anything she couldn't share.

He parried Harriet's question. 'I seemed to lose interest.'

She nodded grimly. 'I'll bet you did . . .'

She got him a drink. 'Do you remember,' she said, 'the night we all sat here and drank to Shakespeare's birthday or something?'

'George Washington's.'

'That was it. Daddy wouldn't let me have sherry.'

'It was the night I met Norah.'

Harriet's face clouded. 'I was *mad* that none of you saw through her – you nor Peter nor Daddy. Men can be so stupid: all they've eyes for is a girl's *legs*—'

'Yours weren't worth looking at in these days, Harriet.'

She wasn't to be diverted. 'I knew in ten seconds she was a bitch and I was dead right.'

'She's not so bad really.' Harriet was too apt to see things in blacks and whites.

'Don't make excuses for her. Look what she's done to you, John; if that doesn't prove she's a bitch . . .'

'What has she done to me?'

Harriet looked coolly at him. 'If you don't know I can't tell you.'

He did know. He had lost hope somewhere along the way.

'Well, I got her to talk last night,' he said. He told her the story.

Harriet was excited. 'I think we're on to something, John. That makes sense.'

'What makes sense?'

'I've never really believed Peter was a thief – it just wasn't in his nature. If Daddy and Norah framed him—'

'Have you considered *why*?'

Her eyes flashed. 'I warned you, John: Daddy's not a murderer . . . I'm sure Peter killed himself, but for some other reason. Some reason so shocking that Daddy had to hush it up.'

'And Norah?'

'She must have been involved too,' Harriet agreed. 'I do know this: it *was* the Monday forenoon before Daddy handed over the suicide note. He said he'd been so upset he didn't remember till then.'

Somewhere in the house a door opened and there was the sound of approaching voices.

'Lord!' Harriet said, 'they're coming in here.'

Prescott's first impression was that Arthur Reece had scarcely changed at all. There wasn't a grey hair in his head, his colour was good, his handshake firm.

He dragged his left leg when he walked, though, and his mouth was slightly twisted. One eyelid had a nervous tic.

He greeted Prescott without warmth. 'After our conversation last week, I'm surprised to find you here,' he said.

'I invited him,' Harriet said untruthfully.

'Did you? Well, just remember that John is *married*.'

Harriet flushed.

Edward Lowson tried pouring oil. 'Isn't Arthur looking well, John?'

'Very.'

Reece smiled sardonically. 'Thank you . . . The fact remains it's past my bedtime. Where's the whisky, Harriet?'

The decanter she had brought out for Prescott was on the piano.

'You're not having a drink at this hour, Daddy. You know what Dr. Hornby said.'

'Hornby's a fuss-pot. Excuse me.' She was standing in front of the piano like Horatio on the bridge.

'Goddammit to hell!' he said. 'Whose house is this?' Crimson, Harriet stepped aside. 'Get a glass, would you?' Reece added mildly. 'Not for me, for Edward . . . Good night, everyone.' He went out.

While Harriet was fetching the glass, Lowson said: 'You have to make allowances, John. He's not well.'

'That's no excuse for treating Harriet like that.' Prescott was angry.

Harriet came back. 'That's how he always behaves with someone new,' she said. 'He thinks they're staring at his mouth and he gets mad. You'd be sorry for him really.'

Prescott didn't think he could ever be sorry for Arthur Reece.

'Help yourself, Uncle Edward,' Harriet added. 'You know how you like it.'

Edward Lowson poured his drink. He was enjoying himself, Prescott could see: storing it all up to tell his wife and Alice. 'You'll never guess who was visiting Harriet to-night . . .'

Now he raised his glass with a flourish and said: 'Your very good health, Harriet . . . John.' He came over and sat on the sofa, produced a cigar from an inside pocket. 'You don't mind, my dear?'

'Not a bit.'

As he removed the band, he said: 'I can truthfully say that in thirty years your father and I have never exchanged an angry word. It's all a question of how you handle him.' He struck a match and embarked on the ceremony of lighting the cigar.

Prescott couldn't resist deflating him. 'I saw you quarrel once. At that engagement party in the Regent.'

'Engagement party?'

'For Peter and Norah.'

'Oh yes!' Harriet said. 'I remember. You and Daddy were going at it hammer and tongs.'

Lowson looked pained. 'I recall the incident,' he admitted. 'But you exaggerate. I was giving Arthur unpalatable news which he wouldn't accept. Alas! later events were to prove my warning justified.' He was staring at Prescott.

'What warning?' Harriet asked.

'Ah no! I'm not one to rake up old scandals.' He crossed one ample leg over the other. 'I must say, Harriet, this is not the most comfortable seat I've ever sat in.'

She nodded. 'The springs dig into your bottom, don't they? Take the arm-chair.'

Lowson winced. Prudery governed his vocabulary, and certain parts of the body had no name. However, he moved to the arm-chair.

Harriet said: 'Have the police been questioning you, Uncle Edward?'

'The police?'

'They've been here twice. Surely they must have been to you too?' 'What about?'

'About Peter. They think he may have been murdered.'

She knew how to harry him. You had to be absolutely direct, to give no opportunity for evasion and circumlocution.

He had brought his spectacles into the battle now and was brandishing them in genial reprimand. 'My dear child, that's utterly preposterous. You've been watching too much trash on television.'

'It's true, isn't it, John?'

'Yes.'

Lowson puffed his cigar, carefully blew a smoke ring. 'Murder? Preposterous,' he repeated. 'And in any case how could I assist the police?'

'You were one of the last persons to see Peter alive.'

'*I* was?'

'Yes. You phoned him after lunch and he went round.'

He didn't deny it. 'How did you know that?'

She shrugged. 'I've been making enquiries . . . Why *did* you send for him?'

But he smiled and shook his head. 'As I said before, there are some things best left buried.' Again his eyes were on Prescott. 'All the same, if the police are talking of *murder*, that puts a different complexion on it. I'll give Lacey a ring in the morning.' He stood up. 'I must go. I told Madge I wouldn't be late. Thank you for the drink, Harriet. When are we going to see a ring on that pretty finger? You're far too attractive a girl to be single . . . Good night, John.'

Harriet made a face when she came back. 'When are we going to see a ring on that pretty finger?' she mimicked.

'Like a caricature, isn't he?'

'He's dangerous, all the same. He has his knife in you, John.'

Prescott laughed. 'He thinks I jilted his daughter years ago.'

'Oh that's it, is it? It's no laughing matter. I'd like to know what he'll say to the police.'

'Does it matter?'

She was angry. 'Of course it matters! Stop burying your head in the sand, John. Inspector Lacey already half believes you murdered Peter.'

Still he couldn't take it seriously. 'What possible motive could I have?'

Harriet looked at him steadily. 'You married his fiancée as soon as he was out of the way . . .'

Oh God! Surely no one could believe that!

'If you want my opinion,' Harriet continued, 'Edward Lowson will say you were carrying on with Norah even while Peter was alive.'

'You don't believe that, Harriet?'

'No. But who am I to contradict Edward Lowson? Norah's rooms were right opposite his house, weren't they?'

Yes, and there had been that *one* night . . .

'Lowson's a windbag,' he said, 'and he can be malicious. But I doubt if he'd deliberately fabricate evidence.'

'I've always understood the most dangerous witness was the one who *believed* the lies he was telling.'

She meant that Lowson could convince himself that what he wanted to believe was true. Was he vindictive enough for that? Perhaps . . .

It was nearly half-past ten; he ought to go. But the prospect of returning to Norah didn't appeal – though perhaps she was with Tim Raven again. The thought made him angry.

'Speaking of legs—' he said suddenly.

'Who was speaking of legs?'

'Yours have developed very satisfactorily. After a slow start.'

Primly Harriet smoothed down her skirt. 'Thank you, John,' she said.

Her tone was not encouraging. Encouraging? What was he trying to do, anyway? He was oppressed by a terrible loneliness, he wanted sympathy, comfort, love. It didn't have to be Harriet, any girl would have done.

He looked at her and knew it wasn't true: no other girl could satisfy him. He had fallen in love with Harriet. Too late.

'Edward's right,' he said. 'It's surprising you're not engaged yet.'

She didn't answer.

'Your doctor friend,' he continued, 'is he—'

Harriet interrupted angrily: 'If you must know, Alan and I have broken it off. That's why I went down last week-end – to tell him it wouldn't work. Satisfied?'

'I'm sorry, Harriet.'

Her cheeks were flushed, her eyes smouldered. 'I really don't see what business it is of yours.'

'I'm sorry,' he repeated. He wasn't: he had the answer he hoped for.

He got up to leave: no point in pressing his luck.

'What are we going to do, John?' Harriet said.

For a moment he misunderstood. 'Do?'

'About this blackmail?'

Oh *that*! 'The police should be told,' he said.

Harriet wasn't happy. 'I think we must leave Daddy to do that. He'd never forgive me—'

'If Peter was murdered—'

'Yes, but *was* he? I still don't believe that.'

'Frank Hornby thinks Dr. Parry knew more than he said at the inquest.' He repeated what Hornby had told him. 'Not that it helps,' he added, 'since Parry's dead.'

'I'm not so sure,' Harriet said slowly.

Dr. Parry had been the Reeces' doctor and friend for many years, she told him. Mrs. Parry was like a mother to her. Since she returned to Cromley, Harriet had been meaning to visit the old lady, who now lived at Shepperton, fifty miles away.

'I think I'll go to-morrow,' she said.

'You don't imagine Mrs. Parry would know anything?'

'They were very close – the kind of couple that had no secrets.'

'How will you go?' She hadn't a car; Reece hadn't brought his over from France.

'Bus, I suppose.' It would be a tedious journey, with several changes.

'If you can leave it till Thursday, I'll drive you.' He had to be in court to-morrow.

Harriet looked doubtful. 'Do you think we ought?'

'I promise not to rape, seduce or otherwise molest you.'

She laughed. 'How disappointing!'

CHAPTER VII

Prescott almost didn't get away on Thursday. He was visited in the office by Chief Inspector Lacey and Ron Williamson.

Lacey he knew only by sight and reputation: a large, soft-spoken man who had achieved some fame last year over the Cromley drugs scandal.

He went over the same ground Williamson had covered in the

club, only more slowly. 'I've answered that before,' Prescott said more than once. 'I dare say, Mr. Prescott, but it won't do any harm to answer it again, will it?'

He had the impression that Lacey was antagonistic, but perhaps this was how he conducted all his interviews. At any rate he was the kind of man most calculated to destroy Prescott's confidence, for there was a solidity about him, an air of inner certainty and moral ascendancy.

It came out most clearly when he asked about Prescott's early relations with Norah.

'You used to visit her at night at her apartment?'

'You mean before Peter's death?'

'Yes.'

'I took her home once from Ash Grove, at Peter's request.'

'Once only?'

'Yes.'

Silence. Clearly they had conflicting evidence.

'Very well,' Lacey said eventually. 'We'll deal with that one occasion. Did you go into her apartment?'

'She asked me in for a drink.'

'What time was this?'

'Half-past eleven.'

'I see. Late at night. And you went in. What happened?'

Suddenly Prescott knew they'd been talking to Norah and he guessed what she'd said. Well, it was her word against his: he could deny it and they'd never prove it. But he was still plagued by a conscience formed in his youth: he didn't lie readily.

'I tried to kiss her. She pushed me away.'

The chief inspector re-phrased it: 'You made advances to her?'

The disapproving line of Lacey's mouth reminded Prescott of

his father. 'Well, dammit,' he said angrily, 'she sat up and begged for it.'

'Then why should she push you away?'

'Because she's a—' He stopped suddenly: the whole office must be hearing this. He said quietly: 'You'd better ask my wife.'

No doubt they had. He glanced across at Ron Williamson, who was taking notes of the interview, head bent over his notebook. This must seem to him a sorry, sordid tale; as indeed it was. But the incident was an isolated one, a moment's madness; and it had been stage-managed by Norah. How could you put that across to an unsympathetic policeman?

The questions were continuing.

'Yes,' he agreed sullenly, 'I went to her flat to break the news of Peter's death. I told Inspector Williamson that too.' Williamson nodded without looking up.

'Quite so,' said Lacey. 'And you stayed until two-thirty, I believe?'

'Look here, if you think we spent the time in bed—'

'Control yourself, Mr. Prescott. I made no such suggestion. Nevertheless, within a fortnight you were engaged, within six weeks you were married. You didn't lose much time, did you?'

He didn't answer.

'How do you think your friend Peter Reece would have looked on that?'

He would have applauded their good sense. Peter had had a logical mind: 'If a person's dead, he's dead,' he had once said. 'Nothing you do can hurt him – so why pretend?'

But again how to convince the conventional mind? Prescott didn't even try.

They left after an hour. The inscrutable Mrs. Welch made no

reference to their visit, although she must have overheard his outbursts.

'Mr. Crawley couldn't wait,' she said. 'I made another appointment for two-thirty this afternoon.'

'I'll not be here. I'm going out of town.'

'There was nothing in your diary.'

'I know. It's not your fault.'

Sandra waited, saying nothing. Her lack of inquisitiveness was inhuman. Prescott, who usually admired the quality, was, in his present mood, irritated by it.

Moreover, her Jekyll and Hyde existence suddenly struck him as peculiar. He couldn't forget that night in the Chilton, when he'd seen Sandra in an expensive evening dress, pearls round her throat, her golden hair shimmering under the lights. The contrast with her office image was excessive: here her hair style was severe, she used hardly any make-up – and surely that black dress was unnecessarily unbecoming?

'When are you leaving, Mr. Prescott?' she asked now.

He was to call for Harriet at 12 o'clock. 'In ten minutes.'

'Mr. Raven wants to see you too,' Sandra said. 'Mr. Raven's here now,' Tim said, coming into the room. Sandra went out.

'Will it take long, Tim?'

'Seconds only.' He twisted his head sideways to peer at a letter on Prescott's desk. No lack of inquisitiveness in him.

The business took nearly twenty minutes, while Prescott inwardly fumed. He didn't want Raven to sense his eagerness.

At last Raven stood up. 'Thanks, John,' he said. 'What it is to have an incisive mind!'

A knowledge of the law, Prescott silently amended. Raven was becoming increasingly slack as the years passed. He was almost as rusty as old Lowson himself.

'Where are you off to, then, John?'

Trust Raven to ask the direct question! At least he hadn't mentioned the visit of the C.I.D. 'Shepperton,' he said.

'Shepperton! I didn't know we had clients as far afield as that.'

'It's not a client.'

Brief pause, then: 'Oh I see! Good hunting, then. If you're not back, I'll keep Norah warm to-night, shall I?'

He must be very confident, Prescott thought, to make cracks like that.

'It's not *my* fault you were late, John.'

'I'm sorry.'

'And another thing: we're not so late that you have to risk our necks. Slow down!' He let the needle slip back to sixty.

Nothing was going right. First that unedifying scene with Lacey and Williamson; the whole office would be sniggering over it now. Then the maddening delay on Raven's problem which made him late in calling for Harriet. And now this.

They drove in silence. As they approached the Anvil Road-house, twenty miles out of Cromley, Prescott said abruptly: 'Will this do for lunch?'

By the time Harriet had orientated herself sufficiently to answer the question, the road-house was behind them. Prescott sighed.

Harriet said: 'Stop the car, please.' He pulled up by the verge.

'Now,' she said, 'either you give over sulking or you drive me straight home. Do you understand?'

He took a grip of himself. 'I'm a fool, Harriet. I was so depressed—'

'Well, I wasn't responsible for your depression.'

'I know. I just wanted to hurt someone.'

'And I was handy? I'll be many things to you, John, but not your whipping boy. So don't do it again. Not ever.'

'No.' He drew her face towards him and kissed her. Harriet allowed her lips to remain on his for a brief moment, then gently pulled away. 'And that's another experiment,' she said, 'that we'll not repeat.' Her voice was shaky.

As he turned and drove back to the Anvil, she said: 'You musn't feel sorry for yourself, John. Self-pity's the meanest of the emotions.'

'You're quoting Peter.'

'Very likely. It's no less true for that.'

Peter also used to say that if every suicide had delayed 24 hours, ninety per cent of them wouldn't have done it: even the blackest mood is ephemeral. So to-day, by the time they were in the bar and had their drinks, Prescott's whole outlook had changed. He was having a day out with a pretty girl (a beautiful girl, he amended, looking at her eager face and dancing eyes and that marvellous black hair) – with a beautiful girl whom he loved and who loved him. The last three words were founded in hope rather than knowledge.

True, there were obstacles. His marriage, for a start; but Norah by her own acts had released him from his obligations. There was also this growing cloud of suspicion over Peter's death: he could no longer shrug that off.

They discussed it over lunch, when Prescott described his interview with Chief Inspector Lacey.

'You admit now,' Harriet said, 'that this is more than a token investigation?'

Yes, Lacey's manner indicated that they had some concrete evidence of murder. Clearly, too, their suspicions centred on

Prescott. Why? Motive and opportunity. Anything else? That depended on what Norah and Edward Lowson had told them.

'All the same,' Harriet said, 'I don't see why you were *quite* so upset by the chief inspector.'

'It was the way he spoke to me. He made me feel—' He stopped: Harriet wouldn't understand.

But she did. 'You're too concerned about what people think of you. Do what seems to you right and to hell with the opinion polls.' It might have been Peter talking.

She continued: 'It's a matter of confidence. You have to believe in yourself, that's all.'

All? It was too much.

'How do you know so much about me?' Prescott asked.

She coloured. 'Peter used to talk about you. I was . . . interested. He had great hopes for you.'

If anyone could have given him self-confidence, it was Peter. If only Peter had lived . . .

Harriet had been thinking on parallel lines. 'If only you hadn't married Norah . . .' she said.

A cluster of houses, a tiny church, one shop: that was Shepperton. Hardly big enough to earn the title of village.

Hawthorn Cottage was set back from the road, with a rose garden in front and a vegetable patch behind. Ivy clung to its white-washed walls.

It was half-past three when they stopped outside the gate.

'It's terribly *tiny*,' Harriet said doubtfully.

'There can't be more than one Hawthorn Cottage in Shepperton . . . I'll wait in the car.'

'No, come in, John. She's expecting you.'

Mrs. Parry was one of those small, apple-cheeked women on whom time makes little impression. To-day she looked no different from six years ago when Prescott saw her at Peter's funeral.

After an affectionate reunion with Harriet (with much clucking over how she had 'filled out') Mrs. Parry greeted Prescott politely but with – he sensed – some curiosity. He wondered what explanation Harriet had given of his presence.

They had tea round the fire. It was a pleasant room, agreeably furnished, but small. Indeed the whole cottage, as Harriet had said, was miniscule.

Prescott noticed, too, that the black dress Mrs. Parry was wearing was shiny from long use. He wondered if, as sometimes happened in elderly widows, frugality was yielding place to miserliness. She didn't look the type.

The same thought had occurred to Harriet, who was delicately probing her financial circumstances. Mrs. Parry answered without embarrassment.

She had received a shock when her husband's estate was wound up: after his debts were paid there was nothing left. She sold the house in Cromley to pay off the mortgage and with the balance bought this cottage. She was living on a not over-generous pension.

Prescott was surprised. Dr. Parry had had a good practice in Cromley, with a fair number of private patients. True, he lived well, but even so . . .

'David was hopelessly unbusinesslike,' Mrs. Parry was saying. 'He thought of his patients, not their money.'

'Daddy's firm did his accounts for him, didn't they?' Harriet said.

'Yes, he'd have been bankrupt, I often thought, but for your father and Peter. He never remembered to send bills . . . And, of course, instead of pulling in his horns when he took a partner, he carried on as if his income was as big as ever. Frank's been terribly kind, incidentally. Hardly a month passes but he comes down to see me. Tessa's having another baby in February, did you know that?'

'That'll make five, won't it?' said Harriet. 'Must be an annual event.'

Prescott's mind was on the Parry finances. 'We were your husband's lawyers, weren't we, Mrs. Parry?'

'We? Oh, of course, you're with that firm. Yes. My dealings have all been with Edward Lowson.'

'He wound up the estate?'

'Yes, very expeditiously too, I must say.'

Harriet noticed the grudging tone. 'You don't like Uncle Edward?'

'Well, I know he's a friend of your father's, my dear, but, really, he's so conceited. And these cigars! He was here the other day and the house stills smells of them.'

'You seem to have lots of visitors, anyway.'

'Yes. Not always welcome ones. I've had the police twice in the last fortnight.'

That saved trouble: she had introduced the subject herself.

'The police, Aunt Lucy?'

'I'm sorry to bring back unhappy memories, Harriet, but I think you ought to hear. It's about Peter's death.'

Inspector Williamson had been the advance party and, when he found there was something worth probing, he brought along the chief inspector a day or two later.

'You must understand,' Mrs. Parry said, 'David was already ill when your brother died. We didn't know then what it was, but he was losing his grip, getting confused.' Prescott had heard that after his retirement Parry's mind and body slowly disintegrated as one tiny blood vessel in the brain after another gave out.

'That was his last police case. He should never have taken it – especially when it concerned Peter. Peter was like a son to him . . . And to me.' She sighed, then continued: 'He was beside himself with worry over the case. And he wouldn't tell me what was wrong. Months later he let it out.' She stopped.

'What was it, Aunt Lucy?'

'He'd found a bruise on Peter's neck.'

'On his *neck*?' Prescott said. 'But the rope would leave marks—'

Mrs. Parry shook her head. 'David didn't think this was done by the rope. Peter had been knocked out before he was hanged. There's a place on the nape of the neck where—'

'So I've heard . . . When your husband told you, Mrs. Parry, why didn't you go to the police?'

She looked at him sadly. 'Because by that time David had Gladstone and Disraeli among his patients and sometimes addressed me as Queen Victoria. Even in his lucid moments you couldn't trust his memory. I'd never have convinced the police.'

'But you believed it?'

'I believed he'd found the bruise – I didn't think it followed that Peter was murdered.'

'And the police? They accept it now?'

'They seem to.'

Harriet said: 'I wonder why he kept quiet at the time?'

'I've told you, Harriet: he was ill. He'd no confidence in himself any longer. Frank had been covering up for him – David admitted that to me. Peter's death was so obviously suicide that he was afraid of making a fool of himself by raising doubts.'

Prescott recalled Dr. Parry's reply to the coroner: 'There was no other relevant injury . . .' The word 'relevant' was probably a sop to his conscience.

It was at that moment that Prescott became convinced that Peter Reece had been murdered. The evidence would never stand up in court: the ramblings of a man in his dotage, reported at second hand. And yet he had no serious doubt of their truth.

'Mrs. Parry,' he said, 'have you ever told this story to anyone else?'

'No.' But there was hesitation in her voice.

'You're sure?'

'Well,' she said, 'there was that reporter a week or two ago . . .'

A woman had phoned, saying she was from the *Globe*. Her paper was doing a series on unsolved crimes and one case they were covering was the death of Peter Reece. They had found evidence, she claimed, that Reece had been murdered, and their theory was he must somehow have been rendered unconscious first. In view of Dr. Parry's obvious signs of stress at the inquest, they wondered if the post-mortem had been more revealing than he admitted. Had he perhaps voiced doubts to his wife?

'I sent her packing,' Mrs. Parry said indignantly. 'The impertinence of her!'

'You told her nothing?'

'Not a thing! She kept suggesting Peter had been struck on the head. I said it was stuff and nonsense!'

Yes, but Mrs. Parry would not make a convincing liar . . . Interesting, though, that the *head* was mentioned: the same mistake as the anonymous letter writer had made . . .

'What sort of voice had this woman?' Harriet asked.

'Educated. Sounded young. Not unlike your own.'

*

Mrs. Parry was unwilling to let them go. She produced an album of old photographs of the Reece family: Arthur and Eleanor Reece on their wedding day, Arthur stiff and tight-lipped, his wife sweetly smiling, a thinner, more delicate version of Harriet; a larger group, taken on the same occasion.

'Who's that?' Prescott asked, pointing to the best man, whose dignified features under a shock of black hair looked familiar.

'That's Edward Lowson,' Harriet said.

'What! With hair!' They all laughed.

There were snaps of Peter as a baby, Peter in rompers, Peter in his first school uniform. Then Harriet in her mother's arms, a fat, contented baby sucking her thumb. And as an angelic young child: no wonder those who'd known her then had predicted that after the gawky teenage period she would be a winner. *Rightly* predicated, Prescott thought, stealing a glance at her now.

The last picture of Mrs. Reece was with Harriet at four, and you could see death in her face. Afterwards the Parrys were increasingly in evidence.

The final page contained a photograph of Peter receiving the cup on winning the golf club championship the summer before his death.

Mrs. Parry closed the book.

It was half-past six when they left. While Harriet was putting on her coat, Mrs. Parry said to Prescott: 'Don't hurt that girl, John.' Her bright little eyes were on him: she hadn't missed much, he thought.

The car was slow to start, and when it did, the engine sounded unhappy. But it picked up.

'Marvellous old lady,' Prescott remarked.

'Yes. She never lets life get her down.' Harriet didn't have to point the moral further.

'You haven't seen her since you left Cromley?'

'No. I wrote, not nearly often enough.'

Silence for a few minutes, then Prescott said: 'Where shall we have dinner?'

'No, John, I said I'd be home.'

'You could phone.'

'What about Norah?'

'I'll phone her too.'

Harriet hesitated, then gave in. 'I suppose Daddy's capable of taking cold meat out of the fridge . . . The hotel at Hazelford used to be quite good.'

A mile or two further on she said: 'What's that funny noise?'

'The engine's misfiring a bit. Nothing serious.'

They phoned from the Hazelford Hotel. Harriet got through to her father, but there was no reply from Norah.

'She plays bridge, doesn't she?' Harriet said.

'Among other things.'

'What?'

He'd made the opportunity and took it. 'I expect she's with Tim Raven.'

He told the story over dinner. Without exaggeration or embellishment – it needed none. Harriet was angry but not surprised.

'You musn't judge her too harshly,' he said. 'I'm not her type at all. I bore her.'

'She worked hard enough to get you. What are you doing about it?'

He shrugged.

'You can't just let things slide, John. You must—' She stopped. 'Sorry. I shouldn't offer advice.'

They lingered over their coffee. Harriet was more relaxed now, as if to-day's expedition had ceased to trouble her conscience.

They left at ten o'clock. Harriet put her arm in his as they crossed to the car park.

The car was again sluggish and this time the signs of stress didn't disappear. Two miles out of Hazelford the engine faltered and died; the car slid to a halt. Prescott opened the bonnet; but in the total darkness he was helpless.

The third car he flagged stopped, and the driver undertook to give a message to a garage in Hazelford. Prescott got back in beside Harriet.

It seemed natural to put his arms round her and kiss her; and this time Harriet responded. The thought flashed through his mind that of all his life this moment – in a dark, deserted road miles from anywhere – was the most important. He had found the means to happiness.

At length Harriet broke away. 'You will divorce her, John, won't you?' She was breathless.

'Yes,' he said. 'I'll divorce her.'

The lights of a car approached from Hazelford. It pulled in behind them and a burly man in overalls got out.

He flashed a torch into the engine of Prescott's car, checked and found no spark from the distributor. Prescott watched while he cleaned out the distributor points and tightened the leads.

'Try her now,' he said.

Prescott pressed the starter. The engine briefly responded, then stalled. He tried again with the same result.

The mechanic tinkered some more under the bonnet, then straightened. 'Can't do anything with that lot to-night,' he said.

'Can you find us a taxi, then?'

'Where to?'

'Cromley.'

'*Cromley*! Are you kiddin'? That's over forty mile. No dice, mate.'

'Is there somewhere else, then?'

'You won't get a taxi in Hazelford at this hour. You were damn lucky to find me working late. This isn't London, you know. It's not the metropolis.'

He grudgingly consented to tow them back to Hazelford. They discussed prospects on the way. They could phone the Central Garage in Cromley for a taxi, but Harriet was afraid it would cause talk.

'We can probably get a couple of rooms at the hotel,' she said.

'We haven't any night things,' he objected.

'You can sleep raw for once.'

Harriet telephoned her father again while Prescott explained their predicament to the receptionist.

'You're in luck, sir. There's a conference here this week, but we do have one vacant room.'

Prescott opened his mouth to correct the woman's misapprehension, thought better of it.

'Fine,' he said.

'If you'd just sign the register, sir . . .'

Another problem. But with scarcely any hesitation he wrote: 'Mr. and Mrs. J. W. Prescott, Fenleigh.'

Harriet reappeared. He explained the position *sotto voce*. She gaped at him.

'And how did you sign?' she asked.

'She was watching. My mind went blank, so I had to write "Mr. and Mrs. Prescott". But I didn't put 'Cromley' I put Fenleigh".'

'Oh that's great!' she said. 'That'll fox them.' Suddenly she began to laugh. 'At least it proves you don't make a habit of this.'

The room was small and very cold and dominated by the double bed. They spoke stiffly, carefully avoided contact. Prescott stared out of the window while Harriet undressed.

'You can turn round,' she said. She was standing in her slip. She giggled nervously. Prescott laughed too and the tension was eased.

'I'll sleep on the chair,' he said.

'You don't *have* to . . .'

'Take temptation out of my way,' he said. He aimed a slap at her and she leapt into bed.

'Ouch, it's icy!' she said as she slid between the sheets.

Prescott settled in the arm-chair, put his feet on the small chair. He was still fully dressed, and had draped his own and Harriet's coat over him. He was almost screaming with desire. But he could wait. He'd divorce Norah, marry Harriet. The future had some meaning at last.

A small voice called: 'John!'

'Yes?'

'I'm frozen!'

'Would you like a coat over you?'

'No.' Short pause, then: 'John!'

'Yes?'

'If you *really* were a tiger . . .'

No man could resist that challenge.

CHAPTER VIII

Harriet returned to Cromley by bus after breakfast. Prescott had a shave and haircut to fill in time until his car was ready at midday. A hair-line fracture in the distributor cover had caused the trouble. He had lunch in the Anvil and drove straight to his office.

His euphoria was already wearing off. He imagined that people were staring at him, that they knew. It was a guilty conscience: he wasn't sufficiently hardened in duplicity.

He was conscious of a sudden hush and of surreptitious glances as he passed through the general office; or was it imagination again? They couldn't possibly know about Harriet.

'Good afternoon, Mr. Prescott.' No questions from Sandra Welch, no sign of curiosity. He ought to have been grateful, but again was oddly irritated.

'Hallo, Sandra. Much doing?'

'I've left notes on your desk. Mr. Crawley—'

'I'll make my peace with Crawley. Anything else?'

'Dr. Hornby rang. He says it's urgent.'

She turned back to her typewriter. Prescott said impulsively: 'Sandra, does nothing ever change the rhythm?'

She looked up. 'I don't understand.'

'Do you never laugh, or sulk, or fly into a temper? Do you never get excited?'

'I'm not paid to get excited, Mr. Prescott.'

He'd asked for the snub. As he closed his door and heard the typewriter go into action, he realised why he was coming to dislike

Sandra Welch: she reminded him of Norah. Not so much in physical appearance, although she had the same build and colouring; but in her attitude to him. Under the camouflage of impersonal efficiency she despised him no less than Norah despised him – he was suddenly certain of it.

A warm inner glow reminded him of Harriet. He wasn't concerned any longer about other people's approval.

Frank Hornby was out on his rounds when Prescott phoned. He rang back at half-past five. He couldn't talk over the telephone, he said: so they arranged to meet in a pub.

When Prescott arrived, Hornby was already there, sitting in an alcove, with an empty glass. Prescott brought over two double whiskies.

Hornby said: 'What the hell are you up to, John?'

'Up to?'

'I've already had it from two sources that you spent last night in a hotel with Harriet Reece.'

Prescott had a sinking sensation at the pit of his stomach. 'What sources?' he said.

'Tim Raven for a start.'

It could hardly be worse: it meant that Norah would know too.

Hornby explained that Raven's cousin, who was attending a congress of bankers in Hazelford, thought he recognised the couple at breakfast. He was sufficiently curious to look up the hotel register and to phone Tim.

Prescott and Harriet had idly speculated this morning on the profession of all those men in dark suits and white collars. Accountants, they'd decided. Not so far out; but what damnable luck that Raven's cousin should have been one of them! Prescott vaguely remembered meeting him once with Norah, although he couldn't put a face to him.

'Why should Tim tell *you*?' Prescott asked.

'You don't suppose I'm the only one he's told? He'll dine out on this for a month.'

'He's in no position to cast stones.'

'What's that supposed to mean?'

Prescott didn't answer, but said instead: 'Who's your other source?'

'Matter of fact, it was Mrs. Parry. Not that she knew you'd actually *slept* with Harriet—'

'I haven't admitted I slept with Harriet.'

'No? "Mr. and Mrs. Prescott": you'll be telling me next it was *Norah* . . . Mrs. Parry's very fond of Harriet, and she didn't trust the look in your eye. So she phoned me to find out the score . . . Same again?' He crossed to the bar.

Prescott swore. Other people could carry on an affair for years without being detected: take Raven and Norah – how long had that been going on? Yet the very first time Prescott cut loose it became public knowledge within hours. It would sound so sordid, too: a convenient breakdown, a word in the ear of the receptionist, the whole squalid seduction prearranged . . .

'Get outside that.' Hornby set down the drinks. 'You look as if you need it.'

Prescott was irrationally angry with Hornby as the bearer of the news. 'What's in it for you, Frank?' he said.

Hornby's jaw tightened, but he answered mildly enough: 'I don't like to see you make a bloody fool of yourself, that's all. If you must have a tumble in the hay, don't advertise it in lights. And don't mess around with a nice girl like Harriet Reece.'

Prescott interrupted. 'Harriet and I are going to be married.'

That pulled him up short. Hornby's religion didn't recognise divorce.

'I see,' he said stiffly. 'And what does Norah say to that?'

'She hasn't been consulted yet.'

Hornby stared at him, then shrugged. 'It's your affair, I suppose.'

They sat in silence for a bit, then Hornby said: 'What took you down to Mrs. Parry anyway?'

Prescott told him.

Hornby nodded. 'Ron Williamson's been telling me about that bruise. Wanted to know if it ruled out suicide.'

'And does it?'

'Not necessarily. Depends how recent it was.'

'Couldn't Parry tell?'

'Probably that's what was bothering him: he wouldn't be sure. His judgment was all to hell. He actually mistook a case of measles for – no, *de mortuis* etc . . . What's the latest about the anonymous letters?'

'Harriet's putting pressure on her father to take them to the police.' She'd promised to tackle him to-day.

'Why wait for Arthur? She should go herself – or you, John.'

'Harriet's afraid the old man might take another stroke.'

'That's a risk, I agree. But there are other risks.'

His voice contained a warning. Prescott sensed that this was the real reason Hornby had contacted him to-day.

He glanced at the doctor's empty glass. 'Will you—'

'No thanks, John. I've a surgery to-night.' He offered his cigarettes. 'The police suspect you of murdering Peter. Williamson practically told me.'

'I know.'

'You *know*! Then what the hell are you messing around for? Concealing evidence—'

'What evidence?'

'Evidence of blackmail. These damned letters. Get in first, tell Ron about them.'

'I can't, Frank. Not before Monday anyway. I promised Harriet.'

Hornby stared at him, shook his head. 'You're a bloody fool, John. Don't you realise – somebody has it in for you. You're playing into their hands.'

Prescott got home at seven o'clock.

Norah called from upstairs. 'Is that you, John?'

He went up. She was at her dressing-table doing something to her eyebrows. A cigarette smouldered on an ashtray.

'Do my zip, darling, would you?' Her silken tone told him that she knew already.

It was a new dress of pale blue material which shimmered as she moved, and when he had done up the zip it fitted like a stocking. His hand brushed her bare shoulder and a feeling of revulsion swept through him.

Norah saw his expression in the glass. She swung round: 'Let me tell you this, Valentino: if you think you'll divorce me to marry Harriet, the harlot, just try, that's all!'

'We're through, Norah – why not admit it?'

She stood up. 'I've no time to argue. I'm going out for dinner.'

'With Tim?'

She laughed. 'Why not?' She stretched her face towards him mockingly. 'Going to slap me again?'

He believed she really wanted him to. He walked away.

Norah laughed again and called after him: 'Sorry I haven't made your supper. One never knows when to *expect* you nowadays.'

Prescott's hopes had crashed round him. What a blundering fool he'd been; When Norah was at his mercy, when he'd surprised her with Raven, he'd turned a blind eye. All because of these ridiculous qualms, the feeling that he was in part to blame. Now he'd let her off the hook: if he sued for divorce now, she'd fight tooth and nail, drag Harriet's name through the mud.

Norah would fight because she was smart enough to see that Tim Raven would never marry her: their affair could prosper only so long as she was safely tied by law to someone else.

At half-past nine Harriet rang.

'John?' Her voice was vibrant with pleasure. 'Thank goodness! I was afraid Norah—'

'Norah's out.'

She was quick to detect his mood. 'What's the matter, darling?'

He told her.

She said: 'You're too volatile. It's not the end of the world. You, my precious, are going to divorce your wife, come hell, come high water.'

'It's not so easy now. She'll defend it; and she'll make a meal of last night.'

Harriet laughed. 'What of it? The whole town knows already of our night of sin. Edward Lowson was kind enough to ring Daddy and put *him* in the picture.'

She sounded cheerful. 'Don't you mind?' he asked.

'Mind? One day we're going to marry – that's all I can think of. I've dreamt of it since my fourteenth birthday. I never thought it would happen.'

'What was so special about your fourteenth birthday?'

'You gave me a present. A great, gaudy brooch. Remember?'

'No.' It seemed an unlikely choice.

'I still have it. Darling, I don't care what people say about me. I'm not ashamed of last night. Are you?'

'No. But it wasn't very wise.'

'Who cares? I really phoned, John, to say I spoke to Daddy about the letters.'

Volatile? She must be right; he was more cheerful already. 'Did he go up in smoke?'

'More or less. He knows who's writing them, he says, and he's taking action.'

'What kind of action?'

'I don't know. I warned him that unless he tells the police by Monday I'm going myself.'

'Did he say what was in the letters?'

'I was scared to ask. He was purple in the face as it was.'

Prescott said: 'Darling, I don't think we should wait until Monday.'

'He made me promise, John. It's only two days . . .'

CHAPTER IX

Norah laid aside her *Express* when Prescott came down. 'I'll get your bacon,' she said. She was in her dressing-gown, a cigarette dangling from her mouth.

Prescott sat down, glanced at the headlines in the *Telegraph*.

Norah laid his bacon and eggs in front of him. 'Take it while it's hot,' she said.

She wasn't normally so solicitous. He noticed she didn't pick up the paper again.

Prescott had a routine at breakfast: front page headlines, stock exchange, sports results. Then his mail; finally back to the newspaper at leisure.

When he turned to the letters on his plate this morning, he sensed Norah's nervous attention.

Letter from his father – that was unusual but wouldn't interest Norah. Bill for £53 from Lyon and Featherstone. That's what would be bothering her: they'd had a row only last week over her extravagance in clothes. He opened his mouth to comment, then realised Norah was staring at the two remaining letters on the plate.

The top one was innocent enough – a circular from the Electricity Board. Underneath was a foolscap buff envelope, postmarked 'Cromley, 3 Nov. 1967,' and addressed to 'JOHN W. PRESCOTT, ESQ., L.L.B . . .' in the characterless letters now so familiar.

He took a bite of toast and a sip of coffee before he opened it. Norah was fidgeting.

Inside the envelope were two sheets of writing paper covered in ink capitals. Prescott read the message:

I KNOW YOU MURDERED PETER REECE. YOU STRUCK HIM ON THE BASE OF THE SKULL, THEN HANGED HIM. YOU GAVE YOURSELF AWAY IN THAT FIRST 'SUICIDE' NOTE. YOU THOUGHT IT WAS GONE, DIDN'T YOU? YOU THOUGHT ARTHUR REECE HAD DESTROYED IT. WELL, HE DIDN'T.

I'M NOT VINDICTIVE, YOU MAY HAVE IT — FOR A PRICE.
PLACE £1000 IN SINGLE NOTES IN THE TELEPHONE KIOSK
OUTSIDE THE ENTRANCE TO THE GOODS STATION ON
SUNDAY FIRST, 5 NOVEMBER, AT PRECISELY 11.30 P.M.
THEN LEAVE IMMEDIATELY.

IF YOU TRY TO IDENTIFY ME, THE DEAL IS OFF AND THE
NOTE WILL BE SENT AT ONCE TO THE POLICE.

BUT IF YOU KEEP FAITH WITH ME IT WILL BE IN YOUR
LETTERBOX ON MONDAY MORNING. I GIVE MY WORD.

'A FRIEND'

Prescott read it twice, folded the sheets, restored them to their envelope, and put the envelope in his pocket. Then he went on with his breakfast.

Norah said: 'For God's sake, John, what does it say?'

'What business is it of yours?'

She made an impatient gesture. 'This is one time we have to work together.'

'You weren't so anxious to cooperate when I wanted to know why Arthur Reece was being blackmailed.'

'I'll tell you now if you like,' Norah said.

'You don't have to: I can guess.'

The idea had been simmering for days. The letter he'd found on Peter's body was not the one read out at the inquest. That one had been forged by Arthur and Norah in Reece's office; and they had also faked the embezzlement.

'That's the truth, isn't it, Norah?'

She nodded sulkily. 'We *had* to,' she said.

'Why? What was in the first note?'

'He accused me of having an affair with his father. That's why he'd decided to kill himself. He must have been *mad*...'

Yes, even Norah was hardly capable of that; and Arthur Reece certainly wasn't. How Peter could for one moment have believed ...

But of course the answer was that he hadn't: the first suicide note was as spurious as the second. Peter had been murdered, and the murderer had planted the note.

'Do you remember the exact words?'

'I never saw it – Reece just told me about it.'

'You're sure he was telling the truth?'

She shrugged. 'I thought so. I was so terrified of him, I just – Anyway, why should he invent a story like that?'

'And now he's being blackmailed. Someone knows about the switching of the notes?'

'Yes.'

Prescott tossed the letter across the table. 'Our friend thinks he knows a hell of a lot more than that,' he said.

Norah read it slowly. Then she said, her eyes frightened: 'Did you?'

'Did I what?'

'Murder Peter?'

'Oh for God's sake!' He snatched the letter back.

'*Someone* did,' she said. 'Someone who was able to—' She stopped.

'Was able to what?'

'I lost my key,' she said. 'My office key. Remember?'

He didn't understand.

'That first note,' she explained, 'was typed on the office machine too. So Arthur said anyway.'

He saw the point now: the murderer must have had access to Reece's office.

'*You* could have—' she began.

Prescott was angry. 'Just cut that out, will you?'

Pointing at the letter, she continued inexorably: 'Then why does it say—'

'I said *cut it out*! . . . What I want to know is who's writing this filth.'

'Reece believes it's his ex-mistress. The woman he lived with in France. Her name's Goddard.'

'Was it her address you were looking up in the directory that night?'

'Yes. It wasn't there, though.'

'And you still don't know where she is?'

'No.'

But he'd spotted the hesitation. 'That's not true, Norah, is it?'

'Ask Arthur Reece if you don't believe me.' She picked up the *Express* and pretended to read.

But as he was going out she said: 'What are you doing about the letter?'

'I'll take it to the police.'

Norah raised her eyebrows. 'Well, it's your funeral.'

Although the office was officially closed on Saturdays, Prescott usually went in: he liked to chew over the week's problems, uninterrupted by the telephone or visitors or the office routine.

Edward Lowson sometimes appeared and, rather more often, Sandra Welch; neither was here to-day. But as Prescott passed Tim Raven's room, he heard Raven's voice on the telephone. It was unusual for *him* to work on a Saturday.

Prescott took out the letter and re-read it. Several curious features were beginning to strike him. First, how was he supposed to raise £1000 in banknotes within twenty-four hours and at a week-end? Like Arthur Reece, he would have had to realise shares or government bonds; but he couldn't do that between now and to-morrow night. The blackmailer must be ignorant of the way the average person manages his affairs.

Secondly, was Prescott expected to disgorge £1000 on the strength of the bald statement 'You gave yourself away in that note'? Suppose he was guilty: wouldn't he want to know *how* he'd given himself away? Wouldn't he insist on learning the evidence against him before he parted with money? Again it seemed as if the blackmailer was surprisingly naive.

Prescott's instinct, backed by his professional training, was to take the letter to the police; but doubts were forming. Something about the letter – he couldn't lay a finger on it – was still more sinister than the specific threat it contained.

When he telephoned Ash Grove, Arthur Reece answered. Prescott asked for Harriet.

'She's not at home. Look here, I want a straight answer: did you spend Thursday night with Harriet in a hotel room?'

'Yes.' No use denying it.

'You haven't heard the last of this. No one does that to me and gets away with it.'

'To you?'

'She's my daughter. She's a Reece.'

Prescott lost his temper. 'Your son was a Reece too. It didn't stop you branding him as a thief to save your own reputation.'

The harsh voice answered: 'My son had taken his own life, he had forfeited his rights.' He didn't seem surprised that Prescott knew.

'But suppose Peter *didn't* take his own life, suppose he was murdered?'

'Murdered? Don't be a bloody fool, man! Goodbye.'

'Would you ask Harriet—' Prescott began, but the line was dead.

As he put down the receiver his door was pushed open and Tim Raven came in.

'Didn't like to interrupt while you were on the phone. Was it old man Reece?'

'Yes.'

'What was that about branding Peter as a thief?' He was, as usual, scanning the papers on the desk; his eye soon riveted on the letter with its block capitals.

Prescott ignored the question. He picked up the letter, folded it and put it in his pocket.

'You wanted to see me, Tim?'

Raven produced his monogrammed gold cigarette case, selected a cigarette and lit it. Everything about him was elegant, from the hair parted with mathematical precision to the suede shoes.

'I thought it was time we had a chat, John. Man to man, you know. Straight from the shoulder.' He laughed delicately.

'About your whoring with Norah?' Prescott had tried these tactics before, of answering the rapier with the axe. It never worked.

Nor did it now. 'What a graceful turn of phrase you have, John! But remember the old saw about people in glass houses. Though I do applaud your choice: Harriet is a most—'

'Get on with it,' Prescott said.

Raven said he was seeking a *modus vivendi*. He admitted ('without prejudice, of course – I'll deny it in the box if necessary') that he and Norah were lovers. ('You'd be surprised how far back it goes, old boy.').

Norah, he implied, was more dependent on him than he on her. He could at any time turn to pastures new; whereas Norah was in love with him.

'What's wrong with pastures new?' Prescott asked.

'Norah in small doses is very agreeable.'

'But you wouldn't want to marry her?'

'God forbid! Look, John, we'll be terribly, terribly discreet. Tongues will not wag, I assure you. And this will leave you free to have your fun with Miss Reece.'

'I'm going to marry Harriet.'

'My dear John, our ridiculous laws allow us only one wife.'

'I'll divorce Norah and name you as co-respondent.'

He noticed perspiration on Raven's brow. Already Harriet had made a difference to Prescott's self-confidence. He no longer accepted his lot as irreversibly decreed by fate: by his own action he could mould the future.

'That would be imprudent,' Raven said. 'Norah's determined to fight; and I think she'd win. And as for poor Harriet—'

Prescott smiled. 'Poor Harriet's spoiling for battle too.' He saw a way out of the wood. Raven was Norah's weak link: he would do almost anything to avoid being named in a divorce suit.

Raven stood up. 'Well, this has been a useful preliminary skirmish.' Abruptly he changed the subject. 'What does Inspector Lacey think of your anonymous letter?'

Norah had been quick off the mark: she must have phoned him while Prescott was on his way to the office. 'I haven't shown him it yet. I'm not sure if I will.'

'No? Norah said—'

'You can't believe everything Norah says, Tim.'

Raven smiled. 'True. By the way, did I ever tell you Peter called on me that afternoon? The day he died, I mean?'

'No, you didn't. Nor anyone else either, as I recollect.'

'I did inform the police at the time, but they weren't interested. They were treating it as a straightforward suicide. However, I happened to mention it the other day to Ron Williamson and in no time the whole of Cromley C.I.D. was hanging on my words.'

Prescott waited for the punch line.

It soon came. 'Yes, Peter looked in about tea time. Margaret was out, so we had a jar together. He seemed a little ... *distrait* – but perhaps that's hindsight. You certainly figured prominently in his thoughts.'

'What do you mean?'

'Apparently he'd heard rumours about you and Norah . . .'

Second round to Raven. Prescott was beginning to see why the police were suspicious.

He phoned Ash Grove again in the afternoon and got no reply. And twice during the evening; Arthur Reece answered both times and put down the receiver as soon as he heard who was speaking. It didn't matter much: Prescott had already made his decision.

He left the house at five to eleven on Sunday night. Norah had been out again all evening and hadn't yet returned. A bridge engagement, she'd said.

The wind had dropped and the predicted rain was imminent. From time to time exploding fireworks illumined the clouds that were massing over the town; but the celebration of Guy Fawkes Night seemed half-hearted.

Prescott parked in the drive outside the main entrance to the Central Station. The station was locked and in darkness: the last train on a Sunday left at 9.30. He took the footpath that tunnelled under the line and joined Trinity Road fifty yards beyond the entrance to the goods station.

Trinity Road was narrow, cobbled and ill-lit. A coal merchant's premises sprawled along the north side; on the south the properties were dilapidated and mostly derelict. A fish and chip shop, its windows boarded up, still carried on business, but had closed for the night. The smell of frying hung round the door.

Prescott stopped in the shadow of the wall where the footpath debouched on Trinity Road. The street was empty apart from two railway lorries parked near the goods entrance. The yellow pools from the widely spaced street lamps served merely to emphasise the darkness.

The cabin of one of the lorries obscured from Prescott's sight the telephone kiosk against the station wall. He moved quietly down the street towards the station until the lighted panels of the box came into view.

When he saw there was someone inside, bending over the directory, he tiptoed back to his vantage point behind the footpath wall. It was 11.10 p.m.

Spots of rain began to fall. Prescott turned up his coat collar but kept a constant watch. Although from here the kiosk itself was hidden, he was bound to see the caller as he came out.

As he waited, he analysed his motives in coming tonight. The anonymous letter could not be taken at face value, no blackmailer would be so naive. All right, assume it was a trick: what, then, was its object? A practical joke? Hardly. No, it must be aimed at inducing Prescott to do something. To do what? Well, the natural course was to go to the police.

So Prescott had concluded that that's what he was *intended* to do, that the letter was one more link in a plot to frame him for Peter's murder. He was not going to fall into that trap.

He came here, he told himself, to prove his theory, to demonstrate that there was no blackmailer lurking by the telephone kiosk. And yet, as the minutes passed, Prescott was increasingly uneasy. Partly it was the atmosphere: there was something sinister about the place. And who was that in the phone box? He'd been a long time.

Prescott looked at his watch. 11.37. A new suspicion dawned. He walked quickly down the street until the kiosk came in view again. The rain was beating a tattoo on the pavement and water was running down his neck.

The person inside the box was still leaning over the directory. Leaning? No, *slumped.*

Prescott broke into a run. As he wrenched open the door, the body slid out, almost knocked him over.

It was a woman. Fair hair, camel coat. 'Norah!' he thought at once.

But he was wrong: it was Sandra Welch.

She was dead. Even in the dim street light he could tell that. Her eyes were open and staring, her skin already cold.

He was supporting her by the shoulders. Now he eased her to the ground. She lay on her back, her feet still inside the box, propping the door open. He noticed, irrelevantly, that she was wearing expensive shoes the same colour as her coat.

There were spots of blood on the floor of the telephone kiosk, more blood on Prescott's clothes; and the sticky wetness of his hands – that was blood too. Now his eye fixed on what it had been subconsciously avoiding: the hilt of a knife protruding obscenely from the front of the camel coat. Round the knife the coat was stained reddish brown.

He grasped the knife and pulled it out: the most fatal of all his foolish acts to-night. It was an ordinary bread knife, but wickedly sharp. It had been driven deep into her left breast.

Prescott went into the phone box, stepping over the body and standing in the blood by Sandra's feet. As he dialled, his brain was alerting him to his own danger. The anonymous letter had been a trap, but a more subtle one than he had suspected.

'Police? I want to report a murder . . .'

When he came out, a taxi was drawing up behind the lorries. A girl jumped out and ran over. It was Harriet.

She gasped when she saw the body, but checked her instinctive reaction to feel for pulse and heartbeat. It was too obviously a corpse.

'There's blood all over you, John,' she said. 'Look at your *hands* . . .'

'I know.' He saw her accusing eyes and added sharply: 'I didn't kill her, Harriet.'

The taxi-driver came across.

'Gawd!' he said, looking down. 'What happened to her?'

Silently Prescott pointed to the knife, now lying in the gutter.

The man edged away. His thoughts were transparent.

Just then a car swung into Trinity Road, followed by another. The police had arrived. The questions began.

The deadliest was one of the first: 'What time did you get here, sir?'

He was ready for it. 'Just after half-past eleven,' he lied. He knew Sandra Welch had been dead by 11 o'clock or very soon after. If he swore he didn't arrive on the scene until 11.30, they'd never disprove it: he was sure he hadn't been seen. As a rule Prescott had an almost fanatical addiction to the truth; but the circumstances justified an exception. He was being framed for murder.

'You're sure of the time?'

'When I parked on the station drive it was eleven twenty-seven – I looked at my watch. Then I came round by the footpath – it's two or three minutes walk. I had an appointment for eleven-thirty.'

'An appointment?'

He handed the chief inspector the letter.

Harriet stood a little apart, bare-headed in the rain, silently watching and listening.

By this time more cars had arrived, the police surgeon was bent over the body. Photographers and fingerprint men were going into action.

Chief Inspector Lacey said: 'If you don't mind, Mr. Prescott, we'll continue this discussion down at headquarters.' He looked curiously at Harriet. 'We'll want a statement from you too, Miss Reece.'

'To-night?'

'Yes. Ron, would you . . .'

Inspector Williamson nodded, ushered them into the back of his Triumph Herald.

'Where did you say your car was, John?' he said as he started the engine.

'Outside the front entrance to the station.'

'May as well pick it up, eh?' He began to whistle.

'How did you get here?' Prescott whispered to Harriet.

She was sitting very straight and rigid. 'I'd been at her flat,' she said.

'Whose flat?'

'Mrs. Welch's. I don't want to talk about it, John. Not yet.'

'At *Sandra's* flat? What on earth—'

'I said I don't want to discuss it.'

The car stopped; they were in the station drive.

'Perhaps you'd follow in your own car, John,' Williamson said. Then in a changed tone: 'What time did you say you parked here?'

'Eleven twenty-seven.'

'The rain came on, I think, before a quarter past.' He was staring at the dry patch under Prescott's Cortina.

God! what a fool! He'd never thought of that. . .

'On second thoughts, Mr. Prescott, we'll leave your car where it is.' He turned the Triumph and set off for the police station.

In the back seat Prescott turned to Harriet and said: 'You must believe me, I—'

But she was cringing from him in horror. 'Don't touch me,' she hissed. 'Don't come near me . . .'

PART III

THE TRIAL

CHAPTER I

The trial was into its fourth day, and still the prosecution case continued. Relentlessly every loophole was being closed, every loose end tied.

It was hard to believe, Prescott reflected, that this was happening in twentieth century England, that so powerful a case, supported by such a mass of evidence, could be built up against an innocent man. Innocent? Well, innocent of the crimes with which he was charged.

Granted, he had contributed to his own plight. To smear himself with Sandra Welch's blood, to implant his fingerprints on the murder weapon, above all to lie about the time of his arrival – these were acts of monumental folly.

Granted, too, that someone – presumably the real murderer – had *fabricated* evidence against him. Given all that, it was still astonishing that witness after witness could stand up and condemn him: Edward Lowson, Arthur Reece, Tim Raven, even his old landlady, Mrs. Jardine. And Norah and Harriet and Frank Hornby still to come.

They didn't consciously lie, they simply allowed their recollection of events to be distorted by the knowledge of Prescott's guilt. It had been proved in the Magistrates' Court, hadn't it? So doubts and qualifications voiced at the preliminary hearing were now discarded: memories had improved . . .

Norah took the stand at half-past ten, a key witness for the prosecution, but a vulnerable one. Julius Rutherford, the defence counsel, who had so far yawned his way through the trial, seldom intervening, and cross-examining only briefly, was keeping his powder dry for Norah.

She was quietly dressed in a grey suit and her voice held just the right trace of nervousness.

Sir Hugh Lympney took her briefly and sympathetically through her early life up to her engagement to Peter Reece in April 1962.

'When did you meet the accused?' counsel asked.

'A month or two before that – February, I think. He was a friend of Peter's.'

'Did you see much of him?'

'Not to begin with. But latterly Peter was working late a lot, and John sometimes took me home from Ash Grove.'

Sometimes? *Once.* She couldn't have forgotten; the mis-statement, Prescott decided, was deliberate.

'What was he doing at Ash Grove?'

'I don't know. He always seemed to be there.'

'When he took you home he left you at your door, did he?'

'Usually. But one night I asked him in for a drink. I shouldn't have, I suppose, but' – she looked appealingly at the jury – 'I was terribly inexperienced in these days and – well, after all, he was Peter's *friend.* I never dreamt . . .'

She was creating the image of the ingenue. Successfully, too:

Prescott saw the thin-faced woman on the jury nod sympathetically. But he also saw Julius Rutherford taking notes.

'What happened, Mrs. Prescott?' counsel continued.

'All of a sudden he put his arms round me and started kissing me and – and pulling at my clothes and – oh it was awful.'

'You didn't encourage him?'

'Encourage him! I soon stopped him. I made it plain I wasn't that kind of a girl.'

'But you continued to see him?'

'Well, it was so awkward: Peter wouldn't hear a word against him. If he could have heard the things John said about him!'

'Such as?'

'He used to say: "If only Peter hadn't met you first. If only Peter was out of the way . . ."'

Sir Hugh paused while that last phrase sank in. Then he turned to the night of Peter's death.

'Who brought you the news?' he asked.

'John. He was terribly nice about it, terribly kind.'

'He stayed till when?'

'Half past two.'

'Did he make any advances to you that night?'

'No. Except' – she hesitated—'well, he insisted on coming into my bedroom to help me dress. I was past caring. And later on, in the car, he kissed me.'

In a detached way Prescott almost admired Norah's technique. Every sordid detail was being manipulated so as to put the blame on him and to build up a picture of him as an unprincipled lecher.

She described her visit to the Reeces' office in the early hours of the morning. Arthur Reece, she said, had told her that the note Peter had left accused his father of having an affair with her.

'Was there any substance in the allegation?'

'Certainly not! Peter must have been out of his mind to believe that.'

'You didn't actually *see* the note?'

'No, but I'm sure Mr. Reece wasn't making it up. He was in a terrible state.'

Reece, she said, was determined to suppress the note and had already drafted an alternative version giving embezzlement as the reason for the suicide. He put a sheet in the typewriter and made Norah type the message, warning her not to get her fingerprints on the paper. He then placed it in the original envelope. Afterwards she helped him doctor the books to square with the confession.

Norah's account tallied with the evidence Arthur Reece had given earlier.

'You say Reece *made* you do all this? You did realise it was wrong?'

She nodded. 'But I was terrified of him. And anyway what harm could it do? Nothing could bring Peter back . . .'

'It didn't occur to you that the first note might have been a forgery too?'

'No.'

'Or that John Prescott might have been responsible for your fiancé's death?'

'Not then. I'd never have married him, would I, if I'd thought that?'

'Perhaps you'd tell us about the marriage . . .'

She made a convincing story of it: grief-stricken and shocked after Peter's death, rejected by his family, not even invited to the funeral, she had turned for comfort to the only person to show her kindness – John Prescott. And he comforted her to such effect that she was at the Registry Office almost before she knew what was happening. It was a marriage on the rebound and as ill-starred as most such unions. It began to crumble as soon as her husband's sexual obsession for her was sated.

'Why did he marry you?' counsel asked.

'I've told you: sex.'

'Yes, but why *marriage*?'

'He knew he couldn't have me on any other terms.'

She tried to make the best of things, she said, but it was hopeless. Her husband soon turned to other women.

'He was unfaithful?'

'I had no proof of it – not till recently. But I *knew* . . .'

'And recently?'

The judge, anticipating an objection, glanced at defence counsel, but Rutherford was stifling a yawn. Give her enough rope . . .

Norah shrugged. 'Let's just say I've ample proof now. The whole of Cromley knows about it.'

Prescott was surprised by the prosecution's tactics. He supposed, in view of the motive alleged for the first murder, it was necessary to paint him as a man of ungovernable sexual passion. It was necessary too, perhaps, to lay the blame for the broken marriage squarely on his shoulders, for juries as a rule are unsympathetic to wives who testify against their husbands. All the same it was a dangerous gambit.

Norah now described her summons to Ash Grove last October. Here again she was corroborating Arthur Reece's evidence. Reece had received a series of letters – the first two while he was still in France – which made it clear that the writer was aware of the substitution of the suicide note. Reece's sole object in returning to Cromley was to find out who was writing them. He enlisted Norah's aid.

The third letter was more specific: it accused Reece and Norah of tampering with evidence in order to conceal a murder and demanded £500 as the price of silence. Norah described how she delivered the money to the blackmailer.

'Was Mr. Reece content to pay this sum?'

'No, he was setting a trap. I was to leave the money, drive away, then double back and watch who went into the phone box.' But the blackmailer had been too quick for her.

'Had Mr. Reece no idea who it was?'

'He was fairly sure it must be Alexandra Goddard, his – his ex-mistress.' Norah managed a blush as she said the word. She was over-playing her hand, Prescott thought.

Reece had earlier testified that Sandra Goddard, a Hastonbury girl, had followed him to France and lived with him there for a year or two. Eventually they fell out and the girl returned to England. He believed she was the likeliest person to be writing the anonymous letters.

Norah made enquiries on Reece's behalf. She discovered that the girl, after a brief and explosive marriage to a travelling salesman named Welch, was back in Hastonbury living – alone – under her married name. And employed in W. B. Clyde and Sons, the lawyers; employed, indeed, as secretary to John Prescott, Norah's husband.

Norah described the letter Prescott himself received the day before the murder.

'I knew it was from the blackmailer,' she said, 'as soon as I saw these funny capitals.'

'What was his reaction?'

'When he read it he went all white.'

'Did he show you it?'

'Only after I asked. He wanted me to tell him who the black-mailer was.'

'And did you?'

Norah hesitated. 'Mr. Reece made me swear never to tell anyone ... He said he would deal with Mrs. Welch himself ... But I did just *hint* to John that it was his own secretary.'

Another lie. She'd told him it was a Miss Goddard, but had given no hint of where she was to be found.

Well, what did it matter? And yet, in spite of himself Prescott's interest was engaged. His feelings might be dead, but his brain still demanded food.

He looked round the court: judge, counsel, jury, clerks, reporters, spectators – not one of them but believed him guilty. Unless possibly his father up there in the gallery. Yet they were all wrong. Someone had so manipulated events, juggled with the evidence, that an innocent man was in the dock and likely to be convicted. No mean performance, even if he was abetted by the half-truths and evasions of the prosecution witnesses.

Who could it be? Perhaps one of those very witnesses. Certainly someone with a knowledge of human psychology, someone who could foresee exactly how he would react to the anonymous letter . . .

Norah was being questioned about the night of the murder.

'I had a bridge engagement,' she said.

'When did you get home?'

'Eleven o'clock struck as I opened the front door.'

'Was your husband at home?'

'No, he wasn't. And he'd taken the car.'

'Thank you, Mrs. Prescott.' Sir Hugh seemed about to sit down, then added unexpectedly: 'One last question. You've told us of your unhappy relations with your husband: has he ever offered any physical cruelty?'

'Yes.'

'Tell us about it.'

'It was a few days before Mrs. Welch was killed. We were quarrelling – I can't even remember what it was about – and without any warning he struck me on the face. Twice.' She illustrated with her hand. 'With all his force. My jaw was swollen for days.'

'Thank you, Mrs. Prescott.' This time Lympney did sit down.

A note was passed to Prescott in the box. 'What was the quarrel about?' Prescott scribbled 'Tim Raven' and passed it back. Julius Rutherford read it, nodded, then lumbered to his feet.

He was a large, paunchy man, with a fat face that somehow lacked cohesive shape: the kind of face you couldn't remember when he wasn't there.

He was bordering sixty, a barrister of the old school, his style declamatory rather than conversational, emotional rather than intellectual. As a lawyer he was not in the front rank: he had a woolly mind and was not at home with the subtleties of legal argument. His reputation – fading now as juries became more sophisticated – was founded on his flamboyant appearances for the defence in the more sensational murder trials.

No one could rival Julius Rutherford in demolishing a dishonest witness. (Unfortunately he was apt to apply the same technique to an honest one, with less satisfactory results). Norah Prescott was a sitting target.

'You told us, Mrs. Prescott, that you married in June 1962.'

'Yes.' Norah looked wary.

'Were you then a virgin?' The question was tossed out casually.

Sir Hugh Lympney exploded: 'My lord, that is a most improper question, entirely irrelevant—'

Mr. Justice Yardley cocked an eye at defence counsel and said: 'Mr. Rutherford?'

Rutherford said: 'With respect, my lord, witness was at pains to impugn my client's character and to set herself up as a model of virtue. I submit—'

The judge waved a hand. 'I will allow the question,' he said in his curious hoarse voice.

Norah stood silent.

The judge said patiently: 'Counsel's question, Mrs. Prescott, was whether you were a virgin before your marriage.'

'Not exactly,' she answered at last.

Rutherford pounced on the phrase. 'Not exactly? Not *exactly*? Pray enlighten us on the degrees of virginity.' He glanced at the jury to share his derision. But he was too soon: sympathy was still with Norah.

She was fundamentally a stupid woman: she should have realised she was walking into a trap. 'When I was working in London, a man – he was my boss, actually – seduced me. It was only the one time. I was very young, you understand and—'

'Only once? My information is that you consorted with this man for more than a year.'

'I—'

'And you were cited as co-respondent in the divorce case?'

Prescott hadn't known this himself until his solicitors had ferreted it out. From Sir Hugh Lympney's face it was clear the prosecution hadn't known either.

Norah's morale collapsed. Rutherford pursued her without

mercy, forced a confession that she'd been Tim Raven's mistress for years, brought into the open the malice towards her husband that had activated her testimony.

By the time he was finished with her Norah was utterly demolished. Sir Hugh's re-examination could not repair the damage.

Rutherford was preening himself. He'd done it again: the front page would belong to him to-morrow.

But Prescott, watching his wife leave the court with bowed head, was sorry for her.

CHAPTER II

Prescott had lunch each day in a little room at the back of the court-house, with a police constable standing guard by the door. Afterwards he usually had a few minutes with his solicitor.

But to-day he was told that his father wanted to talk to him. He knew exactly what to expect.

The old man was crowing over Norah's discomfiture: 'We've turned the corner now, John, eh?'

'It won't make a tittle of difference.'

His father sighed. 'If only you had a little *faith.*'

Faith? In what?

He said: 'You should go home, Father. There's nothing you can do for me here.'

'It's never too late to save a brand from the burning.'

God! The arrogance of it! This was what he had turned his back on years ago.

He wanted to say: 'It's your fault. If there had been an ounce of humanity in you—' But what was the use? His father was as much a prisoner of the past as himself.

Anyway John couldn't be angry with him any more. He looked dispirited, defeated, as if his religion no longer sustained him. He had gone downhill since his wife died.

John said: 'I'm sorry I'm such a disappointment to you.'

The old man sighed again. 'Why don't you *fight*, John?'

'Why don't you fight?' Because there was nothing to fight for, now that he had lost Harriet – now that Harriet had betrayed him, he amended. He was teaching himself to forget her.

But in the court-room after lunch, as they waited for the judge to enter, Prescott was nervous, keyed up, as he had not been at any previous stage of the trial.

'Court!' The hum of conversation died, there was the usual scraping of chairs and feet as everyone rose.

Mr. Justice Yardley trotted briskly in and took his seat; a spare little man, whose robes seemed too heavy and whose wig was always slightly askew. He had a light touch and intervened seldom, but was quick to deflate pretentiousness: he had dealt sharply with both Edward Lowson and Tim Raven.

'Dr. Frank Hornby.'

The name took Prescott by surprise: he had been watching the door for Harriet to come in.

'Frank Hornby!' The words echoed in the corridor outside.

Evidently Sir Hugh Lympney wasn't risking a second debacle so soon after this morning's, and had promoted the reliable Hornby in the batting order.

Frank Hornby had visited Prescott a few days after his arrest;

but it was a meeting that, by tacit consent, was not repeated. Conversation was intolerably strained as they skated round the subject of the murders.

His evidence mainly concerned Peter Reece, who had been both patient and personal friend. A few weeks before his death Peter had consulted him at his surgery, complaining of headaches and insomnia. Hornby examined him, could find no physical cause, and prescribed a mild sedative.

Peter was back the following week: he still wasn't sleeping. The doctor gave him something stronger this time, but probed more closely into the causes. Had he anything on his mind? Peter admitted that he had.

'He was under pressure at the office,' Hornby said. 'But that wasn't the main trouble. Personal problems were worrying him.'

'Did he say what they were?' counsel asked.

Hornby hesitated, turned to the judge. 'Do I have to—'

The judge inclined his head. 'I think it's relevant, yes.'

'Very well. He said his father was making a fool of himself over a girl in Hastonbury.'

'That would be Miss Goddard, I presume.'

'He didn't mention a name.'

'Was that his only worry?'

'He said there was something else, but he wouldn't talk about it because he wasn't sure of his facts yet.'

Exactly what Peter had told Prescott.

'Did you see him again after that second consultation?'

'We met pretty frequently at the golf club. And every Sunday we had a foursome – Peter, John Prescott, Tim Raven and myself.'

'What about the Sunday of his death?'

'I had to call off that day. As a matter of fact, I don't think any of them played.'

'Did you see Peter Reece?'

'Yes. He called at my house about a quarter to six.'

'Why?'

'To renew the prescription.'

'Do you consult on a Sunday?'

'No, but he knew I'd be at home. I've told you: he was a personal friend.'

'And that was the only reason for calling?'

Hornby hesitated. He was a good witness: calm, judicial, authoritative. Only Prescott, who knew him intimately, recognised the signs of strain: the tongue flicking along the lips, the whiteness of the clenched knuckles. His appearance of imperturbability was simply a translation to the witness box of his bedside manner.

'No,' he said at length, 'it wasn't his only reason.'

'Tell us about it, please.'

'He said Edward Lowson had phoned for him after lunch and told him that' – again the tongue ran along the lips – 'told him that John Prescott was trying to steal his fiancée. I said the idea was ridiculous.'

'Did *he* think it ridiculous, Dr. Hornby?'

The court had already heard evidence from both Lowson and Raven that Peter was extremely upset by the rumour. In face of that, it was hard for Hornby to maintain that he didn't take it seriously.

Hornby glanced towards the dock as if in apology. 'Peter was excited,' he said. 'He was seeing John later in the evening to have it out with him.'

'You haven't answered my question.'

'All I can say is, if he believed that story he was more of a fool than I thought him.'

'Was this the second problem, Dr. Hornby?'

'I beg your pardon?'

'The other matter that was troubling his mind? Perhaps he had his facts clearer now . . .'

'I don't know,' Hornby said shortly.

'Are you *sure* you don't know?'

The judge interposed: 'Witness has already given his answer, Sir Hugh.'

'Just so, my lord. When you heard that Peter Reece had committed suicide, Dr. Hornby, were you surprised?'

'Extremely.'

'Why?'

'He wasn't the type. He enjoyed life too much.'

'And yet you didn't inform the police of that remarkable conversation you had with him only a few hours before his death?'

'It didn't seem relevant.'

'No?' Counsel raised his eyebrows.

For the first time Hornby let his irritation show. 'Dammit, it had to be suicide. How do you hang a man who's conscious and able to defend himself?'

'You knock him out first,' Sir Hugh suggested.

'My partner, who conducted the autopsy, assured me there was no other injury.'

'We know now that there was.'

Hornby shrugged. 'We know that *now*,' he agreed.

'When did you first suspect it was murder?'

'Not till last autumn, when Arthur Reece returned to Cromley and I heard of the anonymous letters.'

'Mr. Reece told you about them?'

'No.'

'Who did, then?'

'John Prescott.'

'Did you report *that* to the police?'

'I did advise Mr. Prescott to report it.'

'Did you?' The eyebrows were raised sardonically. 'Very public-spirited of you . . . Thank you, Dr. Hornby.' The cross-examination was brief.

'How long have you known the prisoner, Dr. Hornby?'

'About six years.'

'As a friend or as a doctor?'

'Both.'

'What is your opinion of him?'

Hornby looked across at the dock. 'An extremely sensitive and intelligent man. Very reserved: we only see the tip of the iceberg.'

'You like him?'

'Very much.'

'Would you say he was capable of murder?'

'We're all capable of murder if we're sufficiently provoked.'

Rutherford ignored the red light. 'You're playing with words, Doctor. What I'm asking—'

Hornby interrupted harshly, angrily. 'I'm well aware of what you're asking. I've told you John Prescott is a friend: isn't that enough for you?'

'Thank you, Dr. Hornby.' Rutherford hastily sat down.

Ask a foolish question . . . Did he imagine, Prescott wondered, that Hornby would perjure himself? Hornby, like everyone else in this court, believed Prescott *was* a murderer.

Sir Hugh Lympney's presentation of the case was logical enough. He'd started with medical and police evidence to establish the uncontentious facts of the two deaths; then miscellaneous witnesses – from Edward Lowson to Dr. Hornby – whose testimony cumulatively focussed suspicion on John Prescott; now, finally, Chief Detective Inspector Lacey and others to trace the official investigation, to place the earlier evidence in perspective, to seal the prosecution case. (But what about Harriet Reece? Surely, Prescott thought, they *must* call her.)

The chief inspector told how the file on Peter Reece was re-opened as the result of an anonymous letter last October to Cromley C.I.D. The writer alleged that Reece had been murdered and advised the police to consult Dr. Parry's widow for corroboration.

The letter was produced in court. It was in the notorious ink capitals; and expert evidence would later claim it was by the same hand as the threatening letters to Arthur Reece and to Prescott himself: in other words they were all written by Sandra Welch. A weakness in the prosecution case was the motivation behind these letters: why should Mrs. Welch, who was bent on blackmailing Reece and Prescott, imperil her prospects by alerting the police? The answer was, apparently, that she wanted to have her cake and eat it: to collect her dues but at the same time to shop her victims. An unconvincing answer, Prescott thought . . .

Chief Inspector Lacey described the events of 5th November: the telephone call from Prescott; the arrival of the police and the discovery of the body; the blood on Prescott's clothes and hands; the knife with his fingerprints on it; the letter in his pocket from the blackmailer; his statement of when he arrived at the station, and the dry patch under his car which refuted it.

The chief inspector then read out the statement whose admission the defence had unsuccessfully opposed at the start of the trial. This was the 'confession' Prescott had made at the police station later that night.

' "... I bought the knife in Broadbents', just for emergencies. I carried it to-night in case the blackmailer turned rough. I didn't *plan* to use it. But when I found it was Sandra Welch I saw red. The knife went in very smooth, through her coat, through her blouse, through her body. Like slicing butter. I never guessed it would be so easy." Question: "Did you also murder Peter Reece five years ago?" Answer: "For God's sake, man, you're not taking this *seriously*?" He then retracted his confession.'

'How would you describe his manner, Chief Inspector?'

'Overwrought, sir. Although I'd cautioned him, he seemed anxious to talk, anxious to get it off his chest. They're often like that—'

'Never mind the general observations, Mr. Lacey. You took it as a serious confession?'

'Certainly. But then suddenly he saw his danger and tried to wriggle out ...'

It showed, Prescott thought, how misleading a written record of a conversation could be. Although every word had been conscientiously recorded, the effect was totally false.

'Overwrought' – Lacey's adjective – was an understatement: Prescott had been beside himself with frustrated rage. Rage at the police, at Norah, at himself, at Fate. Above all, at Harriet: he would never forget the loathing in her eyes.

And so he poured all his bitterness into a sarcastic pseudo-confession; and was astounded when the detective took it at face value. They checked with Broadbents and found that they stocked that brand of knife. That clinched it.

Clinched it for the jury too, Prescott guessed, as he watched their reaction to the evidence . . .

CHAPTER III

The sixth morning began with some light relief, when Julius Rutherford, who enjoyed jousting with specialist witnesses, annihilated the prosecution's handwriting expert, Dr. Edward Villars. Villars was tailor-made for him: pompous, touchy, given to wrapping simple ideas in technical jargon. His thesis was that all the anonymous letters were by the same hand; under pressure he so modified and hedged his statements that Rutherford was able to end with the question: 'So your evidence amounts to this: these letters were written either by the same person or by different persons?' And the answer, amid laughter, was 'Yes.'

There was a relaxed air in court, even the judge was smiling; and for the first time Rutherford had the jury behind him: it is human nature to enjoy seeing the expert cut down to size.

Dr. Villars, flushed and petulant, stepped down. A short delay, then: 'Call Harriet Reece!'

A ripple of comment ran round the court; the change of mood was almost tangible. Prescott repeated to himself: 'She is nothing to me.' But his eyes were on the door and his pulse was racing.

As she came in, Harriet's glance flickered over him, passed on without sign of recognition. She was wearing a tan suit and looked thinner, paler than when he last saw her three months ago; and her eyes didn't dance any more.

He couldn't bear to listen at first: the memories her voice evoked were too painful. With fierce concentration he made a pencil sketch of the judge, and tore it up when the face wouldn't come right. He reverted to his favourite doodle, improvising variations on his monogram. Then he signed his name seven times: the psychiatrists would make something of that, he thought. He tried printing it in the style of the anonymous letter: 'J. W. PRESCOTT.' There was something missing. He added: 'ESQ., L.L.B.': it still didn't look right. Then he remembered that the envelope had been addressed to 'JOHN W. PRESCOTT, ESQ., L.L.B.' Vaguely he sensed that this small distinction had significance.

But he couldn't put his mind to it, because the even tenor of question and answer had been broken, sharp words were being exchanged between Harriet and prosecuting counsel. Prescott could no longer ignore the present.

'May I remind you, Miss Reece,' Lympney was saying, 'of your evidence at the inquest on your brother's death?' He stretched a hand behind him and impatiently snapped his fingers. His junior was frantically leafing through papers and eventually passed an open file to him.

Sir Hugh cast his eye down the page. 'Ah yes! I quote: "About a quarter to nine Peter thought he heard a knock at the back door and went to see who it was. I heard the door closing and I never saw Peter alive again. About nine o'clock the front door bell rang: it was John Prescott." You do remember saying that?'

'Yes,' said Harriet.

'Yet now, five and a half years later, you tell us your evidence was – what? – mistaken? – perjured?'

'Neither. Eight-fifty is *about* a quarter to nine; eight fifty-five is *about* nine o'clock. At the inquest the exact times didn't seem important.'

'You recognise their importance now, however?'

'I see that John Prescott couldn't have murdered my brother and been back at the house, all in five minutes.'

'Just so.' Sir Hugh made one last gesture of conciliation. 'Miss Reece, I put it to you that after five years your memory of times cannot be accurate.'

'I don't agree.'

Lympney turned and had a whispered colloquy with junior counsel and the solicitors.

Prescott was watching Harriet, trying to gauge if she was lying. She stood perfectly still, eyes cast down, never glancing in his direction.

One part of her statement was true: it *was* 8.55 when he arrived at Ash Grove that night. She'd told him that Peter had gone out. What were her exact words? 'Not long ago,' he seemed to remember. His impression was that she'd meant rather more than five minutes.

Sir Hugh Lympney addressed the judge. 'My lord, in view of the answers witness has given and her general attitude I ask leave to treat her as hostile, and to lead.'

Mr. Justice Yardley inclined his head.

Counsel hitched his gown over his shoulder. 'How long have you been in love with the prisoner?' he said to Harriet. The veneer of respect was gone from his voice.

She turned her head slowly towards the dock. 'Since my four-teenth birthday,' she said.

There was an excited murmur from the gallery.

'Silence in court!' the judge rapped out.

Counsel continued: 'How many years ago is that?'

'Nearly seven.'

'When did you first sleep with him?'

A renewed buzz of comment brought a further rebuke from the judge.

Harriet said: 'I spent a night with him in a hotel last November. It was the only time.'

Sir Hugh raised an eyebrow disbelievingly and shrugged. Then he said: 'Are you still in love with him?'

Harriet continued to face the dock: it was as if she were looking for a sign from Prescott.

'Yes,' she said in a whisper.

'I didn't hear the answer,' the judge complained.

She repeated firmly: 'Yes!'

God! she was magnificent, Prescott thought: her head held high, eyes steady, expression composed. Only the hectic spots of colour on her cheeks betrayed her emotion.

'Now we know where we are,' said Lympney, smiling. 'Now we see why your memory has so miraculously improved . . . You don't answer?'

'I didn't hear any question,' Harriet said.

'Let me put it bluntly: I suggest you're lying to save your lover's skin.'

'If that's a question, the answer is "No!"'

Sir Hugh stared at her, then shrugged. 'Let the jury form their own judgment,' he said. He shuffled through some papers. 'Turning to another matter, Miss Reece . . .' His voice was neutral again.

Prescott savoured the moment, stored every detail in his memory: the squeak of the judge's pen as he took a note; Sir Hugh Lympney, eloquent and languid, concealing, with the ease of long practice, his irritation over a witness gone sour; Julius Rutherford, yawning, adjusting his wig, equally concealing his satisfaction; the nine men and three women of the jury, briefly jolted from their composite expression of glazed boredom; and, in the witness box, Harriet, the incomparable Harriet.

It was a moment of decision: the decision to fight. From the public gallery his father was staring at Harriet with puritanical disapproval; Prescott no longer cared, no longer felt either resentment or guilt.

And a moment of anger. Waves of indignation came welling up inside him. Someone had framed him for murder . . .

Harriet was being questioned about the anonymous letters her father had received.

'Did you ask him about them?'

'Many times. But he wouldn't discuss them.'

'Did you mention them to anyone else?'

'Yes. To John Prescott.'

'Why Prescott?'

For the first time Harriet smiled. 'Why not?' she said.

Sir Hugh was impassive. 'And then?'

'We found out my father was being blackmailed.' She explained how they'd discovered it. 'John wanted to go to the police, but I persuaded him to wait until I'd talked to my father.'

'I suggest he didn't need much persuasion,' Lympney murmured sceptically.

Her eyes flashed. 'You're wrong.'

'When did you talk to your father?'

'On the Friday.'

'Third November?'

'Yes.'

Her father had admitted he was being blackmailed. He promised to take action by the week-end.

'"Take action"? What did that mean, Miss Reece?'

'I took it to mean he would inform the police himself. I gave him till Monday.'

'One day too long, as it turned out?'

'Yes, one day too long.'

'Wouldn't it have been wiser—'

She interrupted. 'Of course it would have been wiser, as things turned out. But I hadn't a crystal ball, I'm only a nurse. I was concerned about my father's health if I argued any more.'

'Very well. What happened next?'

On Sunday night at 10.15 a taxi had come to the door. Harriet was dumbfounded when she learned her father had ordered it, for he had scarcely been out since his illness, and never at night.

She stood in the doorway and wouldn't let him pass until he told her where he was going, and why.

To see the blackmailer, he said – as, indeed, she had already guessed. He told her it was his former mistress, Alexandra Goddard, now Mrs. Welch. Norah had tracked her down at an address in Hastonbury. Reece was determined to call on her, put the fear of death in her and get his money back.

'But he didn't go?' counsel interrupted.

'He wasn't able to. The excitement was too much, he knew himself he'd never make it. So I offered to go instead.'

'Why?'

'Mainly to pacify him. Also I was curious . . .'

Harriet paid off the taxi outside Mrs. Welch's flat, which was above a chemist's shop on Hastonbury's main street. The front windows were unlit. She climbed the stairs and rang the doorbell: there was no reply. She was already regretting having dismissed the taxi.

Under the doormat she found a key. With it she unlocked the door and went in.

'You expected to find a key there?' Lympney asked.

'Not really. But it *was* there, so I used it.'

'Why?'

'Because the door was locked.'

Laughter in court.

'Do you make a practice of breaking into people's houses, Miss Reece?'

'I'd come all that way to see the woman who was blackmailing my father. I wasn't over-scrupulous, I'm afraid, about her legal rights.'

'What did you find inside?'

It was a small flat – bedroom, sitting-room, kitchen, bathroom. Modestly but attractively furnished: its occupant, Harriet guessed, was a woman of discrimination but no great means.

An aroma of perfume still hung about the bedroom, as if the woman had not long gone out. Harriet found something else of interest: a man's dressing-gown and slippers, and an electric shaver. Evidence of occasional rather than permanent residence; it perhaps explained the key under the mat.

A framed photograph of a young, fair-haired woman stood on a walnut roll-top desk in the sitting-room. It was some time before

Harriet placed it: she'd last seen this girl in John Prescott's office. She was, in fact, his secretary. 'Sandra', he'd called her; a contraction, doubtless, for *Alexandra*.

Harriet's last scruples vanished. The desk was locked and this time there was no key. Inserting her nail-file, she forced the catch and rolled back the top.

In the pigeon holes were cheque book, bank statements, cancelled cheques, receipted bills; on the flat surface letter paper, envelopes (including buff foolscap envelopes), engagement book, ready reckoner, street map of Cromley, blue, red and black biros. Everything was very tidy.

Harriet opened the drawers underneath; here again was evidence of a methodical woman. They contained files, each neatly labelled: 'Car,' 'Rent,' 'Insurance,' 'Income Tax' etc. No personal correspondence.

She flipped through the pages of the engagement book. Mrs. Welch didn't seem to go out much. Most of the entries recorded appointments with the hairdresser or the dentist, although there was one reference to a dinner and one to a wedding. Every few days, the cryptic letter 'R' appeared; Harriet wondered if 'R' was the owner of the dressing-gown, slippers and shaver.

For Sunday, 5th November, '11 p.m.' was written in red, but with nothing opposite it. Harriet had seen another entry like that, and she turned back the pages until she found it. It was a fortnight earlier, Sunday 22nd October: here the red ink said '9 p.m.'

She puzzled over these entries. Presumably Mrs. Welch was keeping the 11 o'clock rendezvous at this very moment. And a fortnight ago? Harriet remembered now that Sunday, 22nd October, was the night Norah paid over the £500. And at 9 p.m.

Her eye caught another splash of red – on the street map which lay open on the desk: two circles in red ink. One was in Howlands Road at the Midland Bank, the other at the entrance to the goods station. There was a telephone kiosk there too, she remembered.

Harriet was suddenly in a panic. Had her father tricked her? Had he intended all along to keep an appointment with Mrs. Welch at the telephone kiosk, not to visit her flat?

The telephone was in the hall. Harriet rang Ash Grove and got no reply. Perhaps he was in bed by now: but she feared he wasn't.

It was 11.25 and rain was pattering on the windows. That settled it: she rang the Central Garage in Cromley and ordered another taxi. . .

Sir Hugh Lympney had let Harriet tell her story almost without interruption. But now she needed prompting. 'When did the taxi come?' counsel asked.

'Eleven forty-five. I knew it was far too late, but I *had* to go.'

'To go where?'

'To the station. I had a feeling – I don't know, I felt if my father had gone there he wouldn't survive it.'

'You went just on the strength of that little red circle?'

'I had a hunch . . .'

'Go on, then.'

'The taxi driver parked behind a lorry on Trinity Road. I got out and went over to the phone box. John Prescott was just coming out. A woman was stretched out on the pavement and I saw she was dead. There was blood on John's hands and on his clothes. And I saw a bloodstained knife in the gutter.'

'What conclusion did you draw, Miss Reece?'

'I thought John had murdered her.'

'Do you still think that?'

She paused. 'No,' she said.

'When did you change your mind?'

A longer pause, then: 'This morning.'

Sir Hugh Lympney pounced on the unexpected gift. 'This *morning*?'

Harriet said: 'I hadn't seen John since that night. As soon as I came into court this morning I knew I should never have doubted him.'

'A sudden, mystical conversion?'

'If you like.'

'Just from seeing him in the dock?'

'Yes.'

Sir Hugh smiled. 'What could be more touching than that?' He turned and faced Prescott. 'Behold him, members of the jury! The embodiment of virtue, the living proof of innocence! A pity some of us' – he waved a hand to embrace the jury – 'some of us are prosaic enough to take account of bloodstained hands and finger-prints and dry patches under cars ... Thank you, Miss Reece.' He sat down.

Mr. Justice Yardley glanced towards defence counsel. Julius Rutherford half-rose from his seat. 'No questions,' he said.

Harriet stepped down. She didn't glance at the dock on her way out.

The prosecution rested.

CHAPTER IV

They had a conference that night – Rutherford and his junior; Elliot Watson, the solicitor; and Prescott himself.

The others had the relaxed air of men who have dined and wined well.

'Damned good witness, that girl,' Rutherford remarked. 'She gave Hugh more than he bargained for, eh?'

Visby, the junior, said: 'You were absolutely right not to cross-examine.'

'Never give the enemy a second chance – the barrister's first lesson.'

'Absolutely right,' Visby repeated. A glittering future was predicted for Maurice Visby; meanwhile his deference to declining stars did his stock no harm.

'Remember the Courteney case?' Rutherford was saying. 'You know, where the M.P.—'

Prescott interrupted. 'I thought we were here to discuss my evidence.'

Elliot Watson looked shocked, but Rutherford laughed and said: 'The boy's right.' He took a cigar from an inside pocket: Visby was ready with his lighter.

'You did yourself a good turn,' he said to Prescott, 'when you latched on to that young woman. I'd say she's doubled our chances . . . Thanks, Maurice' – he lit his cigar – 'Yes, two per cent instead of one.'

Sycophantic laughter. Prescott was becoming angry.

'As for to-morrow, keep it short. Answer "Yes" or "No" wherever you can. Don't give Lympney anything to get his teeth into. You'd agree, Maurice?'

'Absolutely.'

Prescott said: 'I *don't* agree. I've nothing to hide.' Into the pool of silence he threw: 'You think I'm guilty, don't you?'

The other three exchanged glances. Watson said: 'As a lawyer,

Prescott, you should know better. We don't ask ourselves that question – our only concern is to persuade the *jury* you're innocent.'

'To raise a reasonable doubt of your guilt,' Rutherford amended.

'Reasonable doubt?' Prescott said. 'Don't you understand, someone *framed* me: I want him exposed.' Silence again. 'All right,' he added sharply: 'you don't believe me. Then don't expect me to follow the party line to-morrow. Two per cent chance of raising a "reasonable doubt" is not the kind of odds I favour.'

Rutherford laughed comfortingly. 'The two per cent was a figure of speech. Forget it! I've won tougher cases than this in my day, eh, Maurice?'

'Yes, indeed!'

'Just don't be too clever, Mr. Prescott, that's all I ask.'

Just don't be too clever . . . He knew what they meant: curb your tongue, don't give yourself away. They were only putting him in the box because it would be a confession of despair if they didn't.

To raise a reasonable doubt was the summit of Julius Rutherford's ambition. If the jury were even half convinced by Harriet Reece, they might acquit Prescott of the first murder. And if they even half believed Leonard Finch, who was now taking the stand as the first witness for the defence, the second charge might be thrown out too. If . . . if . . .

Mr. Finch was tall and emaciated, with a large head balanced unsteadily on a long, scrawny neck, which bobbed and weaved like a snake to the music of the charmer. He wore a brown suit and green bow tie; a button of his shirt was undone.

He gave his age as 48 and his profession as dental mechanic, temporarily unemployed. He lived in Keiller Street, off Trinity Road. On the night of Sunday, 5th November, shortly before eleven o'clock he took his dog for its nightly walk. He turned into Trinity Road, intending to cut down by the footpath fifty yards short of the station.

He noticed two people standing by the telephone kiosk against the station wall. One was a fair-haired woman in a light coat, the other was half hidden by her and in shadow. The woman was talking rapidly and sounded 'either angry or frightened.'

'The second person – was it a man or a woman?' Rutherford asked.

'It was too dark to make out.'

'You say the woman wore a light coat. What colour?'

'Not white – yellow or fawn, maybe.' Good enough description of a camel coat.

'Thank you. Go on.'

Finch branched off by the footpath. He had gone a few yards when he heard a strange noise from the direction of the station, now cut off from view. Like a shriek of laughter. But afterwards he wondered if it might have been a scream.

He followed the footpath under the railway line and emerged on the drive outside the main entrance to the passenger station. When he was well down the drive, a car passed him and parked under a lamp near the station entrance. A man got out.

'Would you be able to recognise this man?'

'No. I didn't see his face. But he was quite tall, well-built. He wore a raincoat but no hat.'

'Was it raining?'

'No, it was still dry.'

'What time would this be?'

'I reckon about five-past eleven.'

'Could you describe the car?'

'I'm ignorant about cars. This one was medium-sized, dark green, maybe blue, with a white roof.' Prescott had a two-tone Cortina: white roof, lime green body.

'Did the man see you, do you think?'

'Probably not. I was already past him, you understand. I looked back because I was surprised to see a car park there at that time on a Sunday. The last train was gone.'

'What did he do after getting out of the car?'

'He took the path under the railway – the one I'd just come from.'

'Leading to Trinity Road?'

'That's right.'

Finch continued his walk. But about 11.15 the rain came on and he turned towards home. He took a different way back, avoiding the station and Trinity Road. He was home shortly after half-past eleven.

He was an odd man, Prescott thought, an eccentric, but he gave the impression of honesty. And if his story was true, it practically let Prescott off the hook. Even if you discounted the scream, there was still this second man talking to Sandra Welch, *quarrelling* with her. Who was he? And, if he was innocent, why hadn't he come forward?

However, there were questions to be answered about Leonard Finch also; and Sir Hugh Lympney was asking them.

'The day after the murder, Mr. Finch, did you have a visit from the police?'

'Yes. They went to all the houses round about to see if—'

'Quite so. Did you tell them the story you've just told the court?'

'No.' The gyrations of his head were becoming more rapid, and his adam's apple was moving up and down in distress.

'Why not?'

'My – my wife wouldn't let me. I wasn't well, you see.'

'But you were well enough to go walking?'

'That was the previous night. *Next day* I was ill. I had to go into hospital.'

'Which hospital?'

'Southcraigs.' The local mental hospital. 'As a voluntary patient,' he added hastily. 'A slight nervous condition.'

'I see . . . You're a dental mechanic, Mr. Finch. When did you last work at your trade?'

'Well, you see—' The eyes were staring now, there was perspiration on his brow.

'Come, come, it's a simple question . . .'

It was twelve years since he'd worked. A story of one breakdown after another emerged: Finch's answers became progressively more incoherent, his voice more shrill.

It was painful even to watch and listen to him; for Finch himself it must have been hell. When Lympney finally released him, he was reduced to a gibbering caricature. He had contradicted his evidence-in-chief a dozen times.

And yet, Prescott thought, his original story of the walk with the dog might still be true, every word of it. And he wasn't sure that the jury might not think so too. Prosecution counsel's tactics were suspect: it is seldom wise to humiliate a witness, especially one so pathetically defence-less.

It was 11.25 when John Prescott was sworn. The court was packed in anticipation of drama, the press bench crowded, the gallery full.

A week ago, two days ago even, Prescott had been apathetic, indifferent to his fate. A single word from Harriet Reece had changed all that. (' Are you still in love with him?' 'Yes.')

Harriet's other service had been to engage the sympathy of the jury. They had liked her, they had disliked Norah; and some of their goodwill towards Harriet had rubbed off on Prescott. They probably still – most of them – believed he was guilty, but they no longer looked at him as if he had horns . . .

Julius Rutherford's questions were geared to his declared policy; defensive questions, eliciting a string of denials. Whenever Prescott tried to elaborate an answer, counsel cut him short and moved on.

From time to time Prescott stole a glance at the jury. He was depressed by what he saw: they weren't with him. Once or twice during the last day or two – especially during Harriet's evidence – the pendulum, he thought, had swung towards him. But it was right back now – he read the signs in the disapproving mouth and contemptuous eyes of the thin woman in spectacles.

He knew what the jury were thinking: 'If he didn't do it, who *did*?' They weren't being offered any feasible alternative. Rutherford didn't offer one because in his heart he believed none existed. Well, if Rutherford didn't, Prescott would: he would *have* to. Stonewalling wasn't enough, counter-attack was the only hope . . .

Rutherford ended with a flourish. In ringing tones he asked: 'Did you murder Peter Reece?'

'No.'

'Did you murder Alexandra Welch?'

'No.'

'*Thank* you, Mr. Prescott.'

The court adjourned for lunch.

'Keep it up, Prescott,' Elliot Watson said to him. 'You're doing nobly.'

Nobly? The foreman of the jury had actually fallen asleep before the end. Never mind, he wouldn't get much sleep in the afternoon.

*

Sir Hugh Lympney's first question set the pattern: 'When did you begin to covet Peter Reece's fiancée?'

'Even before she *was* his fiancée.' You had to think fast with Lympney: hesitation was more dangerous than an ill-judged answer. Lympney's weakness, however, was intellectual arrogance: sometimes he underestimated his opponents.

'You admit you coveted her?'

'I find it an odd verb. I was attracted by her, I was envious of Peter.'

'And you tried to steal her from him?'

'No.'

'You made advances to her . . .'

And so he went on, establishing the motive for the first murder. Making bricks with little straw, for it was the weakest part of the prosecution case.

On, then, to the night of Peter's death. Sir Hugh cast doubt on every statement Prescott had made in his evidence-in-chief.

'You found the "suicide note" on the deceased's body?'

'Yes.'

'Isn't that a remarkable coincidence?'

'I don't understand.'

'That you of all people found the note? The very person accused of the murder?'

'That's a logical fallacy,' Prescott said. 'If I'm guilty, naturally I pretend to find the note; if I'm innocent, I do find it. It proves nothing.'

'Please confine yourself to answering my questions.'

'I did.'

The judge smiled. 'I think he did too, Sir Hugh.'

Counsel managed a smile. 'Yes, my lord.'

Julius Rutherford was frowning heavily, shaking his head. Prescott ignored the warning. For the first time in his life he felt supreme confidence in himself. He was fortified by the knowledge that Harriet believed in him . . .

Now counsel was moving on to the second murder.

'Tell me, Mr. Prescott, what is the normal reaction to a blackmailing letter?'

'Anger, I suppose. Fear perhaps.'

'Yes, but suppose the victim is innocent of the crime the letter accuses him of. What would you expect him to do?'

'Take it to the police.'

'Precisely. That wasn't your response, though, was it, to the letter you received on fourth November last? You didn't take *that* to the police.'

'No.'

'Why not? Was it because the charge it contained was true? The charge that you murdered Peter Reece?'

'No.'

'Why not, then?'

There was an easy answer: because Harriet had begged him to keep quiet about the blackmailer until she'd had it out with her father.

Prescott didn't give the easy answer, he gave the true one: 'Because I was already conscious that a trap was being sprung for me. I was being framed.'

Lympney smiled: things were going his way now. 'Ah! you were being framed. By whom?'

'By the writer of the letter.'

'By the unfortunate Mrs. Welch?'

'No, not by Mrs Welch. Mrs. Welch wrote the letters to Mr.

Reece. She didn't write the one to the police, she didn't write the one to me.'

Rutherford was glaring at him, but Prescott didn't care. This was his chance: he had to take it before the prosecution realised their error and clamped down.

'You fascinate me,' said Lympney. 'We have *two* anonymous correspondents who favour these weird capitals?'

'It's not coincidence, if that's what you mean. One was imitating the other.'

'You heard the evidence in this court that the letters were all by the same hand?'

'I found it singularly unconvincing.'

'You wouldn't yourself claim to be an expert on handwriting?'

'Not on handwriting. But Mrs. Welch was my secretary, I know how she would have addressed a letter to me.'

'Please explain.'

'I always sign myself "J. W. Prescott." The envelope was addressed to "John W. Prescott." It would have been as unnatural for Sandra Welch to write that as—'

Counsel interrupted scornfully. 'I doubt if the jury will be impressed by *that* argument.'

'If they've ever worked in an office, they will . . . Besides, since I *know* I didn't murder Peter Reece, Mrs. Welch couldn't possibly have found proof that I did. Therefore it wasn't a genuine blackmailing letter. Therefore she didn't write it.'

'Then who did?'

'The person who murdered Peter Reece and who was already planning to murder Sandra Welch.'

Prescott glanced at the jury. He couldn't read their expression, but at least the foreman was awake.

Sir Hugh plunged on, employing his favourite weapon of irony. 'You can't, however, put a name to this master criminal?'

'No.' But he added impulsively: 'Except that it's someone who's given evidence in this trial.'

That made people sit up. But it was a tactical error, since he couldn't substantiate it. Something had been said in the course of the last week that jarred on his subconscious. Someone had told a lie, an unnecessary lie, a revealing lie. If only he'd been taking more interest early on . . .

Lympney had struck oil at last, and was making the most of it. 'A witness? Well, in the true tradition of detective fiction it ought to be the least likely one. Chief Inspector Lacey, perhaps? No? Well, how about Dr. Villars, our handwriting expert? And what, pray, is the motive for this elaborate plot?'

It was the opening Prescott had been waiting for. 'The very motive you say I had. You see, Mrs. Welch did write one more blackmailing letter. But it wasn't to me – it was to the real murderer. She made a rendezvous for Sunday night, the 5th November, for eleven o'clock, not eleven-thirty; and she gave long enough notice for him to lay his plans . . .'

'Sheer fantasy,' counsel said derisively. 'Not a tittle of evidence for it.'

'The entry in her engagement book said eleven o'clock. The letter to me said eleven-thirty.'

But Lympney was talking through his answer, brushing it aside as an irrelevance. If he was flustered, he didn't show it.

The rest of the cross-examination was anti-climax. The damning facts of the night of the murder couldn't lightly be explained away: Sir Hugh Lympney extracted his last ounce from them.

Rutherford's re-examination was perfunctory. He didn't touch on the alternative explanation of the murders that Prescott had advanced.

As Prescott stepped down and returned to the dock, the thin-faced woman on the jury was talking to her neighbour, the stout woman in the green suit. He strained his ears and caught the words '. . . Majorca this summer . . .'

CHAPTER V

Julius Rutherford's closing speech lasted an hour and a half. It was a characteristic piece of bombast, studded with emotive and headline-catching phrases. The main theme – the dire consequences of convicting an innocent man – had lost its dramatic impact with the abolition of capital punishment.

His rehearsal of the facts was slovenly: he got details wrong, missed points favourable to the defence, emphasised others he would have done better to slide over.

His defence in a nutshell was that the testimony of Harriet Reece and Leonard Finch cast sufficient doubt on the prosecution's case to justify an acquittal. He did refer, although without enthusiasm, to the theory that Prescott had been framed. The only evidence he cited in support was the conflict between the time mentioned in Mrs. Welch's engagement book – 11 o'clock – and the summons to Prescott for *11.30*.

Rutherford built up to an embarrassingly emotional peroration. He was like an old-style actor in a modern play, Prescott thought; strutting the stage and over-acting grotesquely.

Sir Hugh Lympney's manner was in total contrast. Speaking

quietly and conversationally, he went over the evidence in logical sequence, correcting Rutherford's errors of fact in passing. He conceded that Miss Reece's testimony, if accepted, would raise doubts about Prescott's opportunity to commit the first murder; but Miss Reece had the best of all motives for misremembering (he avoided the word 'lying'): she was, on her own admission, in love with the prisoner. As for the unfortunate Mr. Finch, the jury could judge for themselves the worth of his evidence.

The reference in the engagement book to 11 o'clock Sir Hugh dismissed as of no importance. True, Prescott had been summoned for 11.30; but Mrs. Welch would want to be there early, watching for his arrival, making sure there was no police trap . . .

He ended, still on a quiet note: 'Ladies and gentlemen of the jury, my learned friend has adjured you to heed the danger of convicting the innocent. And rightly so: it is a cardinal principle of British justice that the prisoner is not required to prove his innocence; the onus is upon the prosecution to establish his guilt. And to establish it beyond reasonable doubt. But "reasonable doubt" does not mean some far-fetched, fanciful distortion of plain facts. Would you, as reasonable men and women, accept for one moment the bizarre theory advanced by the prisoner, and, if I may say so, almost apologetically taken up by my learned friend, that some unknown person committed the murders and fabricated evidence to incriminate him? I venture to suggest that you would not. I need only remind you of the statement the prisoner himself made on the night of Mrs. Welch's death, while the blood was still hot: I refer, of course, to his confession of murder. I say to you that the evidence against John Prescott on both these charges is so over-whelming that there can be no other verdict than "Guilty".'

Mr. Justice Yardley began his summing-up after lunch on the

ninth day. He rarely referred to the notes in front of him. The dry, husky voice flowed smoothly on, every sentence perfectly modulated, no dependent clause stranded from its principal verb. Linguistically it was a *tour de force*; and as an impartial summary of the evidence it was masterly too. If anything, Prescott thought, he leant towards the defence, perhaps to redress the balance which had been tilted by the inequality of the two counsel. He pointed out that Sir Hugh Lympney's explanation of the entry in the engagement book ignored the fact that a fortnight earlier the time in the book corresponded exactly with the time specified in the blackmailing letter to Arthur Reece.

Commenting on some of the witnesses, the judge hinted that the evidence of Leonard Finch should be given little weight. On the other hand he had been impressed by Harriet Reece and reminded the jury that her motive for perjury was not in itself proof of perjury – or even of 'misremembering.'

In careful, lucid phrases he explained the issues the jury had to decide, re-defined 'reasonable doubt,' and sent them on their way.

The jury retired at 4.15.

Julius Rutherford had a word with Prescott. 'That summing-up should shorten the odds.'

'We're up to three per cent now, are we?'

Rutherford grinned. '*Touché* . . . Was I all right?'

'Heart-rending.'

The big man nodded happily and lumbered away; he took it as a compliment.

Maurice Visby said: 'If they're out more than an hour, we've won.'

Prescott recognised it as the kind of remark which sounds profound but is superficial. Nevertheless as the hands of his watch crept round towards the hour he was almost biting his nails in suspense.

5.15 came and went. At 5.30 there was a stir, the court reassembled, the jury filed back in.

It was a false alarm. They wanted to know on what date, according to his testimony, Arthur Reece had received the first anonymous letter. The shorthand record was consulted, the answer was given, they retired again.

Prescott wondered what possible relevance that information could have. It demonstrated once more how wayward are the mental processes of a jury. The evidence so carefully presented, the arguments of counsel, the explanations and guidance of the judge – all these could count for nothing beside the irrational prejudices and misconceptions of members of the jury. If the system worked at all, it could only be because the errors tended to cancel out . . .

As the minutes ticked agonisingly on, Prescott recalled one of Peter Reece's aphorisms: 'Never worry over what you can't control.' Easy to say.

At five minutes to seven the jury returned. Prescott could tell from the solemn faces that the moment had come.

It is said that if the jury don't look at the prisoner as they come in, the verdict is guilty. Prescott was watching: some glanced at him, some didn't.

'Members of the jury, are you agreed upon your verdict?'

'We are.'

'Do you find the prisoner guilty or not guilty on the first charge?'

Savouring his moment of drama, the foreman paused and looked round him. Then he said firmly: 'Not guilty, my lord.'

A murmur rose in the court. Someone hissed.

'And on the second charge?'

'Not guilty.'

'And that is the verdict of you all?'

'It is.'

The judge's words were drowned in the hubbub. Prescott caught only '. . . discharged.'

People were shaking him by the hand. Rutherford, jubilant, said: 'By God, that was a chestnut pulled from the fire!'

Prescott was scarcely listening. His only thought was of Harriet. She hadn't been in court but she would be waiting outside; he *knew* she would.

In the corridor his father came up, tears streaming down his face. 'Thank God, son!' he said. 'Thank God!'

Don't go soft, Prescott told himself. Not again. Not ever again.

'Thanks, Father,' he said briefly. 'Excuse me a moment – I'll see you outside.'

He hurried along the corridor, dodging reporters, down the steps, out through the swing doors. A camera flashed.

It was dark and it was raining. A small huddle of people under umbrellas were on the pavement outside. When they saw him they booed. Someone shouted 'Murderer!'

There was no sign of Harriet.

PART IV

CHAPTER I

The train swept through the derelict Hastonbury station and began the long descent into Cromley. John Prescott put on his coat, lifted his suitcase from the rack.

It was a grey, cheerless February morning. A pall of smoke hung over the town.

'Cromley Central!'

John Prescott jumped out, his eyes scanning the platform. Harriet wasn't there. Perhaps she hadn't got his wire in time.

Two young men came up; he recognised one as a reporter on the *Cromley Advertiser*.

'No comment,' he said automatically, as he'd said yesterday outside the assize court, and again last night in Fenleigh.

'But, Mr. Prescott—'

He walked past them. A bill outside the station bookstall proclaimed: 'Prescott Trial Verdict'.

Taxis were lined up where he'd parked that night three months ago. He took the first one. 'Nelson Avenue,' he said. The driver glanced at him with interest.

As the taxi nosed into the traffic and the familiar streets opened out ahead, Prescott was conscious that the testing time was imminent. Had he really changed? Or was it another mirage? . . .

Norah answered his ring. She was dressed – inevitably – in blue dressing-gown and slippers, cigarette in her mouth.

'I've been expecting you,' she said.

Prescott hung up his coat, went into the sitting-room. Norah followed.

'I heard it on the radio last night,' she said. When he didn't answer she added shrilly: 'What are you staring at? Why don't you *say* something?'

He continued to study her. He was wondering how he could ever have loved her, how he could ever have accepted even part of the blame for their broken marriage. She was mean, twisted, rotten. A bitch, as Harriet had said from the beginning.

She looked frightened. 'You can have your divorce, John. I'll not fight it.'

He spoke then. 'I don't give a damn whether you fight it or not . . . And another thing: you'll get out of this house. By to-night.'

'But—'

'By *to-night*. You understand?'

Now he was talking, her fear receded. 'Shall I make up the bed for Harriet?' she said.

A blind rage came over him. He gripped her by the shoulders and shook her till her teeth rattled and she gasped for breath. Then he threw her down like a rag doll. She lay on the floor sobbing and panting, massaging her neck. Her dressing-gown was ripped open down the front.

He looked down without compassion. This was the woman who'd lied to convict him of murder.

Norah struggled to her feet, never taking her eyes from him. 'By God, John,' she gasped, 'if only you'd done *that* a bit oftener . . .' Her face was flushed, with excitement more than fear.

Prescott turned away. 'Put some clothes on,' he said. 'You're disgusting.'

Silence apart from Norah's breathing. Then she said viciously: 'Have you met Harriet's fiancé yet?'

He telephoned Ash Grove for the third time; he'd rung twice last night from his father's house in Fenleigh.

Again it was Arthur Reece who answered. 'Yes,' he said, 'I gave her your message.'

'I sent her a wire this morning.'

'She got that too.'

'I'm coming round to see her,' Prescott said.

The harsh voice vibrated in his ear: 'I shouldn't advise it. Harriet doesn't want to see you.'

'I'll believe that when she tells me herself.'

'Anyway she'll be out all afternoon. With Alan.'

'Alan?'

'Alan Studley.'

Prescott thought he heard a chuckle at the other end of the line. 'Tell her I'll be round to-night,' he said, and rang off.

Three days ago in court Harriet had sworn she was still in love with John Prescott. She couldn't be as fickle as that. Not Harriet . . .

It was 1.15 and he was hungry. Norah was moving about upstairs; packing, he hoped.

He called to her: 'I'm going out for lunch.' She didn't answer.

There was a deep scratch on the offside rear door of the Cortina and the bumper was dented. Norah had always been a rotten driver.

He drove to the Regent Hotel. Although there was no one he

knew in the dining-room, all through the meal he was conscious of being stared at. He was a celebrity, a nine days wonder: the man acquitted of double murder.

On his way out Prescott glanced into the bar and saw Frank Hornby at a table by himself with a drink and the *Times* crossword. He went over.

Hornby looked up. Then he was on his feet, vigorously pumping Prescott's hand. 'Good to see you, John.'

Absence, even for a few months, Prescott thought, made you see your friends with new eyes. Hornby looked middle-aged. The great strength of shoulder was still there, but now it was the paunch you noticed, the incipient double chin, the plumpness of the hands.

Tessa was in hospital, Hornby explained. Their fifth child – a boy – had been born on Tuesday.

'Cheers, John!' he said, raising his glass. Then, in a lower tone: 'I can't say how pleased I am.'

'Thanks . . . And for your effort in the witness box.'

'I did my best.'

'It helped. I want your advice, Frank.'

Hornby looked round. Conversation in the bar had frozen; all eyes were on them. 'Yes, well, not here,' he said. 'Come back with me.'

They finished their drinks and left.

Hornby had a new car, a Rover, which he drove as he had driven a succession of Zephyrs – expertly but too fast. Prescott lost him at the Tunnicliffe lights, where the Rover swept round on the amber.

As he waited at the lights Prescott recalled the night Frank Hornby had driven him home from the engagement party in the Regent Hotel. They'd stopped at these very lights; and later they'd had an accident. It was the night his mother died, the night—

The driver behind blasted his horn: the lights had changed to green. Prescott eased forward and turned west into Tunnicliffe Road.

He was driving mechanically. He was back in the Regent six years ago, with Peter and Norah, Arthur Reece, the adolescent Harriet. Again – like the other day in court – he felt on the threshold of discovery; something had happened at that party that foreshadowed and explained the murder of Peter Reece. If only he could *remember* . . .

The Hornbys had a pleasant modern villa on Hurst Park Avenue, with Frank's surgery tacked on at the back.

Drinks were already laid out in the study when Prescott arrived. It was a small untidy room adjoining the surgery and its furnishings included two comfortable leather arm-chairs.

'Where are the rest of the family?' Prescott asked.

'At Tessa's mother's. When did you get back, then?'

'Just before twelve. I went down to Fenleigh with my father after the trial yesterday and stayed overnight.'

'Talked to anyone here yet?'

'Only you. And Norah, of course.'

'Ah yes, Norah . . . You're going to divorce her, I suppose?'

'Yes.'

'She's not well, you know.'

'My heart bleeds for her.'

'She's my patient. If you kick her out now, she'll end in the gutter. Nothing surer.'

'It's where she belongs.'

Hornby frowned. 'She's your wife. You married her.'

'Our marriage is dead, Frank.'

'It takes two to kill a marriage.'

For a man so tolerant in most things Hornby had rigid views on the sanctity of marriage. His own was an example of one that had survived in the face of odds. His wife was selfish, rude, a spendthrift, a liability to him professionally. And yet they were devoted to each other and to their family.

Hornby said: 'And what then? Harriet Reece?'

'I hope so.'

The doctor opened his mouth to comment, thought better of it. He began to fill his pipe. 'These people in the bar this afternoon, John – how did they strike you?'

'I thought they were hostile.'

'That's an understatement. Your name's a dirty word in Cromley. Everyone believes you did it.'

'The jury didn't; and they're the ones who count.'

Hornby looked at him thoughtfully. 'You asked for my advice, John, and I'll give it: clear out of Cromley, start afresh somewhere else. Especially if you're going to involve Harriet Reece.'

'Run away, you mean?'

'You have to be realistic. Things will be rough for you here – and even more so for Harriet.'

'Frank, someone framed me for murder. Would *you* run away in these circumstances?'

'No . . . But then I'm not you. I'm tougher, less vulnerable.'

No one would impose on Frank Hornby. His genuine warmth and friendliness did not conceal the flinty core of self-interest. If threatened, he would bite, and bite hard.

Prescott said: 'I've changed, Frank. I'm nobody's doormat any more. I'm going to fight.'

Hornby smoked his pipe in silence. Then he said: 'What do you mean by "fight"?'

'Find out the truth about these murders.'

'You'll get no cooperation from the police. Ron Williamson was saying—'

'I can guess.' Their file was closed: they had arrested the guilty party, had brought him to trial; and he had got off. They could do no more.

Hornby said briskly: 'All right, how can I help?' He refilled the glasses.

'I'm looking for a motive. *Why* was Peter murdered?'

'I don't know any more than I told the court, John, but I can *guess*. What struck you as unusual about Peter in the last weeks of his life?'

'His irritability.'

'That, yes, but I meant his *actions* rather.'

'Working late?'

'Exactly. Alone in his office night after night. Why?'

'Cooking the books' had been the accepted answer; but that was now ruled out.

Hornby continued: 'He did the Income Tax accounts. Suppose he found one of his clients was swindling the Inland Revenue and threatened to report him?'

Possible, yes, although the motive seemed inadequate for murder. No great moral stigma attached to tax evasion.

'I'll look into it,' Prescott said. He could get from Arthur Reece a list of his former clients. Or from Norah.

'Another suggestion, John – you should check on Mrs. Welch.'

'Check on her?'

'Find out where she got her information.'

'That's easy: she was Reece's mistress for years.'

'Yes, I dare say she had access to *his* secrets. No doubt that's how she discovered the suicide notes had been switched. But your theory is she was killed because she'd smoked out the real murderer. That right?'

'Yes.'

'Well, how did she do it? Where did she find her evidence . . . Unless, of course—' He broke off.

'What?'

'No, it was a sudden thought. Quite impossible . . . Pity no one's seen that first suicide note. Except Arthur Reece, of course.'

'And he destroyed it.'

'So he says. I wonder . . . Another drink, John?'

'No, thanks. I must go. By the way, is that the Medical Register up there?'

'Yes. Want to see it?' Hornby took down two fat red volumes from his bookshelves. 'It's last year's.'

Prescott opened the second one, turned to the letter S. Yes, there it was: 'Studley, Alan Hunter, 27 Cliveden Road, Southampton. M.B., Ch.B., 1960, Leeds.' *Southampton* . . . It was the same man.

CHAPTER II

It was beginning to drizzle as Prescott left Frank Hornby's; and at four o'clock almost as dark as in mid-December.

Where now? Ash Grove? No, Harriet wouldn't be home yet.

He parked in Selwyn Place and crossed the street in the rain, turned in by the familiar brass plate, 'W. B. Clyde and Sons.' As he climbed the stairs qualms of doubt assailed him, the old indecision returned, the fear of giving offence, of being conspicuous. The antidote was anger: he reminded himself that but for the perversity of a jury, he would be serving a life sentence now. The plot against him had miscarried, but only just. On the evidence they *ought* to have convicted.

The same musty smell of varnish and old books greeted him. On the stairs a red-haired, mini-skirted girl passed him carrying the bag with the mail. Must be new – he didn't recognise her.

He looked into the general office. There was a crashing silence.

Prescott said: 'Good afternoon. Is Mr. Lowson in?'

Miss Burroughs, the filing clerkess, was the first to find her voice. 'He's out of town to-day.'

'Mr. Raven, then?'

'Yes. Betty, take Mr. Prescott—'

'I remember the way.'

There had been an undercurrent of hostility. But what of it? A pity he hadn't learned years ago that other people's thoughts can't hurt. Unless you let them.

He noticed in passing that his name on the glass door of his office had been obscured by an oblong of white gummed paper, on which was printed: 'MR. GUNSTONE.'

Tim Raven rose from his chair with outstretched hand. 'My dear fellow, how nice to see you! You look fit.'

'Thanks. You, too.'

'One struggles on.' At forty Raven was as slim and well-groomed as ever, not a grey hair on his head, not a line furrowing his brow. His clothes always looked new.

'May I say, John, how delighted I was by the verdict.'

'Your evidence didn't suggest it.'

'Alas, one has to tell the *truth* on such occasions.'

Prescott let it pass for the moment. 'Who's Mr. Gunstone?' he asked.

'We needed extra assistance, John. Gunstone's a very sound chap – I heard of him through a chap I was at school with.'

'And you put him straight into my room?'

'Temporarily. Of course, if you were to come back—'

'There's no "if", Tim.'

Raven smiled uneasily. 'We thought you might want – well, a holiday – first, you know.'

'I don't. You can tell Mr. Gunstone to start moving out to-night.'

'I think you'd better talk to Edward. I mean, personally I'm delighted, but you know how stuffy he is.'

'I only know I'm a partner in this firm.'

Raven put his cards on the table. 'Look, John, I'll accept the jury's verdict. Maybe Edward will too. But we'll be the only people in Cromley who do. We can't afford to have a suspected murderer – double murderer – in the business.'

'Don't worry, Tim: it won't be for long. I'll find the murderer, I promise you that.'

Raven shrugged, unconvinced. 'You'll have to talk to Edward,' he repeated.

'I will.' Prescott changed the subject. 'I'm divorcing Norah.'

'I expected that.'

'And naming you as co-respondent.'

'That's no surprise either.' He smiled ruefully. 'You'd never have proved it, you know, if the stupid woman hadn't gone to pieces in the witness box . . . I've told Margaret. She's upset, but she'll get over it.'

'Are you still seeing Norah?'

'After that? Not on your life!'

Prescott had prepared the ground carefully; now he sprang the question: 'So you've lost them both? Norah and Sandra?'

'Sandra? What the hell are you talking about?' Although his recovery was swift, the shock had registered in his eyes.

'I think,' said Prescott, 'that Mrs. Welch's estate owes you a dressing-gown and a pair of slippers . . . Oh, and an electric shaver.'

Raven shrugged his admission. 'How did you guess?'

It wasn't difficult. An attractive woman like Sandra Welch was bound to be a temptation, especially when she was a lone wolf in the office. No danger of complications.

'She was using you,' Prescott said.

'What?'

'She didn't share her bed with you because of your natural charms.'

Tim Raven was ruffled. 'That girl enjoyed her sex. She knew a trick or two . . .'

'Maybe so. But she was using you all the same. If she'd had any interest in you as a person, she'd have put "T" and not "R" in her engagement book. I can think of few things more insulting than that "R".'

Prescott was enjoying himself. He had scores to settle with Tim Raven.

'What did you talk about, you and Sandra?' he said.

'What do you think?' Raven said archly, trying to salvage his self-respect.

'I'll tell you what I think: you talked *ad nauseam* about the Reeces, father and—'

'Well naturally. She'd been Arthur's mistress.'

'—and son. Especially son. She squeezed you dry of everything you knew about Peter's death, didn't she?'

Raven didn't answer.

'By the time she was through she'd be word-perfect in that last conversation you had with Peter. Why *did* he call that day, Tim?'

'I've told you – it was about you and Norah.'

'Don't be a bloody fool. He'd never have consulted you over that.' When Raven said nothing, he added: 'Listen, Tim: somehow or other Sandra Welch found out who murdered Peter. It may have been from you, it may not. But—'

'It couldn't have been from me: I don't *know* who murdered him.'

'You may have given it away without realising it. I want to know exactly what you said to her.'

Raven took out a handkerchief and mopped his brow. He had been shaken out of his composure.

Peter, he said, had been excited to the point of incoherence that afternoon. He couldn't stop talking: about his father and the office and professional standards and legal and moral duties.

'He seemed to want my opinion as a lawyer,' Raven said. 'But he wouldn't be specific, I couldn't make out what his problem was. I told him I couldn't answer a hypothetical question. Then right at the end he came out with that tale about you and Norah. He said he'd just heard it from Edward Lowson.'

'And you jumped to the conclusion that that's what was worrying him, that's what he wanted your advice on?'

'Well, it was the natural assumption, wasn't it?'

There was no point in recriminations. 'Think carefully, Tim. You say Peter mentioned his father and Edward Lowson and Norah and me. No one else?'

'I don't think so.'

'And when you reported the conversation to Mrs. Welch, did *you* mention any other name?'

'She went on about it so damned often I can't be sure what I told her. She was hellish persistent.'

'Didn't you think it odd she should be obsessed by something that had happened years before?'

'I decided she was morbidly fascinated by death and suicide and so on. She was all right in other ways, I can tell you. A little eccentricity was excusable.'

On his way out Prescott asked Miss Burroughs for the office file on the Reece inquest; and after some hesitation she produced it. She showed further reluctance when he announced he was taking it home. Prescott stared coldly at her, until, flustered, she handed it over.

Tim Raven, he reflected, as he drove home, released information like a sponge: you had only to squeeze him to get it out. He wasn't sure if he had yet squeezed hard enough.

The local reporter who had met Prescott's train this morning was now waiting for him in the rain at his gate. Prescott's automatic response was forming, when he changed his mind. 'You can say I've found evidence that will lead to the conviction of the murderer.'

No one would believe it, of course; except, just possibly, the one person with a guilty conscience: it *might* provoke him into rashness.

'What evidence?' the reporter asked.

'I can't disclose that yet.'

The young man nodded sardonically, put away his notebook. 'Thanks. By the way, your wife left in a taxi half an hours ago with a load of suitcases. Is she off on holiday?'

'No, we're separating. I'm going to divorce her.'

'Can we print that?'

'Why not?'

The notebook had promptly reappeared. 'How about afterwards, Mr. Prescott? Any plans for the future?'

'Plenty. But not for publication.'

He brushed aside further questions and let himself into the house.

Norah had left a note:

> 'I'll collect the rest of my stuff to-morrow. You can get in touch with me at Mother's, though I hope you won't.'

Prescott tore it up.

He studied the file he'd brought home. It was the file Sandra Welch had once borrowed, a slim folder covering the inquest on Peter Reece in May 1962. The day after his son's death Arthur Reece had asked Clyde and Sons to hold a watching brief for him at the inquest.

The file contained an exchange of letters between Reece and Lowson, the senior partner; a draft of the evidence Reece was to give; a photostat of the 'suicide note'; and cuttings from the *Cromley Advertiser* containing a full account of the inquest. Each paper was numbered in Miss Burroughs' neat hand and the numbers corresponded with the index: nothing was missing.

Prescott read through the papers twice and found nothing he didn't know already. Unless he was overlooking something, Sandra Welch hadn't acquired her fatal knowledge from the file.

CHAPTER III

It was eight o'clock. The rain was dancing on the pavement under the street lamp as Prescott reversed out of the drive. Colin Mortensen, his neighbour, was approaching his gate, umbrella into the wind. Prescott tooted his horn in greeting; the umbrella was not raised.

The streets were dark and empty. The only sound was the swish of the wipers and occasional splash as the wheels went through water.

There was an old Lanchester outside the door of Ash Grove. Edward Lowson's. Prescott rang the bell.

The door was opened by Arthur Reece.

'I've come to see Harriet,' Prescott said.

'She's not here.' There was no welcome in the voice.

'When will she be home?'

'I don't know.' A pause, then, grudgingly: 'You'd better come in.'

He led Prescott upstairs to the study, hardly dragging his leg at all.

'She's seeing young Studley off,' he said. 'He goes back by the night train.'

The 8.19. She shouldn't be long, then.

Edward Lowson was taking his ease in an arm-chair: brown plus-fours, red bow tie, spectacles, cigar – all the props in evidence.

He pulled himself to his feet, came forward, beaming, 'My dear boy!' he said. 'My dear boy!' He turned to Reece: 'Arthur, this calls for a celebration. I confess my palate yearns for that exquisite brandy—'

Reece grunted and went out again.

'I went to the office this afternoon,' Prescott said.

'Yes, Timothy phoned. Sorry I wasn't there.'

'Tim had the odd idea I should stay away for a bit.'

Lowson laid his cigar on an ashtray, removed his spectacles and began to polish them. 'One must take account of public opinion, John,' he said. 'I'm bound to say your stock is not high just at present.'

'The partnership agreement's still valid, though.'

The spectacles described an arc. 'I'm sure we can come to an arrangement. Ah here we are!' Arthur Reece had reappeared carrying a tray. 'Hasn't he thrived on bread and water, Arthur?'

Reece didn't answer. He poured the brandy, handed them their glasses.

Reece himself looked better, Prescott thought. His eye no longer twitched, and he had put on weight.

'I'm glad to find you both here,' Prescott said, 'because—'

'Pity Harriet's not here,' Lowson interrupted. 'But she's otherwise engaged, eh, Arthur?'

Prescott refused to be drawn. '—because,' he continued, 'I have questions to ask about Peter's death.'

Lowson frowned. 'We musn't upset Arthur.'

'Don't mind me,' said Reece. He lit a cigarette.

Prescott said: 'You sent for Peter that afternoon, Edward?'

'I asked him to call, yes.'

'How long did he stay?'

'Half an hour. But I told all this in court, John.'

'You tried to persuade Peter I was having an affair with Norah?'

'I gave him the facts, that's all.'

'And he laughed at you, didn't he?'

'My dear John, as I told the court, Peter was very angry—'

'He *laughed* at you, Edward. Peter knew me: he'd never have believed that story. Especially coming from you.'

'Why especially me?'

Prescott stared at him. 'You think I don't know why you had your knife in me? You think Peter didn't know?'

Lowson's spectacles were being polished again. 'Naturally,' he conceded, 'Peter didn't just take my word. He said he would investigate it.'

'At any rate he wasn't incoherent with rage when he left?'

'He was indignant—'

'The word I used was "incoherent".'

'Certainly not that. He was perfectly calm . . .'

It was the admission Prescott had been seeking. For Peter was far from calm two hours later, when he called on Raven. What had happened in the interval?

Mentally he reconstructed Peter's movements that afternoon. 2.15 to 2.45: at Edward Lowson's. 4.30 to 5.30: with Raven. 5.45 to 6.30: with Frank Hornby. 6.45: home. The critical gap was from 2.45 to half past four.

Prescott recalled the note Peter had left for him at Ash Grove: 'Sorry – can't make it to-day. I've just realised I didn't let you know' – or words to that effect. Which meant that Peter had known earlier he wasn't to be free. Therefore it wasn't Lowson's last minute summons that put off the golf: Peter already had an appointment for that afternoon.

With whom? Prescott felt he ought to know, that he had at one time been told. But it was all so long ago . . .

He asked Lowson: 'Did Peter say where he was going when he left you?'

'It's six years ago – one can't remember every detail.' No, only the ones that suited him . . .

Prescott turned to Arthur Reece, who was savouring his cigarette as if it were forbidden fruit. 'Do you know, Mr. Reece?'

'No, and I'm not interested.'

'You don't want to know who murdered your son?'

Reece stared at him with dislike. 'I know already,' he said.

Downstairs a door opened and closed. Arthur Reece guiltily stubbed out his cigarette. But Harriet didn't come up; presently Prescott heard the first notes of a Schubert impromptu on the piano.

Reece said: 'If the inquisition is over, you can see Harriet and go.'

'It's not over.' The urge to go down to Harriet was almost irresistible. But he stayed. 'How much did you tell Sandra Welch about Peter's death?'

Reece's eyelid began to twitch. 'What the hell business is it of yours?' Prescott continued to stare and Reece added gruffly: 'I told her nothing.'

'You must have done—'

'I told her *nothing*.'

Lowson was shaking his head warningly; Prescott ignored him. 'Then where did she get her information?' he continued.

Reece said impatiently: 'She found the suicide note, that's where she got it. She found it and put two and two together and made seventeen.'

'The original note? The one I found on Peter's body?'

'Yes.'

'But you said in court last week you'd destroyed it when you substituted the other one.'

Reece shrugged, didn't answer.

'I want to see it,' Prescott said.

'You're too late: I've destroyed it now.'

'I don't believe you.'

'Nobody calls *me* a liar—' Reece's face was purple and his voice trembled with anger.

'Control yourself, John!' Edward Lowson was flapping his arms ineffectually. 'Arthur's a sick man . . .'

'I don't give a rap,' Prescott said. 'I want the truth.'

Reece shouted: 'Get out of this house, you bloody murderer!'

Downstairs the piano stopped.

Prescott stood up, holding Reece's stare. 'Just suppose for one minute,' he said quietly, 'that you're wrong. Just suppose someone else murdered your son. Do you want him to get away with it?'

The door burst open. 'What's going on here?' Harriet said.

Arthur Reece seemed not even to notice. His eyes had never left Prescott's. He said flatly: 'I don't know who Peter was meeting that afternoon. And as for the note, I told the court exactly what was in it.'

'I still want to see it.'

'You can't. It's in France.'

Harriet said sharply: 'That's enough! If you don't mind, Uncle Edward . . .'

'Surely.' Lowson swallowed the last of his brandy, put his spectacles in their green leather case. 'I can't say how sorry I am, my dear. But you understand—' He glanced at Prescott.

'I understand perfectly,' Harriet said. The hard, contemptuous tone gave Prescott his answer. ('Are you still in love with him?' 'Yes.' Had she *really* said that?).

'Coming, John?' Lowson was already at the door.

'I'm not going till I've talked to Harriet.'

She went over to her father's chair, offered him her arm. 'Bed time,' she said, ignoring Prescott.

Reece was still breathing heavily, but the high colour was subsiding.

He said: 'I think you ought to talk to him, Harriet.'

'Ten minutes,' Harriet said. 'No longer.'

They were in the sitting-room. Arthur Reece was in bed, Lowson had departed.

Prescott was conscious of little irrelevant sounds – the ticking of the clock, rain gusting on the window panes, a door banging upstairs.

He didn't know how to begin. A stranger faced him – a beautiful stranger in an orange and pink striped dress, sitting erect, immobile, unsympathetic. She moved, and it was Harriet again; pushing back her dark hair in the gesture he knew so well.

'No ring?' he said.

She glanced at her left hand. 'Not yet.'

'Are you in love with him?' And when she didn't answer: 'How could you, Harriet? How *could* you?'

In a whisper she said: 'I still see the blood on your hands. Bending over that woman's body with blood on your hands . . . And I think of Peter, strung up like—'

'I didn't kill them.'

'—like a carcase in a butcher's shop—'

'*It wasn't me*, Harriet!'

She said dully: 'I think it was.'

'Harriet, can you believe I would murder Peter? In your heart can you believe it? No, look at me!'

But she got up and crossed to the window, drew back the curtain. 'It was a night like this, remember?' she said, staring out into the blackness. 'Wet and stormy . . . You went down the garden alone through all the rain – just because Peter was late . . .'

'Because you were *worried* about Peter.'

'No! It was because you knew he was there, you wanted to be the one to "find" him.'

'That's not true.'

Harriet sighed, let the curtain fall back. She took a cigarette from the box on the piano. Prescott got out his lighter and offered it.

Their hands touched, and Harriet recoiled as if she'd been struck. Angrily Prescott flicked off the flame and tossed the lighter to her.

'If I'm so loathsome,' he said, 'why did you give that evidence in court?'

She lit her cigarette. 'It was seeing you in the dock,' she said. 'You looked so – so helpless. And I thought—'

'Yes?'

'I thought – "he *can't* be a murderer, because I love him." But afterwards I saw that was silly: every murderer must have *someone* who loved him.'

She sounded as if she were quoting. 'Is this Alan's diagnosis we're getting?' Prescott asked.

'Don't sneer at Alan!' she snapped. She looked at her watch. 'I think you should—'

Prescott interrupted: 'Harriet, suppose I *proved* it wasn't me, suppose I found the real murderer—'

'No!' Her vehemence pulled him up. She added more quietly: 'Don't pretend, John. Not to me. Just be thankful you got away with it.'

'Have you considered, Harriet, that a man who strikes twice may strike again?'

He saw fear in her eyes. She put out her cigarette, half smoked. 'Please go, John,' she whispered. 'Please go.'

'All right . . . Good-bye, Harriet.' Before she could stop him his arms were round her and his lips were firmly on hers. She drummed her fists on his chest, then gave up and relaxed. She began to weep.

Prescott raised his head. 'Tell me about it, Harriet,' he said.

'Go away!' she moaned. 'Please go away!'

He released her gently. She was still sobbing as he went out.

He had established two things: Harriet was still in love with him; and she did not believe, never had believed, he was a murderer. The whole performance to-night had been a charade.

A third discovery too: Harriet was frightened.

CHAPTER IV

Nothing in the *Telegraph*, nothing in the *Express*: the Prescott case was no longer national news. But the *Cromley Advertiser* carried a report of yesterday's interview under the clumsy headline 'I WILL UNMASK KILLER' – PRESCOTT.

Prescott had sat up till two o'clock the previous night. He was reading the papers over a late breakfast when the telephone rang.

It was Tim Raven. 'You'll not be in this morning, John, will you?'

'No point in starting on a Saturday. Why?'

'Well,' – Raven's voice was hesitant – 'I've been thinking over our conversation about Sandra Welch. I've remembered something that might be significant.'

'What's that?'

'You know she lived with old man Reece in France?'

'Yes.'

'I asked her about it once, when we were on the usual subject of the Reeces. She described the house, and then she laughed and said there was buried treasure there for anyone with eyes to see. She'd known of it for years but had only just recognised its full value; and she was going to cash in.'

'When did you have this conversation?'

'Two or three weeks before she died. It was the last time I visited her flat.'

'The last time? She threw you over after that, did she? She had no further use for you?'

Raven was offended. 'There's no need to be offensive. I'm trying to *help*.'

'Sorry, Tim.' But he had his answer; the pieces were beginning to fit.

'You're not coming in, then, John?'

'Not for a day or two. I'm going to France.'

'Why?'

'To catch a murderer.'

Silence, then: 'You sound very confident.'

'I am.' He replaced the receiver.

When he turned round he saw Norah standing in the doorway in her fur coat, two suitcases at her feet. He hadn't heard her come in.

She threw him a copy of the *Advertiser*. '"Mr. and Mrs. Prescott have agreed to separate",' she quoted. 'Why didn't you tell them the truth? Why didn't you say you'd kicked me out?'

'I did. Apparently they didn't risk putting it in.'

She shrugged, lifted the suitcases. 'I'm going up to pack some more of my things.'

'Just a minute, Norah . . . No, put these *down*.'

She laid the cases on the floor.

'Give me your house keys,' he said. And, when she hesitated, added sharply: 'You're not wandering in and out when it pleases you.'

Norah took the keys from her coat pocket and tossed them on the table. 'How does the tough line go down with dear Harriet?' she sneered. 'Does she like the new model?'

'Cut it out, Norah,' he said. He wasn't even angry – only anxious to see the last of her.

Still she lingered. 'She's always schemed for you,' she said venomously. 'Right from the start . . . I never had a chance.'

There was one service Norah could still do him. He showed her the list he'd made out late last night.

'Which of these?' he said, 'were clients of the Reeces?'

She examined the list: it contained the names of those, other than police, who had given evidence at Prescott's trial.

'Only your partners,' Norah said.

'Lowson and Raven?'

'Yes. Peter did their income tax for them.'

'None of the others?'

'Not so far as I know.'

'Suppose, Norah, the Reeces' business was in some way crooked: would you have known?'

Norah sniffed. 'Me? I was just the dumb blonde in that office. I didn't know anything.' She picked up the cases and went upstairs.

Prescott returned to the telephone and rang Frank Hornby.

'You were right,' he said. 'Arthur Reece didn't destroy the suicide note.'

'I wondered . . . You've seen it, have you?'

'Not yet. It's in France. Frank, remember when we were discussing this yesterday, you had a sudden idea, but you wouldn't tell me—'

'Yes, because it was so implausible—'

'Was this it?' Prescott explained: it took a long time. Hornby said: 'That's it exactly.'

'You still think it's implausible?'

'I'm not sure . . . But even if it's true, how could we ever prove it?'

'The proof lies in that house in Brittany.'

'Will Reece let you go?'

'Just let him try and stop me!'

Hornby said: 'Watch yourself, John You're dealing with someone without scruples. We don't want a third murder . . .'

He was at Ash Grove by eleven o'clock. The daily woman answered his ring.

'Mr. Reece?' he said.

'He's in bed, sir. He's not very well to-day.'

'Miss Reece, then?'

'She's on the phone, but I'll tell her—'

'Don't bother. I'll find her.'

Harriet was in the sitting-room, curled on a rug, telephone in her left hand, pencil in her right poised over a pad on her knee. As Prescott came in she looked round and frowned.

She was wearing those tight black jeans again, this time with a bright yellow sweater, and every graceful line of her body was delineated. My future wife, he thought with pride.

She seemed to be talking to a travel agent and was noting times on the pad.

'See what you can do,' she said finally, 'and ring me back. Cromley 22471.' She replaced the phone and stood up.

'Going on a journey?' Prescott asked.

Harriet said coldly: 'I warned you not to come back.' Then she shrugged and added: 'Daddy's talking of returning to Fouesnant. I'm going ahead to see what state the house is in.'

'When?'

'Monday or Tuesday, I hope.'

He looked at her curiously. 'Why the sudden panic?'

'Panic? There's no panic.'

'Your father can't be in *that* much of a hurry to get back.'

'It's no business of yours.'

'That's where you're wrong . . . I'm coming with you.'

'Are you out of your mind?'

'No I must see that suicide note.'

'I'll bring it back.'

'That's too late. Damn it, Harriet, there's a *murderer* on the loose.'

'You're not coming with me,' she repeated stubbornly. Prescott turned to the door. 'I'll speak to your father—'

She caught his arm. 'No, John!' Then, her face dark with anger and frustration, she said. 'All right, come with me; but don't you *dare* say anything to my father.'

They left on Tuesday afternoon by car; there was a cross-channel car ferry on Wednesday morning, and they'd be in Fouesnant before midnight. Prescott hadn't tried over-zealously for plane reservations, for there were compensations in the slower journey . . .

Harriet was stiff and uncommunicative at first. But as they roared down the M.6, he could sense her thawing out. She was by nature gregarious: sulking was foreign to her.

By the time they stopped for tea in Kenilworth they were conversing on neutral subjects: books, music, films, travel. Harriet had refreshingly individual views: she took nothing on trust or reputation.

There was one unhappy incident. As they got back into the car after tea Prescott remarked: 'Have you noticed the date, Harriet?'

She looked at him oddly. 'Why?'

'Thirteenth February. Only nine days to Washington's birthday.'

'Oh for God's sake!' Harriet muttered and lapsed into a silence that lasted half an hour.

They were in Southampton by seven o'clock. Prescott stopped at a hotel in the High Street.

'Now remember, John, *two* rooms. I'll walk the streets rather than—'

'Don't flatter yourself. I want my sleep to-night too.' She didn't smile.

At dinner they might have been strangers. Harriet had withdrawn into her shell; she looked tired and worried.

He didn't force the pace. To-morrow was another day.

It dawned wet and cold, as much of February had been. Harriet came down dressed in ski pants and a thick sweater.

She barely returned Prescott's greeting and they took their seats in the dining-room in silence. As Harriet studied the menu, Prescott slipped the package on her plate.

She laid down the menu, lifted the package and slowly undid the wrapping. A card fell out.

Prescott had spent much thought on the message. In the end he wrote simply: 'To Harriet on her twenty-first birthday, with all my love – John.'

'Oh John, you *did* remember!'

'Of course.'

'And that nonsense about George Washington—'

'I was teasing you.'

Tears brimmed her eyes.

'Aren't you going to open it?' he said.

He had chosen the present with care: a gold bracelet.

'Oh it's beautiful, John!' Then in a changed tone: 'But of course I can't possibly accept it.'

Prescott said *sotto voce*: 'You don't have to tell the whole dining-room.' An elderly couple at the next table were showing interest.

'Darling,' Harriet said loudly, 'how absolutely *divine* of you!' She leant over and kissed him lightly on the forehead, then fixed the bracelet on her wrist.

They discussed it on the car ferry, as Southampton was receding into the rain and mist.

'I've told you, John, I'm not going to marry you.'

'Marriage isn't a condition of the gift . . . Keep it on,' he added as she made to remove the bracelet. 'Just for to-day.'

Harriet fastened it again. 'Well, just so long as you know the score.'

'You also told me,' Prescott said, 'that you believe I murdered your brother. That's not true, is it?'

She was twisting the bracelet round her wrist. 'No, it's not true,' she admitted shortly.

'Then *why*—'

'Don't ask questions.'

But it was his opportunity. 'You're going to marry Alan Studley?'

'No! Alan's an irrelevance. He's just a nice boy who won't take no for an answer.'

'Then what's wrong? Is it Norah? She's not going to contest—'

Harriet turned and faced him. 'Will you shut up?' she said fiercely. 'We're *through*, you and I. Can I make it any plainer?'

They were late getting into Cherbourg, and it was half-past five before they were through the Customs. It was already dark; and still raining.

'*Tenez à droite*,' Harriet said as they nosed out from the docks.

'*Oui, ma chérie.*'

Soon they were zigzagging up the steep hill out of Cherbourg to the south.

He swung out to overtake a battered Citroen.

'Not so fast, John!' Harriet said.

'How far to Fouesnant?'

'Nearly five hundred kilometres.'

'We haven't time to burn, then.'

'We don't have to make it *to-night*.'

But Prescott only stepped harder on the accelerator. He was suddenly oppressed by a sense of urgency . . .

On Harriet's insistence they stopped for a meal in Coutances. They found a pleasant hotel on the town square, right opposite the cathedral.

'Why not spend the night here?' Harriet said after they had eaten. She was fondling a little dachshund that belonged to the hotel.

He wondered if it was an invitation. She seemed as reluctant as he was anxious to get to Fouesnant to-night.

'No,' he said and called for the bill.

Harriet eyed him speculatively. 'You're very determined, John. You've changed.'

'Yes.'

'Tiger wakened at last?'

'Growling.'

The waiter brought his bill. Prescott paid it, exchanged a few words. The man went off, grinning.

'And that's another thing,' Harriet remarked as they went out-side. 'Your French is atrocious, yet you don't mind airing it. When did you stop worrying what people think of you?'

'Last week in court when you gave evidence.'

'When *I* gave evidence?'

'Yes. I decided nothing else mattered except that you loved me.'

He started the engine, turned out of the square into the steep descent to the Avranches road.

'Keep to the right,' Harriet reminded him mechanically. Then she said: 'Don't fool yourself, John. I'm not marrying you. Ever.'

He didn't answer. He knew what was wrong with Harriet, why she was rejecting him. It was a problem, but not insuperable.

He knew everything now – who the murderer was, his motive, his methods. Well, *almost* everything: one or two little points remained stubbornly intractable. But they would fall into place too.

Avranches, Dinan, Loudéac, Pontivy. He ripped through the towns, ate up the kilometres between. Rain lashed the almost deserted roads.

Harriet had long been silent; he hoped she was asleep. But as a car approached, flicked its lights and swished past, spraying water, she said: 'Why do they do that?'

'What?'

'Wink their lights at you.'

'They don't like the white headlamps. I should have had them masked.'

'I wish you'd slow down, John.'

He let the needle slide back fractionally.

Harriet said: 'It's beautiful here in summer. Orchards and pine woods and rivers . . .'

They crossed one of the rivers. A signpost said 'Quimperlé 12 km.' 8 miles; then another 30. It was twenty-past eleven: they wouldn't quite make it by midnight. Although he'd never been on this road before, he'd memorised the route last night, learned the place names, the road numbers, the mileages. He'd always been good with maps.

Harriet was chattering to cover her nervousness. Prescott enjoyed the music of her voice although he was only half-listening.

She was reminiscing about Peter. He caught the words 'engagement party . . . standing there receiving the guests . . .' It conjured a picture.

He saw the bend too late. Harriet screamed as the car mounted the embankment. Prescott wrenched the wheel round, the offside wing grazed the fence, the car slithered down, regained the road and came to a shuddering halt fifty yards on.

'Are you all right?' Harriet said. (Not 'I told you so': even now he noticed that.)

'Yes,' he said. He got out and surveyed the damage: a dent on the bumper, a long scratch on the wing. They'd been lucky.

'I'm sorry,' he said.

Harriet was watching him. He closed the door to extinguish the light.

He wondered if she'd guessed that her words had caused the accident, if she too now saw their significance. No, she couldn't possibly . . .

But to Prescott all was blindingly clear. He had allowed himself to be led insidiously up the wrong path; had underestimated the enemy again; hadn't paid enough attention to the niggling doubts . . .

At twenty-to-one they emerged into the straight from the twisting Concarneau road.

'That's Fouesnant ahead,' Harriet said. 'Turn left at the sign.'

The sign said 'Antiquités' and pointed to a narrow tree-shadowed lane. Prescott turned into it.

'It's about half a mile along,' Harriet said.

The lane was tortuous and in places flooded. His headlights occasionally picked out houses through the trees.

'Next gate on the right. Watch it: it's an awkward turn.'

As he was negotiating the entry, he heard Harriet catch her breath.

He took the car up the short drive and parked outside what seemed to be a white bungalow.

'This it?' he said.

Harriet didn't answer. He repeated the question.

'John,' she said in a frightened voice, 'did you see when you turned in there—'

'What?'

'There was someone behind that tree at the gate.'

Prescott had seen nothing. 'There's a torch in the glove compartment,' he said.

Harriet gave him the torch. 'Be careful, John.'

He walked back down the drive, with the torch unlit; the rear lights of his car gave just enough illumination. Although the rain had stopped, the ground was sodden and squelched under his feet. The air carried the scent of pine.

A thick hedge abutted the road; and just inside the gate, to the left of the drive, was a large tree.

Prescott switched on his torch and cautiously circled the trunk of the tree. There was no one there. But in the mud were confused marks that might have been footprints. He went out the gate, shone the torch up and down the road, saw nothing.

'I must have imagined it,' Harriet said when he returned. 'Let's get inside. This place gives me the creeps.'

CHAPTER V

The house was warm and smelt fresh: there was none of the mustiness of a house locked up for six months. Harriet had phoned a neighbour yesterday morning and asked her to put on the heating and open the windows.

Mme. Leroux had done more than that. The house had been swept and dusted; there was even a little bowl of snowdrops on a table in the hall.

'Nice place,' Prescott remarked, opening doors and switching on lights. He hadn't expected a modern house with light painted walls, polished wood floors and contemporary furniture. The kitchen had a refrigerator and the bathroom a shower.

'My guess is Sandra had a say in it. It's not really Daddy's style.'

Harriet went into a bedroom. 'Oh the poppet!' she called. 'She's even made up the bed.'

Prescott looked in. It was a large double bed.

Harriet caught his eye. 'You, John, will occupy the other bedroom. You can have my sleeping bag.'

'That's generous of you,' he said and went out to bring in the cases from the boot of the car.

When he returned, Harriet was making Nescafé.

She yawned elaborately. 'I'm flaked out,' she said in a brittle voice.

The kettle boiled. She switched it off and filled the cups.

'There are biscuits in the green shopping bag—'

'I'm not hungry,' he said.

'Nor I . . . You'll have to take it black.'

'Thanks. Where did he keep his papers, Harriet?'

She yawned again. 'Not to-night, John.' She didn't look tired: she looked nervous.

'It shouldn't take long . . .'

'Not to-night. I wouldn't know where to begin.'

He gave in.

When they had finished their coffee, Harriet opened a case and handed him a blue sleeping bag.

'Good-night, John.' She shivered.

'Cold?'

Harriet nodded. But she looked frightened rather than cold.

'I'm a very effective hot water bottle,' he said.

'I'm aware of that. Keep your distance!'

'But it's so silly, Harriet. I mean, if it were the *first* time . . . But—'

'Last time was different. I thought then we were going to be married.'

He let her go. She took a suitcase into her bedroom and closed the door.

Prescott found the spare bedroom, laid the sleeping bag on the bare mattress of the single bed, removed his jacket and shoes and climbed in.

He switched off the bedlamp. He was too comfortable, so he dispensed with the pillow. He must keep awake.

He rearranged in his mind the jigsaw pieces to fit the new pattern of the murders: they slid smoothly into place and there was none left over. Curious how he'd been so blind. Mental laziness, that's what it was. He'd been satisfied with a theory that accounted for only ninety-five per cent of the facts. If Einstein had thought like that, relativity might never have been evolved.

Not that he was an Einstein. But he'd always prided himself on his clear, logical thinking. It was in *character* that he'd hitherto been deficient, lacking the confidence to back his own judgment. It had needed Peter to show him the way, and now Harriet . . . Drowsily he let his imagination play on Harriet, with her dark, unruly hair and laughing eyes . . .

He almost didn't hear the handle of the door turn, the footsteps pad across the floor. Then she was bending over him, he could smell her fragrance, sense her nearness.

'Are you awake, John?' she whispered.

Digging his nails into his palms, he kept his eyes closed, breathed evenly and deeply.

She waited a moment longer, then glided away. The door closed gently, a key turned in the lock.

A key! Damnation! He hadn't thought of that. He struggled out of the sleeping bag, ran to the door.

'Harriet!' he called. He rattled the handle. 'Harriet!' he shouted again.

No answer. She was moving about in the little room across the hall. A lumber room, he'd thought, when he glanced into it earlier.

He banged on the door and shouted: 'Don't do it, for God's sake! You're wrong, you've got it all wrong!'

He heard a click and a metallic squeaking, and guessed it was a safe being opened.

In despair he lunged with his shoulder at the bedroom door. It held; but there was a splintering noise from the area of the lock. At the second assault the lock gave and the door burst open.

Harriet, still fully dressed, was on her knees beside an open safe. She was applying a lighted match to papers on a metal tray on the floor.

Prescott thrust her aside, stamped on the papers till they stopped smouldering. Some were already badly charred.

Harriet launched herself at him in fury, fingers clawing at his face.

He held her off. 'You're a silly bloody fool,' he shouted. 'He didn't do it! Your father didn't do it! And you're destroying the evidence that could prove it!'

Harriet went limp. 'Oh God!' she said, covering her eyes. 'Oh God!' Then: 'You're not just saying that?'

'No. I thought it was him too, until last night . . .'

'Then who?'

He told her. She clung to him, shivering.

He felt her hands. 'You're frozen,' he said.

She smiled wanly. 'I could do with a hot water bottle now . . .'

Prescott lifted the tray in one hand, put his other arm round Harriet and led her into the sitting-room. He switched on an electric radiator and installed Harriet in front of it.

'That better?' he asked.

'It wasn't exactly what I meant.'

Prescott grinned. 'We've work to do . . .' He started looking through the charred papers.

Harriet said: 'How do you know it's not Daddy?'

He countered that. 'Why did you think it was?'

For much the same reasons as Prescott. If Peter was upset to the point of insomnia by some dishonesty he'd discovered in the office, it was more likely his *father* was implicated than a mere client. And Arthur Reece's actions after Peter's death were very suspicious: the substitution, with Norah's aid, of the suicide note, the immediate engagement of counsel to protect his interests. Why too did he lie at Prescott's trial and say he'd destroyed the original note?

As for the second murder, it was *known* that Sandra Welch was blackmailing him. Who more likely to want her dead?

'And on the night of the murder,' Harriet said, 'he practically pushed me out of the house. And when I phoned him later, there was no reply.'

In truth Arthur Reece was simply a cantankerous old man, pigheaded to the point of eccentricity; the kind of man whose every action, once you became suspicious of him, could seem sinister.

'Frank Hornby's point was the strongest of all, though,' Prescott said. 'It was easy for Sandra Welch, as your father's mistress, to discover *his* secrets; but where did she find her evidence against the murderer? Unless your father *was* the murderer . . .'

'Where did she get the evidence?'

'Possibly from this.' He gently extracted a scrap of paper from the pile. 'Here's the famous note,' he said, 'or what's left of it.'

It was the first few lines of a typed letter:

"My dear Father,

"When I heard about you and Norah I . . ."

'There may have been something in this that gave the game away,' Prescott said. 'Or else—'

Harriet stopped him. 'Did you hear anything?' she said urgently.

They sat rigid, listening. They sat almost too long. There was no further sound, but Prescott glimpsed a shadow move across the half-open door.

He threw Harriet to the ground, launched himself across the room. There were two shattering explosions, then he encountered solid flesh and grabbed for the arm that held the gun. There was great strength in the arm, but Prescott was strong too. Inexorably he twisted the arm back until there was a grunt of pain and the gun dropped to the floor.

Now Prescott was astride the other and pounding savagely at his face, all his pent-up anger released.

From a great distance a voice called: 'Stop it, John! You'll kill him!' He went on smashing his fist into the face until Harriet put her arms round his neck and made him stop.

Prescott slowly picked himself up. 'If he hadn't gone flabby,' he said, 'he'd have beaten me. He'd have killed us both.' He was gazing down at the pulpy, bleeding, unconscious face of Frank Hornby.

CHAPTER VI

'For a woman,' Prescott said, 'you drive quite passably.'

'At least I keep off the embankment. How's the arm?'

'Aching.' He had a bullet wound in his upper arm, unsuspected at the time.

It was Sunday afternoon, four days after their arrival in France. Days of unreality: tortured sessions with the bewildered local gendarmerie; an interrogation by officials of the Sûreté; finally the arrival by plane of a disgruntled Chief Inspector Lacey.

Lacey was hard to convince of Hornby's guilt; and then grudging in his apology. A small man . . .

'Speaking of the embankment,' Harriet said, 'what caused the swerve? Something I said?'

'Yes, about Peter receiving the guests at his engagement party, remember?' It had touched a chord, brought back a long-forgotten snatch of conversation between Peter and Dr. Parry: arranging to meet the following Sunday afternoon. The Sunday Peter died . . .

It was in itself a tiny, almost insignificant clue. But it forced others to the surface, released the flood of suspicion of Frank Hornby that had been building up in Prescott's subconscious. If he hadn't been mesmerised by the case against Arthur Reece, he'd have seen the truth much sooner.

Spots of sleety rain were falling. Harriet switched on the wipers. 'We haven't much luck with the weather, have we?'

'We'll come back in the summer.'

The 'we' was a trial kite. Harriet ignored it.

'Why did he do it?' she said.

'Frank Hornby? Little sins lead to bigger ones. He lived above his income, got into debt; I dare say his wife was partly to blame. She's always been a spendthrift. So he swindled his partner, was found out, and couldn't take it.'

'Peter had rumbled him?'

'Yes. He found something wrong when he audited the partnership accounts. Old Parry had no business sense and anyway was in his dotage. I imagine Hornby didn't put through the books some of the fees he drew from private patients. Something like that. Incidentally, later on, when Parry retired, he must have been sold down the river. You heard what his widow said about their finances. I mean, Parry *ought* to have been well off.'

'But that was *after* Peter died?'

'Yes. The embezzlements Peter discovered were probably quite paltry.'

Professionally Peter was meticulous: he wouldn't lightly accept the evidence of fraud. Hence the frantic nights in the office, checking and re-checking. Hence, too, the visits to Hornby's surgery – to discuss the discrepancies in private.

Dissatisfied with Hornby's explanations, Peter invited Dr. Parry to his office that Sunday afternoon. Parry's answers finally convinced Peter that Frank Hornby was an embezzler. He decided to turn the facts over to the police.

'But, being Peter,' Prescott said, 'he called on Hornby first to let him know his decision. It couldn't have been easy, knowing as he did that it would blast his friend's career. When Hornby saw he was adamant, he made up his mind to murder him. As soon as Peter left, Hornby went to the office and typed the suicide note—'

'How did he get in?' Harriet interrupted.

'With Norah's key. He'd pinched it a few days before. Norah was in bed ill that week, remember? And Hornby was her doctor.'

'You mean he'd *planned* the murder in advance?'

'Yes. Provisionally, depending on Peter's decision . . .'

Harriet shivered. 'It's so . . . appallingly ruthless'

Ruthless, but in character. Prescott recalled the car accident, when Hornby's immediate reaction was to try and shift the blame to his passenger.

'How could he be sure Peter wouldn't go straight to the police?' Harriet asked.

'I expect he made him promise to talk to me, as a lawyer, before doing anything drastic. He knew I was calling at Ash Grove at nine o'clock. Peter had to be dead before then.'

'How did he do it?' Harriet's knuckles were white on the wheel.

'He went round at 8.45, knocked on your back door—'

She interrupted. 'If only *I* had gone to the door . . .'

Would it have stopped him? Or would he have killed Harriet too?

Anyway Peter went. Hornby enticed him down the garden on some pretext, knocked him out, karate style, put the note in his pocket, and strung him up with the rope he'd left for the purpose. He'd taken the rope – and the chair – from the toolshed.

'Poor Peter,' Harriet whispered. She drove in silence for a bit, into worsening weather.

They stopped for coffee and a Pernod in a cafe in Josselin and watched the sleet turn to snow. The sky was yellow.

'I'm divorcing Norah,' Prescott said.

Harriet seemed not to hear. 'He was incredibly lucky,' she said.

'Why?'

'Suppose Dr. Parry had mentioned at the inquest his interview with Peter . . . In fact, why didn't he?'

'Because although he suspected the truth, he was terrified of public ridicule. He was losing his grip; he'd been making mistakes in diagnosis; he'd lost confidence in his judgment. And Hornby was enough of a psychologist to play on his self-doubts. Parry would consult his partner – he always did in police cases – about the bruise on Peter's neck below the marks of the rope, and would allow himself to be reassured. But Hornby made one slip there.'

During the trial Prescott had been vaguely aware of a jarring piece of evidence, an apparently motiveless lie . . . It was much later before it came back to him. Hornby had testified: 'My partner, who conducted the autopsy, assured me there was no other injury.' Yet earlier he'd said to Prescott himself that Dr. Parry had refused to discuss the case with him: 'Not one word would he say about it.'

'I don't see the point of that,' Harriet said.

'It was inconsistent, that's the point. Once you start telling lies it's very difficult to be consistent. Of *course* Parry discussed the case with him – he always did. But when Hornby was talking to me it suited him to say he hadn't. Later on, at the trial, he forgot he'd told a lie '

'Trust you to work that one out,' Harriet said.

'What's that supposed to mean?'

'A tribute to your powers of deduction or something.'

'It didn't sound very complimentary . . .'

Harriet finished her Pernod. 'We'd better be on our way,' she said, eyeing without enthusiasm the wintry scene outside.

'No hurry.' Prescott summoned the melancholy youth in black jeans who had served them.

'*Encore deux Pernods, s'il vous plaît,*' he said.

Harriet giggled.

'Well, at least he understands.' He added: 'It's a change to see you smile again. Did I ever tell you, when you smile there's a dimple—'

The smile was gone. 'We were talking about Frank Hornby,' she said. 'If he wanted people to believe Peter had hanged himself, why did he put such an unlikely story – I mean, about Daddy and Norah – in the suicide note?'

'It was the best he could think of. And your father evidently thought people would believe it – that's why he switched the notes.'

Arthur Reece didn't destroy the original note. He kept it in his safe in Fouesnant, where in course of time his mistress, Sandra Welch, came across it.

When, later, they fell out, Sandra took a copy back to England; not the original, because Reece would have missed it. She wasn't yet in a position to make capital of it: all she knew was that there was more to Peter Reece's death than came out at the inquest.

Back in Cromley she took a job in Clyde and Sons and cultivated Tim Raven in the belief that he might have inside knowledge.

Her breakthrough came when she phoned Mrs. Parry, posing as a journalist. Mrs. Parry, under pressure, as good as admitted that Peter Reece had been murdered; and also let slip a hint of how it was done.

Sandra, convinced that Arthur Reece was the murderer, sent him a couple of threatening letters, which brought him home from France.

But meantime she had stumbled on the truth.

'How?' Harriet asked.

'From what Tim Raven said, it could have been from the internal evidence of the letter itself; Hornby may have somehow given himself away in it. Thanks to your fire-raising we'll never know . . . Or perhaps she made intelligent deductions from what Mrs. Parry said. Anyway, one way or another, she now knew Frank Hornby had murdered Peter.'

Sandra Welch continued to put pressure on Arthur Reece. He

paid £500 for her silence about his substitution of the suicide note. But she also blackmailed Hornby; and thereby signed her death warrant. He determined to eliminate her.

'And to incriminate you?' Harriet said.

'Yes. It no longer suited his plans to have Peter's death accepted as suicide. So he spread doubts – he even tried to convince *me* Peter was murdered. And he sent the police an anonymous letter in the style of Sandra Welch. It advised them to talk to Mrs. Parry . . .'

When the stage was set, Hornby sent Prescott a message, ostensibly from the blackmailer, summoning him to a rendezvous half an hour after Hornby himself was to meet her.

'And left you holding the body?' Harriet said.

'Precisely.'

'How could he be sure you'd keep the appointment?'

'I told you – he's a good psychologist. He knew me too well.'

A man, too, of considerable resource. After Prescott's acquittal it could only be a matter of time till he discovered the truth. So Hornby delicately focussed suspicion on Arthur Reece and on the house in Fouesnant; threw dust in Prescott's eyes just long enough for the trap to be set . . .

'Suppose he'd succeeded,' Harriet said. 'Suppose he'd murdered us both back in Fouesnant: how could he have talked his way out of it? The police would be bound to discover he was there.'

'He'd have a story ready. He'd heard we were coming over here, suspected I was up to no good, followed us out, arrived just too late. Found I'd shot you then killed myself. Remember the police still believed I was guilty.'

Harriet shivered. 'Let's get on,' she said.

Prescott paid the bill and they left the cafe. It was perceptibly colder, and wet snow had already filmed the road.

'Can you manage?' Prescott asked Harriet as she got into the driving seat.

'I'll have to.' They were aiming for to-morrow's car ferry at Cherbourg.

She drove confidently. Even when the back wheels skidded as they overtook a lorry on one of the short stretches of dual carriage-way, she didn't panic: she used the accelerator, not the brake, and they were safely past. She weaved her way through the traffic of Rennes like a native.

Prescott feasted his eyes on her. Marvellous profile she had: its perfection almost enhanced by the rebellious wisp of hair that strayed over her brow.

Impulsively he said again: 'I'm divorcing Norah ... You will marry me, won't you?'

Harriet didn't take her eyes from the road. 'We'll talk later,' she said.

For days she'd evaded the issue, parried his questions. He knew why she'd rejected him last week: she believed then she was the daughter of a murderer. But now, with that impediment removed, she still held aloof ...

They were in Avranches by six o'clock. It was dry now, the snow was crisping under the car wheels, patches of ice were forming. Harriet dropped her speed; they took ninety minutes to do the fifty kilometres to Coutances.

They had dinner in the same hotel as on the night they arrived. The same little dog ingratiated itself at Harriet's feet in the dining-room.

Through the window they saw a car turn into the square, waltz on the glittering snow and pile up against the wall of the *Mairie*.

'We're going no farther to-night,' Prescott said.

Harriet nodded.

Now was his opportunity. The setting was heaven-sent: the Christmas card scene outside, the soft lights and warmth of the dining-room, a leisurely, intimate meal, a bottle of wine.

But still Harriet procrastinated. 'You'd very little evidence,' she said.

'What?'

'For pinning it on Frank Hornby.'

'Never mind it now, Harriet. Have some more wine.'

'No, thank you.' She put her hand over the glass.

She continued: 'Was it just that Peter was meeting Dr. Parry? Did you deduce it all from that?'

'You're very beautiful, Harriet,' he said. He put a hand on hers; she disengaged it.

Prescott sighed. 'No, it wasn't only that. There was his evidence at the trial.'

'You mean that little slip he made?'

'That, yes, but also the whole drift of what he said. I mean, he was supposed to be my *friend* . . .'

Hornby's evidence had been subtly slanted to appear to be a defence of Prescott when in fact it was damning him. In particular he'd conveyed, with every appearance of reluctance, a picture of Peter boiling with rage over John Prescott's treachery.

That appeared to tally with the evidence given by Lowson and Raven. Nevertheless it was false; or at best, grossly exaggerated. But why should Hornby lie? Unless he *wanted* Prescott to be convicted . . .

'And another thing,' Prescott added. 'Remember the letter you showed me? The one from the blackmailer to your father?'

'Yes.'

'Do you remember what it said?'

'It said Peter hadn't committed suicide, he'd been murdered. He'd been struck on the back of the head and—'

'"The back of the head": these were the actual words?'

'Yes . . . But Sandra wouldn't know it was on the *neck*.'

'That's not the point. I told Hornby about that letter and I distinctly remember saying "base of the skull" instead of "back of the head." One tends to use medical jargon when speaking to a doctor. The letter I received later, supposedly from the blackmailer but in fact from the murderer, also described how Peter died; and used the words "base of the skull" . . .'

The waiter brought coffee. Harriet was silent now, drained of questions.

Prescott said: 'I ask you again: will you marry me?'

She looked at him sadly. 'You've changed, John. You don't need me any longer. The tiger has wakened.'

'I expect you're right,' Prescott said. 'Anyway, I'm too old for you.'

Harriet bristled. 'You're nothing of the sort.'

'Nine years. It's too big a gap.'

She glared at him.

'I might,' he said, 'try once more to make a go of it with Norah.'

Again she rose to the bait. 'John Prescott, if you *dare* . . .' She saw his expression, blushed and laughed. 'You've a perverted sense of humour.'

'You still haven't given me your answer.'

She said quietly: 'I could never marry anyone else . . .'

Across the square the cathedral bell chimed nine o'clock.

Harriet said: 'You haven't asked about accommodation yet.'

'Accommodation': a neutral word, neither singular nor plural.

As Prescott hesitated, Harriet added, her eyes dancing: 'And see if you can get a hot-water bottle for me, will you?'

THE END